# The Happy Onion

# Look for these titles by
## *Ally Blue*

### *Now Available:*

*Bay City Paranormal Investigations Series:*
Oleander House (Book 1)
What Hides Inside (Book 2)
Twilight (Book 3)
Closer (Book 4)
An Inner Darkness (Book 5)

*Print Anthologies:*
Hearts from The Ashes
Temperature's Rising

Willow Bend
Love's Evolution
Eros Rising
Catching a Buzz
Fireflies
Untamed Heart
Where the Heart Is
Adder

# The Happy Onion

*Ally Blue*

A Samhain Publishing, Ltd. publication.

Samhain Publishing, Ltd.
577 Mulberry Street, Suite 1520
Macon, GA 31201
www.samhainpublishing.com

The Happy Onion
Copyright © 2009 by Ally Blue
Print ISBN: 978-1-60504-293-0
Digital ISBN: 1-60504-124-6

Editing by Sasha Knight
Cover by Anne Cain

First Samhain Publishing, Ltd. electronic publication: July 2008
First Samhain Publishing, Ltd. print publication: May 2009

# Dedication

To the local grocery store chain whose back-of-the-delivery-truck ads starring anthropomorphic foodstuffs birthed this particular plot bunny. You know who you are. Never change! And as always, to the JAWbreakers, for their support, their guidance, and their unwavering friendship in the face of all my usual whining and moaning. I could never manage to complete a book without you girls! Love you!

# Chapter One

"I'm sorry, Mr. Stone," sniffed the woman in the blue power suit. "But there's nothing I can do. Our backers on this project are withholding funds until this matter can be resolved."

Thomas Stone gaped at her, wondering if he'd heard right. "Ms. Duncan, I came here all the way from Santa Fe for this job. Now you're telling me there *is* no job?"

"That is not what I'm saying at all."

"Then what exactly *are* you saying?" Thom leaned forward, giving her his best icy glare. "Because I could've sworn you just told me that Bradford & Lehrer is tied up in a legal dispute over who owns part of the land you're building on, that you have no idea how long it's going to last, and that you therefore can't hire me right now."

"I said no such thing. The position is still there."

"You said you can't pay me yet. And since I'm not offering my services for free, I'd say that's pretty much the same thing."

Ms. Duncan's face flushed. Her expression suggested she'd bitten into a particularly sour lemon. "You are more than welcome to find a temporary position elsewhere until we are able to resolve this matter and regain our backing."

"Nice to have your permission." He almost managed to keep the sarcasm out of his voice. Rising to his feet, he smoothed the folds from his suit. He hated wearing suits. "Well. If you could tell me where I'm staying, I guess I'll get settled in and start hunting for a temporary job."

Thank God they'd offered to put him up for a while. After paying off his debts back in Santa Fe and making the two-day trip here on his Harley, he barely had enough money for a couple of meals and one more night at the Best Western.

The woman's flush deepened, and Thom's stomach lurched. *Oh fuck. Please don't say what I think you're about to say.*

"The thing is," she began, hands winding together in a nervous knot, "we haven't the funds to house you at the moment either."

Nodding, Thom clacked his tongue stud against the back of his teeth. He counted eleven metal-on-enamel clicks before he felt able to speak calmly instead of screaming in the woman's face. "You do realize I have nowhere to stay, right?"

She had the good grace to look guilty. "Yes. And as I've said, I'm very sorry. We expected to be able to house you at a local hotel for at least a month, but you must understand what we're facing here. There have been many unforeseen setbacks on this project already, and we were running dangerously close to the red even before our backers froze the funding."

"Oh, I understand what that's like." Sighing, he ran a hand over his carefully gelled and tied-back hair. "Why didn't you call me?"

Not that it would've made a difference, really. But dammit, this wasn't the kind of shit you just sprang on a guy out of nowhere.

"We just found out this morning. I didn't think there was much point in calling since you were already on your way here."

Another nod. Fifteen tongue-stud clacks this time. Thom stuffed both hands into his jacket pockets, reasoning that if they were balled inside those deep polyester pouches, they wouldn't be wrapped around Ms. Dumbass Duncan's scrawny neck and he wouldn't end up in jail on assault charges. After all, it wasn't really her fault. She was just the poor sap the company bigwigs had sent to break the news to him.

He'd met the two owners once, in Santa Fe, when they first hired him. Dickless wonders, the both of them. He could well believe Ms. Duncan got all the shit assignments.

"I truly am sorry, Mr. Stone." Ms. Duncan stood and held out her hand. "I do hope you will still come to work for us once this...misunderstanding is resolved."

*Like hell I will.*

He swallowed the words, as well as a whole string of less savory words which wanted to follow. Experience had taught him to never, ever, *ever* make important decisions when angry.

Taking his right hand out of his pocket, he forced himself to reach across the desk and shake her hand. "Call me when you're solvent again. You have my cell number."

He turned and strode out of the office before his composure had the chance to shatter. No matter how much he hated Bradford & Lehrer right now—and he did, oh *God* did he hate them at this moment—he couldn't afford to burn the only bridge he had in this town. Being homeless again was *not* on his agenda.

*You're already homeless. Or you will be tomorrow, when you have to check out of the hotel and hit the street.* He scowled as he stalked down the short hallway, shoved the front door open and emerged into the blistering August afternoon. "What the hell do I do now?"

Two men in jeans, work boots and hard hats stood talking on the sidewalk outside the small building. One of them gave Thom an odd look but didn't comment. Sliding his sunglasses on, Thom cut an appreciative glance at the older of the pair. Too bad most construction workers were either straight or aggressively closeted, at least in his experience. Nothing like a nice, no-strings fuck to work off some tension.

He walked across the small parking area to his Harley Fat Boy, parked in the shade of a young tree. Maybe after he got back to the hotel he could scan the local paper for work. From what he'd seen of Asheville so far, it was a vibrant, thriving town. There were bound to be at least a few positions he qualified for. While he was at it, he'd find out where a gay guy could go to get laid around here.

Strapping on his helmet, he straddled the Fat Boy and started the engine. With any luck, in a few hours he'd have at least a couple of leads on either jobs or hook-up joints. Preferably both.

∽

Four hours and nine phone calls later, Thom flopped onto the hard hotel-room mattress with a sigh. The *Asheville Citizen-Times* contained almost three hundred job listings, several of which Thom was, in his opinion, perfect for. But most of them wouldn't be making a decision on who they were hiring for at least a couple of weeks. He didn't have that long. He'd set up interview appointments with five different businesses in the next few days, but dammit, he needed work *now*. Didn't anyone just hire people on the spot anymore?

"Did they ever, really?" he inquired of the water-stained ceiling. Just because that was how he'd gotten his last couple of jobs didn't mean most companies operated that way.

After brooding on the bed for a while failed to make him feel any better, he got up and shuffled into the bathroom to fix himself up. The downtown area was chock-full of bars and restaurants. He could walk around, see if any of them could use a bartender. Sure, it was the same job he'd left behind in Santa Fe, but he didn't mind. Tending bar was fun in a lot of ways, and the tips were usually good. A guy could definitely make a living at it.

Tugging the leather tie from his hair, he dampened his brush and ran it through the fine, pale strands which hung thick and straight to his shoulders. When it was as tamed as he could make it, he gathered it into a short ponytail once again and secured the strip of leather around the base.

Stepping back, he gave his reflection a critical once-over. His suit was a little rumpled, but it would have to do. He didn't have another one. Hadn't thought he'd need it. His hair was better than usual, actually, only a few wisps falling out of the ponytail. There was nothing to be done about the baby face and enormous blue eyes that made him look like jailbait even though he was almost twenty-seven. He'd learned a long time ago to always carry his I.D.

"Okay," he said to his twin in the mirror. "Let's do it."

Thus decided, he grabbed his suit jacket, slid his sunglasses on and headed out into the city.

౭౦

Thom wasn't sure why he followed the sidewalk along the narrow one-way street which veered off the main road four blocks from the Best Western. It just seemed so inviting, with its row of colorful storefronts curving into the distance. Inviting, mysterious, full of the potential for adventure...

*Nope. It's the shade.* Leaning against one of the trees lining the road, he let out a sigh of pure pleasure. The cool shadows cast by the leafy branches were definitely what had lured him here. It felt like heaven after the hellish heat on the main thoroughfare.

*That's what I get for walking around in a fucking suit in the middle of the afternoon in August.*

After a few minutes, he pushed away from the tree trunk and strolled down the brick sidewalk. So far, he hadn't found any businesses hiring. Or rather, he hadn't found any businesses hiring for any positions he was qualified to fill, and which might actually cover food and rent.

Rent. Scowling, he brushed away the lock of hair that had fallen into his eyes. He had to check out of the Best Western tomorrow. Even if they could give him the room for a while longer, he didn't have the cash to pay for more than one more night.

Which brought him back to the reason he was out here trudging the crowded summer streets. Finding a source of cash flow, since the one he'd counted on had unexpectedly dried up.

"Stupid fuckers," he muttered. "Should've known it was too good to be true."

In fact, that was the first thing he'd thought when Don Bradford of Bradford & Lehrer first offered him the position managing the on-site nightclub at their newest condominium complex, Rosewood, in downtown Asheville, North Carolina. It had certainly *seemed* too good to be true. Men, whose companies built and managed upscale "residential resorts", as they called them, just didn't walk into grungy bars in the unfashionable part of Santa Fe and offer the shift supervisors management positions in classy nightclubs. Especially not when said men were falling-down drunk and obviously too rich for the neighborhood. But Mr. Bradford had come back the next day with his business partner in tow and made the same offer sober, and Thom had begun to hope it might actually happen. It was the sort of opportunity he'd always wanted but hadn't been able to dig up for himself.

Three weeks and a flurry of phone calls later, all the details were finalized, and Thom had packed what little he'd wanted to keep into a duffle bag, strapped it to his Harley's passenger seat and made the drive to Asheville. And now, here he was, homeless and damn near broke in a lovely but unfamiliar city.

It was exactly how he'd arrived in Santa Fe—with nothing but his bike, some clothes and a couple hundred in cash. At least this time, he didn't have a psychotic ex-boss-and-lover after him—that he knew of, anyway—and he'd gained a lot of useful skills at his former job. With any luck, he'd be able to find something that paid well enough and wasn't too hateful. Hell, maybe the Rosewood job would still come through, though he wasn't about to count on that.

Lost in thought, Thom walked right past the "Help Wanted" sign before it registered. A couple feet past the window where the hand-lettered piece of cardboard leaned, Thom stopped, turned and went back.

"Bartender," he murmured, reading the rest of the sign. Perfect.

Walking the few steps back to the entrance, Thom studied the door. Someone had painted an onion in violent yellow on the smoked glass. The cartoon bulb sported a pair of huge blue eyes and a toothy grin. Spindly brown arms ending in white gloves were flung wide from the round body. It stood on a pair of equally delicate legs, shod rather improbably in biker boots. A tuft of green tendrils erupted from the thing's tapered top to form a verdant arch spelling out "The Happy Onion".

The overall effect was both amusing and disturbing. Thom

shook his head. It didn't look much like a bar, but what the hell. A job was a job, and he was desperate.

He pushed open the door and walked inside. The place was long and narrow, with brick walls and a stained wood floor. The high ceiling featured beautiful white carved tiles. A wood-topped bar lined one wall. Music pounded from a tremendous boom box on a shelf among the bottles of wine and liquor, the beat pulsing and infectious. Small tables topped with colorful mosaic tiles sat along the opposite wall. The room appeared to widen in the back, making space for more tables. A doorway in the far wall led to what was most likely the kitchen.

One couple sat talking and eating at a table near the back, and a young man with green hair and a face full of metal was busily tapping the keys of his laptop at another table. Two middle-aged women huddled on barstools, heads together. Not much business, but then again most bars didn't start getting busy until after dark.

A girl in an eye-crossing red, yellow and orange plaid dress came hurrying out from behind the bar, a plastic menu in her hand. "Hi," she greeted him, flashing a sweet, friendly smile. "Just one today?"

For a moment, Thom had no idea what she meant. Then he got a better look at the menu. It sported the same onion which graced the front door, but underneath it was written *The Happy Onion Vegan Kitchen.*

The light dawned. This wasn't a bar, it was a restaurant.

He almost left. The tips just weren't there for restaurant bartenders. But he couldn't afford to be picky right now. They needed a tender. He could mix drinks and chat up the customers with the best of them.

"Actually, I'm here about the bartender job," he said, gesturing toward the window.

She let out a little squeal. "Cool! C'mere."

Hurrying behind the bar again, she tossed the menu aside and started rummaging through a pile of papers beside the cash register. Thom followed, amused. "Are you the manager?"

"Naw, we don't have one. Phil—that's the owner—he does his own managing usually, but he's taking a couple weeks off so I'm kind of in charge right now." She snagged a crumpled sheet from the stack and turned back to Thom. "Phil says anybody who can mix these is hired, as long as you're at least twenty-one and not a complete nutball."

Thom blinked. "Really?"

"Uh-huh. I can tend bar pretty well, but I can't do that *and* wait tables. Plus Phil says the customers love me so he wants to keep me on as waitress." She dimpled at him, brown eyes wide and innocent. "So, let me see you mix those, and if they're right then you can start tomorrow."

For a moment, Thom stood there debating with himself. The part of him which had managed bars in the past wanted to remind her that it's never a good idea to hire someone without references or at least asking if they had a criminal background. But the part of him that wanted food to eat and a place to live sealed his lips. Pulling off his jacket and laying it across the bar, he set to work mixing the drinks.

There were a dozen on the list, all popular concoctions that anyone calling themselves a bartender should be able to make in their sleep. The bar was well organized and well stocked, so it only took a few minutes for him to get through the list. When he'd finished, he stepped back and looked at the young woman, waiting for her verdict.

She nodded. "Looks perfect. I guess you're hired."

Thom felt like a load of bricks had been lifted off his back. He smiled, holding out his hand. "Thank you very much, Ms..."

"Oh, no 'Ms.'" She took his outstretched hand and shook. "It's just Circe."

"Circe. I'm Thomas Stone. Call me Thom."

"Nice to meet you, Thom." She let go of his hand and hurried past him, rounding the bar to head toward the back of the room. "Come back to the office, you can fill out the paperwork."

Thom trailed after her, feeling a million times better than he had twenty minutes ago. The green-haired boy glanced up as Thom passed. He gave the young man a smile and a nod. The scowl he got in return didn't even make a dent in his good mood. He was young, he was good-looking and he was once again gainfully employed.

*Thom, you are so getting laid tonight.*

# Chapter Two

As usual on a Friday night, Belial's Basement was packed and busting at the seams with sexual energy. Philip Sorrells swiveled his stool around and leaned his back against the bar, sipping his second whiskey and watching the parade of horny men strutting past. Or maybe he should say *struggling* past, since the crowd was so tight any movement at all was an achievement.

Most of the faces were depressingly familiar. Belial's was a fun, lively place, but there wasn't much variety here. The regulars and staff all knew each other, in a Biblical way as often as not. For those nights when he wanted someone who already knew his tastes and who he could still be casual friends with later, it was great. Tonight, however, he had a craving for new blood. Or to be more exact, new cock.

"Well, helloooo there, handsome!"

Phil winced at the sound of the familiar singsong from his right. Of all the guys in his personal "wish I hadn't" file, this was the one Phil always dreaded seeing the most. *My own fault. If I'd been paying attention, he wouldn't have sneaked up on me like that.*

"Hi, Brad," he said, forcing a smile. "How are you?"

"Much better now." Brad leered, his eyes glowing with lust. Or maybe that was just the weirdly bright green contacts he wore. "So. Phil-licious. Wanna come back to my place and play Hide the Sausage?"

Phil clamped his mouth shut to prevent spewing out the mouthful of whiskey he'd just taken and ended up coughing most of it onto the floor anyway. "Good grief," he wheezed when he could breathe again. "What are you, twelve?"

Brad tossed a lock of neon pink hair out of his eyes and grinned. "Why, you want me to be twelve?"

Phil set his whiskey glass on the bar before Brad could choke him to death with any other appalling comments. "Go away, Brad."

Brad crossed his arms and pouted, lower lip sticking out. On a thirty-one-year-old, the effect was a little disturbing. "Well. Who pissed in *your* coffee this morning?"

Sighing, Phil rubbed his temple with two fingers. After a long day of laying tiles in his new bathroom, all he wanted was to get fucked good and hard by someone other than Brad, then sleep for about ten hours.

He opened his mouth to tell Brad in terms even *he* could understand to Go The Fuck Away, when across the room the door opened and in walked a vision. Forgetting all about Brad, Phil stood with his mouth hanging open and stared.

All he could see at first was a face, but what a face it was. Heart-shaped, milky pale, with a sweet rosebud mouth and gigantic eyes the color of a tropical lagoon. Gleaming platinum hair fell in straight shoulder-length layers to frame those angelic features.

As the man slipped catlike through the crowd to the bar, Phil caught glimpses of a slim, compact body clad head to toe in black leather. The open vest revealed well-toned arms and chest and a hard, flat belly. A line of fine golden hair bisected the man's abdomen and disappeared into the snug pants hanging low on his slim hips.

Phil gulped. The urge to run over, fall to his knees and follow that treasure trail with his tongue was hard to resist.

"God, they don't even bother to card people anymore, looks like." Brad dug an elbow into Phil's ribs. "You really *are* into the young stuff, aren't you? Close your mouth, before you start catching flies."

Phil's eloquent and detailed reply, in which he listed all the reasons the beauty who'd just walked in *had* to be legal, got lost somewhere between his brain and his mouth. Not wanting to waste any more time on a guy he wasn't ever going to bed with again in this lifetime, Phil pushed Brad aside and stalked toward the pretty little thing he'd decided he *had* to get between the sheets as soon as possible. Brad's declaration that Phil was a sanctimonious bitch barely registered, except to make Phil wonder where a party slut like Brad had learned such a big word.

"Baileys on the rocks," Blondie shouted to the bartender over the thumping music just as Phil sidled up to him.

"It's on me," Phil declared, counting out the right number of bills and laying them on the bar. "And give me a Maker's Mark," he added when he realized he'd left his whiskey on the other end of the bar.

Turning sideways, Blondie tilted that adorable face upward and gave Phil a heart-thumping smile. "Thanks."

"My pleasure." Phil smiled back, mentally working out the logistics of getting Blondie's cock up his ass. The man was at least eight inches shorter than Phil's six-foot-one-and-three-quarters, but Phil was determined. He had a thing for men who looked delicate and pretty yet were willing and able to fuck him through the mattress.

*God, please let him be a top.*

Blondie's smile widened. "What's your name?"

"I'm...uh, Drake." It wasn't a complete lie. Just because he only used his middle name for one-night stands didn't mean it wasn't on his birth certificate.

"I'm James. Nice to meet you." Instead of offering a hand to shake, Blondie—James, rather—raked a sharp, appraising look up and down Phil's body. "You think we're gonna fuck, just because you bought me a drink?"

Like the answer to *that* question wasn't glaringly obvious in the way "James"—not his real name, Phil would've bet, but who was he to complain?—eyed the crotch of Phil's body-hugging jeans. Phil grinned. "Yep."

James laughed, the sound full-throated and surprisingly childlike. "You're right, as it happens."

"Cool." Leaning an elbow on the bar, Phil picked up his glass of Maker's Mark and took a sip. "We should probably talk first."

James's pale eyebrows went up. "Yeah? Okay." He lifted his own glass and took a long swallow, licking the creamy liquid off those gorgeous lips in a marvelously suggestive way. "I'm clean, I always use condoms until I know my partner's clean too, and before you ask, yes, I really am legal. I'm twenty-six. I prefer to top, but I've learned to enjoy getting my ass pounded once in a while. When you look like this, it's either that or go without a lot of times. What about you? Top, or bottom? And if you want to go bareback tonight, better find someone else."

Phil gulped half his glass down in an effort to be cool. Crowing in triumph usually didn't endear him to strangers.

"I can do either, but I'm mostly a bottom." Setting his drink down again, Phil moved closer to James, catching a whiff of leather, shampoo and musky cologne. "That wasn't really what I meant about talking, though."

James gave him an inscrutable look. Draining his glass, he put it down and slipped a knee between Phil's thighs. Phil could feel the man's heat even through the leather. He clutched at the bar, fighting a dizzying wave of lust.

"So. Drake." James stretched an arm up and around Phil's neck, fingering the thick golden brown braid hanging down his back. "What's your favorite color?"

"Blue," Phil answered, staring down into James's brilliant blue eyes. "Yours?"

"Black." Leaning closer, James pinched Phil's nipple through his threadbare Powerpuff Girls T-shirt. "My favorite movie's *Die Hard*, what's yours?"

Phil licked his lips. "Uh. *The Terminator*." His growing lust guided his hands up under James's leather vest. He pushed it aside and rubbed his thumbs across the little pink nipples, which hardened at his touch. "What's your favorite TV show?"

"*Mythbusters*." Rising on tiptoe, James ran the tip of his tongue up the underside of Phil's chin, stirring the hairs of his close-cropped beard. "You?"

"Check the T-shirt." Phil groaned as James's mouth latched onto his neck and sucked hard. "Shit. Can we go fuck now?"

A chuckle vibrated through James's chest and into Phil's. "Your place or my hotel room?"

"Your room close by?" Phil pushed his hips forward so James could feel the erection trapped behind his zipper. "My house is too fucking far."

"Best Western it is." James unwound his arm from Phil's neck and slid both hands down to squeeze his ass. "I already have lube, but I need to buy condoms. Is there a drugstore or something nearby?"

The feel of James's fingers kneading his butt cheeks made

it damn hard for Phil to keep talking, but he managed. "Um. They sell 'em one at a time in the bathroom vending machine, or by the box at the bar. Just ask the bartender."

James laughed, his head dropping down to rest on Phil's shoulder. "Wow, I don't think I've ever been to a bar that sells whole boxes of rubbers before."

Phil couldn't answer. Having James's sweet little body pressed against his was causing all sorts of pleasant havoc inside him. Following a sudden, overwhelming urge, he slid a hand into James's hair, tugged his head back, bent and kissed him hard.

James responded with gleeful enthusiasm, mouth opening wide and lean hips rocking his erection against Phil's thigh. Moaning, Phil held James's head still and swept his tongue between those pretty lips. The creamy sweetness of the Baileys lingered in James's mouth, almost as intoxicating as his leather-and-lust scent.

Something hard and rounded rubbed Phil's soft palate as the kiss went deeper, and Phil realized with a jolt that James had a pierced tongue.

Sweet Jesus.

Phil's knees turned rubbery. He clutched at the lithe body molded to his, hoping to God he wouldn't embarrass himself by actually *swooning.*

James pulled back, those big eyes gleaming in the low light. "You like the tongue stud, huh?"

Phil nodded, wiping the sheen of sweat from his brow. "I bet that feels amazing when you go down on a guy."

"That's what I'm told." James's soft pink lips curved into a filthy smile. His hand snaked between Phil's legs to cup his balls through his jeans. Phil squeaked, and James chuckled. He stood on tiptoe, pressing his cheek to Phil's. "I bet you're dying for me to suck you off, aren't you? So you can see what that piece of metal feels like on your cock."

"You better believe it." Planting both hands on James's leather-sheathed ass, Phil lifted him right off his feet and kissed him again. "I took a cab here. You got a car?"

"No. Just a bike, and it's back at the hotel. I walked." James bit Phil's lip and wriggled out of his grip. "It's only a couple of blocks. Let me get the condoms and we can go."

Phil eyed James's taut rear hungrily as he bent over the bar to summon the tender. God, the man had the cutest little butt. It was all Phil could do to keep from yanking down those sinfully tight pants to see what it looked like bare.

*Patience. In a few minutes, you'll get to look your fill. Maybe he'll even let you have a taste.*

The thought made Phil's mouth and his prick both water. He pressed a hand to his crotch, not even bothering to be discreet. Every guy here was looking to get laid, and more than a few of them had paired off and were making out in the middle of the floor, so what was the point in trying to hide his excitement?

James stepped away from the bar, a box of extra-thin Trojans in his hand and a lustful gleam in his eyes. His gaze turned heavy when it zeroed in on Phil touching himself. "Shit. Let's get out of here. I need to fuck you before I explode."

Grinning, Phil let James clamp a hand around his wrist and pull him through the crowd to the door. He *loved* it when the short, cute ones took charge like that.

The walk to the Best Western was brief, but supremely uncomfortable. Phil had worn his tightest jeans because they displayed his ass to perfection, but they weren't made for walking any distance in. Especially not with a raging hard-on. He breathed a sigh of relief when they reached the hotel.

25

Inside the empty elevator, James shoved Phil against the wall and sank his teeth into Phil's chest. Phil moaned, burying both hands in James's fine, soft hair. "God, you're hot."

"Thanks." James's warm, wet tongue dragged across Phil's collarbone, the metal stud digging in and sending sparks racing over Phil's skin. "So are you."

Phil was starting to wonder how much trouble they'd get in if they just fucked right here in the elevator when a soft *ding* sounded. He and James jumped apart just as the door slid open. James snagged Phil's wrist again and led him into the hall, brushing past another couple who were entering the elevator as they exited. Phil caught the woman's gaze following James and couldn't help a smug smirk.

*He's all mine, sweetheart.*

For tonight, anyway, which was all he was looking for.

For a second, Phil's inner mom popped into his head to tell him he really should find a nice man and settle down. Give up the bars and the one-night stands in favor of nights at home with someone who knew him at his best and his worst. Someone he would know just as thoroughly. They could shop for organic vegetables together on Saturday mornings and attend war protests hand in hand. Maybe this faceless someone would even share Phil's penchant for action movies and weird cartoons.

"Here we are," James said, stopping in front of room 415. He let go of Phil's wrist to stick the keycard in the slot and open the door to his room. Pulling Phil inside, he let the door swing shut and pressed their bodies together. The box of condoms dropped to the floor along with the keycard. "So. You want my cock up your ass right away, or do I have time to educate you on the delights of fellatio with a tongue stud first?"

The longing for domestic bliss melted like snow in the heat

of James's gaze. Sliding his hands underneath James's leather vest, Phil pushed it over those hard white shoulders, down the strong, lean arms and off. It hit the floor with a faint thump.

"Suck my cock," Phil demanded, staring right into James's fiery eyes. "But don't make me come. I want to come when you're fucking me."

One pale eyebrow arched up. "You think your control is that good, do you?"

"Yep. You think your cock-sucking skills are that good?"

"I *know* they are."

The ring in James's voice and the glint in his eyes said he was absolutely sincere. Phil grinned. In his experience, being little and pretty tended to either turn a guy into the uber-submissive doormat people tended to expect him to be, or give him the impetus to become as strong and confident as possible. Clearly, James had taken the latter route.

Phil was delighted. He *loved* being taken by a man who knew what he was doing and didn't mind saying so.

Taking hold of James's nipples, Phil pinched them hard enough to make James gasp. "Show me, then. I'll tell you when you need to stop."

Licking his lips, James sank to his knees. Phil leaned against the wall and slid his feet apart until his zipper was level with James's mouth. His gaze glued to Phil's crotch, James opened Phil's snug jeans and pulled out his cock and balls. His slim fingers wrapped around Phil's shaft, thumb gently pulling back the foreskin. Leaning forward, he rubbed his face on Phil's balls and up his prick, inhaling deeply.

"God, I love the smell of sweaty cock." He glanced up at Phil, a faint pink flush staining his cheeks. "Tastes good that way too."

Phil agreed, though he had to express his concurrence with a vigorous nod since his voice didn't seem to be working.

As he watched, James's pink tongue came out, swiping a wet trail up Phil's shaft. Phil let out a whimper which would've been embarrassing if he hadn't been so lost in the feel of that damn tongue stud dragging over the sensitive underside of his prick. He dug both hands into James's hair, concentrating on the cool silkiness between his fingers to keep himself from shooting like a teenager.

James noticed Phil's difficulty, if the look on his face was any indication. With a swift, wicked smile, he opened wide and let Phil push his head downward.

Phil stared, mesmerized, as his entire cock disappeared inch by inch into James's mouth. He hadn't even dared to let himself hope James could deep throat this easily. Not when the man was already his fantasy come to life. This night just kept getting better and better.

James pulled off with an audible *pop* and gazed up at Phil, eyes wide and hazy with lust. "Can you take it, Drake?"

Phil swallowed twice and managed to answer with surprising coherence. "Yeah. Do that again."

Licking his lips, James gulped Phil down until his face was buried in Phil's pubes. In the glare of the overhead light, Phil could just make out a faint sprinkling of golden freckles on that adorable snub nose.

Phil narrowed his eyes. James's deceptively innocent face, the blond hair and porcelain skin and huge blue eyes, reminded him of something. Or rather, some*one*. He couldn't quite put his finger on it. Figuring the mental exercise would keep him from coming before he was ready, he studied the cherubic face currently buried in his crotch with an eye to figuring out who James reminded him of.

Hopefully it wouldn't be anyone whose memory would kill the mood. Lord knew Phil had been with his share of pretty-but-forceful men in his search for The Perfect Lay.

It was the way James drew back and beamed up at him, lips red and swollen and eyes glowing, that finally did it. When the connection hit him, Phil didn't know whether to laugh or cry, it was so unexpected. Bunching his hands in James's hair, he drew the shining strands into two short ponytails. The resemblance to his favorite Powerpuff Girl was uncanny, in spite of the leather outfit and unmistakably male body. Laughter won out, and he giggled in a most unmanly fashion.

James did not seem amused. He surged to his feet, one hand clutching Phil's sac, and squeezed hard enough to make Phil yelp. "What's so fucking funny?"

Phil blinked. God, the dangerous glint in James's eyes was enough to make him come all by itself. Thankfully, his fingers were just tight enough on Phil's balls to be painful, which had the fortunate effect of keeping his orgasm at bay.

"Bubbles," Phil panted, fighting back another attack of the giggles. "You're Bubbles."

James stared at him like he'd grown a second head. "Bubbles? What the fuck are you talking about?"

Unable to articulate it any better, Phil pointed at the picture of the three kindergarten-age cartoon heroines on his T-shirt. James looked down. His eyes went wide, that sweet, sexy mouth falling open, and Phil knew he'd seen the similarity.

James's pale face flushed deep pink. He pressed closer, fingers kneading Phil's testicles. "Listen here, you freak," he growled, his gaze boring holes into Phil's skull. "I am *not* a little girl. Plenty of people have made that mistake in the past. They've learned their lesson. Am I clear?"

*Perfectly clear,* Phil's brain enthused. *Just because you're small and blond and blue-eyed and have that precious, innocent little face, doesn't mean you can't fuck me till I can't walk straight. I realize this, and look forward to you showing me just how much of a man you are.*

What actually came out was a high-pitched squeak. Phil couldn't bring himself to care.

James's mouth curled into a feral smile. "Undress, and get on the bed. On your back with your legs spread." He let go of Phil's balls and stepped back. "Now."

Phil scrambled to obey. He toed off his sneakers, wriggled out of the tight jeans and tore off the T-shirt, his spirit singing the Hallelujah Chorus the whole time. *Hell,* he thought, sprawling on his back on the bed and opening his thighs wide, *if calling him Bubbles makes him this dominant, I'm gonna do it all night.*

James kept his blazing gaze trained on Phil's face as he took off his boots and skinned out of the leather pants. Naked, the box of Trojans in his hand, he stalked to the bed and crawled between Phil's splayed legs. His skin gleamed in the light.

"Get ready for the fuck of your life, Drake." The look in James's eyes suggested he could read Phil's mind, and his next murmured words confirmed it. "And don't you dare call me Bubbles, or so help me I'll kick your ass right out of my bed."

Phil grinned. *We'll see about that.*

# Chapter Three

In Thom's dream, he lay naked on his stomach on top of the bar where he used to work in Santa Fe. Something large, warm and furry was wrapped around his body, making him feel safe and comfortable in spite of being nude on a bar with strangers crowded all around. And there were plenty of strangers. The room was packed. The voices of the patrons sounded like rushing traffic and pounding footsteps.

An old woman turned to him, cat's-eye glasses glinting in the surprisingly bright light, and shrieked like a toddler. Thom frowned and squirmed. The old woman's voice was annoying. Thankfully, she sniffed and went back to brushing the tiny dog on her lap. Thom pulled the big, heavy blanket tighter around himself and snuggled in with a sigh.

To his supreme disappointment, the blanket stirred and peeled itself off of him. He whimpered. The blanket rumbled at him and slithered down his back. Something soft brushed Thom's skin. The blanket must have fringe, he figured. The fringe tickled Thom's butt, and his dream self giggled, something he never allowed himself to do when awake.

The blanket pushed Thom's thighs apart and huddled between them. It felt good, Thom decided. He hadn't realized the blanket was *alive,* but what the hell. It was a dream. He'd learned to enjoy the good ones when they came.

31

He bent his left knee and wriggled until his ass was pressed tight against the firm, somewhat scratchy material. Then he wriggled some more, because the movement rubbed his erection against the unusually soft and springy bar and that felt *really* good.

"Mmmm," the blanket growled from between Thom's legs. "Nice."

A puff of warm air accompanied the words, making his balls draw up. Now that was odd. Blankets, Thom had found, did not generally speak.

Blankets also did not generally spread a guy's butt cheeks apart and lap at his hole with a slick, wet tongue.

*This is one hell of a blanket.* With a low moan, Thom lifted his hips to meet the eager coverlet's unexpected oral appendage.

"Fuuuuck," the blanket moaned, drawing the word out by several syllables. "I knew this sweet little ass would taste good." Another lick, followed by something scratchy rubbing up and down Thom's crack. "Goddamn, Bubbles. So fucking hot."

Bubbles?

He'd heard that before. Last night. The tall, rangy man with the easy grin and the weird T-shirt and the spark of wickedness in his hazel eyes. The man who'd dubbed him Bubbles in that honey-and-whiskey drawl. The man whose hungry ass and "I'll try anything twice" attitude had saved him from being kicked out into the street after pointing out Thom's resemblance to a cartoon kindergarten girl.

The man who was definitely *not* a blanket, and was currently devouring Thom's asshole with impressive enthusiasm.

*Oh, my God. I'm not dreaming anymore.*

Thom's eyes flew open. He was in his hotel room, sprawled facedown on top of the tangled bedclothes. Outside, traffic whizzed past. Footsteps pounded past the door of his room, and a child shouted something about going to the pool.

He took in the sunshine pouring through the window and the inside-out clothes scattered across the floor in the space of a breath. Then Drake's tongue wormed itself inside him, and he decided he could berate the man for calling him Bubbles later, when he wasn't this close to shooting his load.

Thom raised his rear into the air and grabbed his cock, pumping hard and fast. "Yes. God. Almost."

Drake made that delightful rumbling noise again, his beard rasping against Thom's ass cheeks. "Yeah. C'mon, sweet thing."

The final word emerged sounding like "thang". For some reason, Thom found it unbearably exciting. He came with a keening wail, rubbing his ass shamelessly on Drake's face.

His orgasm seemed to last for ages. He rode it to completion, shuddering from head to foot. Drake kissed him on both buttocks as the last of the semen dribbled from his cock. Thom felt the mattress move, Drake's warmth disappearing from the insides of his legs.

"Shit, Drake." Thom flopped onto the mattress, forgetting all about the wet spot. Thick, warm liquid squelched under his stomach. Grimacing, he rolled to the side. "Hell of a way to wake a guy up."

"Couldn't help myself." Drake's face came into view above him, grinning like the cat that got the canary. His hair, freed from the braid at some point during the night's romp, fell in wild waves around his shoulders and spilled down to tickle Thom's chest. "You just looked so damn sweet, lying there with that pretty ass just begging me to take a taste." The grin widened, the hazel eyes twinkling. "Don't tell me you didn't like it, Bubbles, 'cause I *know* you did."

*Christ on a fucking pogo stick, not again.* Thom felt his face flush, his scalp tingling like it always did when he was angry. "I thought I told you not to call me that," he ground out, frowning up into Drake's smiling face.

Drake's gaze turned hot and heavy. "God, you're cute when you're mad."

Thom wanted to protest. He despised being called cute, mostly because he knew it was true and wished it wasn't. And since when did "cute" make any normal person look the way Drake did right now, anyway? Intense, hungry. Like he wanted to eat Thom alive.

To his surprise, Thom felt his anger drain away in the heat of Drake's lust. That *never* happened. The only reason he could figure for his inability to sustain his righteous fury was Drake's undeniable hotness, and the fact that he was a fantastic fuck.

Thom took a good look at Drake's nude body, appreciating it all over again in the daylight. It was a nice body, for sure, all sleek muscle and tanned skin. Light brown hair downed the wide chest and flat, rippled belly and formed a thick pelt all over those long, lean legs.

*Fuck, he's hot.* Setting aside (for the moment) his indignation over being dubbed Bubbles, Thom snatched a handful of Drake's shining golden brown tresses and tugged him down into a deep kiss.

Drake groaned. One strong arm snaked beneath Thom's body, pulling him tight against Drake's chest. He rolled, ending up on his back with Thom on top of him.

"You got me hard as a fucking rock, pretty baby," Drake whispered against Thom's mouth. One big hand cupped Thom's ass, the other slid into his hair. "Are you too pissed off to take care of me?"

"No." Thom lifted up enough to curl his fingers around Drake's shaft. God, it was thick. "Just don't call me...you know, *that.*"

That infuriatingly appealing I'm-up-to-no-good grin curved the corners of Drake's mouth. "You got it, angel face."

Thom wrinkled his nose, but didn't protest. This was probably the best he was going to get, and he found he didn't want to kick Drake to the curb. The man revved his motor like no one had in years.

*As long as he doesn't call me* that name, *he's gold,* Thom promised himself, pressing a fingertip against the slit in the tip of Drake's cock and basking in the resulting moan.

Settling his knees on either side of Drake's hips, Thom sat back on the man's thighs and started stroking his prick. Drake groaned and pushed up into Thom's touch.

"Mmmmm," Thom purred, watching the waves of pleasure roll over Drake's face. "Your cock feels so good in my hand. So hot. I can smell it." He bent down, planting his free hand on the mattress to hold his weight, and stared straight into Drake's eyes. "Did it turn you on to eat my ass, Drake?"

Drake nodded, his breath coming quick and short. "Uh-huh."

"Thought so." Thom stroked faster, harder, rubbing his thumb across the head of Drake's prick. "You want to come?"

Drake's eyes went unfocused. "God. Yeah."

Leaning closer, Thom brushed his lips against Drake's. "Come, then. Come on my hand."

A tremor ran through Drake's body. "James," he moaned, and came, his hips bucking so hard he nearly threw Thom off.

Thom was so enthralled by the sight of Drake caught up in the rush of orgasm that he almost didn't notice what the man had called him. His brow furrowed. Why had Drake called him James?

It took him a moment to remember that was the name he'd given Drake last night. He shoved the flash of guilt quickly away. So what if James wasn't the name he generally went by? It's not like it wasn't his name at all. It was just his middle name, not his first.

A low chuckle drew him out of his thoughts. He blinked and focused on Drake's flushed, sweat-dewed face. Those sexy bedroom eyes gazed into his, making him feel hot and squirmy inside. Damn, the man really was gorgeous, in a flower-child sort of way.

"What're you thinking, sweet thing?" Drake trailed his fingers down Thom's cheek. "You look awfully damn serious."

Thom caught himself just in time to keep from rubbing his cheek against Drake's palm. The tenderness in Drake's caress seemed wrong somehow. One-night stands never touched him like that, and the fact that he *liked* it so much frankly freaked him out.

Glancing sideways, Thom got a look at the clock, and found his automatic excuse to get out of this uncomfortably comfortable situation.

"It's almost nine thirty. I have to go to work in an hour." He sat up, ignoring Drake's hands clutching at him, and scooted off the bed. "What about you? Don't you have to work?"

"Naw, I'm off for a couple of weeks. I'm renovating my house." Drake slid to the edge of the bed, stood and stretched. "But I get what you're saying. Time for me to hit the road, huh?"

Thom almost said no. What he really wanted to do right then was tackle Drake to the bed and explore every inch of golden skin with his tongue.

If the teasing gleam in Drake's eyes was anything to go by,

he knew exactly what Thom was thinking. Which ultimately was what stopped Thom from giving in to his libido. Mornings after usually found Thom either already alone, or quite anxious to become so. He didn't like the unfamiliar urge to *keep* this one.

"Sorry," Thom said, giving Drake a bland smile. "I'm starting a new job today and I can't afford to be late."

"I hear you." Plopping onto the edge of the bed, Drake snagged his jeans off the floor. He shot a curious glance at Thom as he unwadded the jeans and pulled them right side out again. "So, are you new in town? That why you're staying in a hotel?"

"Uh-huh." Thom sauntered over to the closet, opened it and perused his limited wardrobe with a critical eye. He could feel Drake's gaze on him, making his skin tingle, and fought the urge to cover his naked butt with his hands. It wasn't like Drake hadn't already seen—and touched, and now licked— every inch of him.

Silence. Thom stood there, half of his brain deciding what to wear and the other half wondering what Drake was doing. After a moment, he heard a rustling behind him as Drake dressed, then the sound of a zipper being drawn up. Footsteps whispered across the carpet. Long arms wrapped around his waist, pulling him snug against Drake's chest.

Thom let himself lean into Drake's embrace. It felt good. Natural. Which was *wrong,* dammit. He shouldn't feel this comfortable with a one-nighter.

"I'd ask for your number, but something tells me you wouldn't give it to me." Drake bent and mouthed the shell of Thom's ear. A hank of his wavy hair fell across Thom's chest. "Maybe I'll see you around?"

"Mm. Maybe." Turning in Drake's arms, Thom stood on tiptoe, wound both arms around his neck and kissed him. "Last night was great, Drake. So was this morning. Thanks."

"My pleasure, believe me." Drake pulled away with a smile. "You're a hell of a lay, Bubbles."

Thom grimaced. "Goddammit, I told you not to call me that."

"Oh yeah? Whatcha gonna do about it, sweet baby?"

For reasons Thom didn't want to examine, Drake's taunt made Thom forgive him at once. Grinning, Thom lunged for Drake, intending to give him the spanking he clearly craved.

He scampered out of reach, laughing. "You want to play some more, come to Belial's any Friday night. I'll be there." He opened the door and stood there for a second, his gaze burning holes in Thom's skull. "See you around, Bubbles."

Drake strode out into the hall without looking back. Thom stared at the door, his guts churning with a weird mix of emotions. In a way, he was relieved to see Drake go, because the things the man made him feel did not sit well with him. But the hollowness in his chest made him want to run after Drake and ask if they could see each other again.

He didn't understand why he felt this way, and he didn't like things he didn't understand.

Scowling, he stomped into the bathroom and started the shower. There was no time for soul searching this morning. He had a new job to go to, and then he *had* to find a place to live.

*Fuck, I don't have a place to live.*

He sighed as he stepped under the warm spray. Maybe Circe could point him toward an available place, preferably one with a low-to-non-existent deposit. Or maybe she could advance him enough money to reserve another hotel room. At the worst, he'd have to stay in the homeless shelter until he built up enough money to rent a place.

"You've survived worse," he reminded himself. "Where there's an income, there's a way."

Shoving the nagging worry to the back of his mind, he set about washing Drake's musk-and-sweat scent off of his skin.

# Chapter Four

Ten days after the most mind-blowing sex of his life, Phil woke to the joyous realization that today was the day he returned to The Happy Onion.

"Finally," he muttered, heaving himself out of bed and shuffling toward the bathroom.

Phil knew most people didn't look forward to going back to work, especially after being off for two weeks. He even understood it. After all, the vast majority of the country's workforce seemed to be stuck in jobs for which they had no real enthusiasm. Phil, however, *loved* The Happy Onion. Being away from The HO, as it was affectionately known around town, made him twitchy even under the best of circumstances. And the past ten days had definitely *not* qualified as the best of circumstances.

The back-breaking labor of renovating an eighty-year-old house wasn't the problem. If he'd been allergic to hard work, owning and managing a restaurant would've killed him years ago. No, it was the persistent memories that made him unable to stand his own company for one more day. Memories of gleaming platinum hair and lust-hazed blue eyes and the sweetest body Phil had ever had the pleasure of clutching between his legs.

From the moment he'd left James's bed, Phil hadn't been

able to think of anything else, and it was driving him crazy. Painting and laying floors didn't provide nearly enough mental distraction. Hopefully The HO would.

By eight o'clock, Phil was peddling his bike away from his Montford-district home toward his restaurant in the heart of downtown Asheville. He could've taken his car, but he much preferred to reduce his personal carbon footprint when he could. Besides, the level of concentration needed to make it to work alive in the morning rush hour kept him from mooning over James.

He glided down the narrow alley running behind The Happy Onion with a profound sense of relief. After chaining his bike to the red metal rack, he dug his keys out of the messenger bag slung over his shoulder and unlocked the back door. He stepped inside with a big grin on his face and bumped the door shut with his hip.

"Hello, HO," he exclaimed, dropping his bag on the floor and flinging his arms wide. "Did you miss me, baby? I sure as fuck missed you."

The cluttered storage room, predictably, did not answer. Phil didn't mind. This cozy little place never failed to speak to him in its own way.

Picking up his bag, he unlocked the tiny office in the corner, tossed the bag on the chair behind his desk and checked his voice mail. There were three messages. He scribbled a note to Circe to call her dentist's office and confirm her appointment for the next day, deleted the message from the giggling drunk wanting to know if someone named "Jay-Dawg" could call him back, and shook his head at the one from Circe apologizing for giving her dentist the work number.

Laughing, he sauntered out of the office and through the kitchen. Damn, it was good to be back.

Out in the restaurant, he put Clap Your Hands Say Yeah on the boom box and started setting up the place for the lunch crowd. Circe would probably be arriving soon, so he could've gone back to the office and hit the books—should have, most likely—but he didn't want to. If he tried staring at a spreadsheet right now, his mind would wander like it always did when he wrangled numbers, and he'd end up jerking off to the memory of James's cock up his ass. He kind of doubted Circe would appreciate walking in on that.

If she *did* appreciate it, he definitely did not want to know.

He was bouncing along to "Satan Said Dance" when Circe arrived. She shimmied up to him, grinning. "Hey, Phil. Welcome back. How're the renovations coming along?"

"Great. Got all the painting and most of the flooring done." He hooked an arm around her waist and whirled her across the floor, laughing when he nearly tripped over a chair. "I'm glad to be back though. So what's been happening here? Anything exciting?"

"I hired a bartender." Letting go of Phil's hand, Circe bopped around behind the bar. "He's good. The customers love him."

"Awesome." Phil perched on a barstool, watching Circe pour herself a glass of water from the tap. "What's his name? Is he working today?"

"Thom Stone, and yes. Should be in soon, as a matter of fact. He's shown up early practically every day and works 'til after closing."

"A guy with a solid work ethic. Sweet." A sudden thought made Phil frown. "Wait, I'm not paying him overtime, am I?"

"Yes, you are. And he's worth every penny, so don't complain." Sipping her water, Circe strolled out from behind the bar and hopped onto the barstool beside Phil's. "Tory's been sick this week, so I've been short one during lunch and through the afternoon. Thom's been filling in for her. When she gets back he'll be working exclusively evenings and nights."

"So the overtime's only temporary?"

"Yep."

"Good."

"Scrooge," Circe accused, wrinkling her nose.

Phil laid a hand over his heart. "Ouch."

Laughing, she jumped off the stool and planted a kiss on the top of Phil's head. "Go take care of all the boss stuff I know for a fact is waiting for you in your office. I'll finish up out here."

"Yes, ma'am." Phil stood and headed toward the back of the restaurant. "Let me know when Thom gets here, okay?"

"Sure thing."

"Thanks."

Circe waved at him before disappearing into the tiny nook which served as a wait station. Chuckling, Phil sauntered through the kitchen. The head cook, Helene, had arrived while Phil was out front. She nodded her usual taciturn greeting in response to his cheerful hello.

Humming under his breath, Phil pushed open the swinging door from the kitchen to the back room. He felt it hit something. A muffled curse sounded from the other side.

*Shit.* Who in the hell had he hit?

Easing the door open, Phil slipped through. "Hey, I'm sorry, I didn't mean to—" He stopped, his mouth falling open. "Oh, sweet holy hell. Bubbles?"

Enormous blue eyes fixed him with a glare that could kill at fifty paces. "Do. Not. Call. Me. *Bubbles*. Asshole."

The growl in James's voice made Phil's knees weak. He

clutched at the door for support, hoping James wouldn't notice the sudden swelling at his crotch. "Sorry. You okay?"

"You jammed my finger with the door." James held up one slender finger. The tip was already bruising. "I'll live. What the fuck are you doing here, anyway?"

"This is my place." Phil took James's hand and inspected the injured digit. "You want some ice for that?"

"No thanks." James snatched his hand back. The death glare turned into something rather more cautious. "What do you mean, 'your place'?"

Phil took James's hand again, lifted it to his lips and kissed the bruised fingertip. "My place, as in I own it."

James's face went an unhealthy shade of grayish white. "You're fucking with me."

"Nope. Though I wouldn't mind you fucking with *me* again." Tilting his head, Phil studied James's shocked face. "So why are *you* here? Coming in through the back door, yet?" He grinned. "So to speak."

James just stared. He didn't even try to retrieve his hand.

Worried now, Phil stepped closer. "James? What is it?"

James swallowed. "I... I'm...uh..."

At that moment, the door swung open again, hitting the backs of Phil's legs. Phil stepped aside and Circe emerged. "Oops, sorry, Phil. I didn't know you were there." She caught sight of James, and her face lit up. "Oh, I see you've met Thom!"

Phil turned to "James", eyebrows raised. "Thom?"

The man didn't even have the good grace to blush. He twisted his hand in Phil's and shook it. "Thomas *James* Stone. Circe hired me for the bartender job." A sly look slid through his eyes. "Let me guess. Philip *Drake* Sorrells."

Phil cringed. Circe gasped. "Oh my Goddess, Thom, how'd

44

you know that? I never told you Phil's middle name."

"Lucky guess." James—no, *Thom*—pulled his hand from Phil's and stepped back. "Now if you'll excuse me, I'll just go make sure the bar's set up for lunch."

With one last icy glare in Phil's direction, Thom stalked through the kitchen door. It swung back and forth in his wake.

Frowning, Circe turned to stare after him. "What the heck's got into him?"

Phil shrugged. "I hit him with the door. It was an accident, but still. I'd be pissed too, if it was me."

She narrowed her eyes, apparently unconvinced by his attempt at nonchalance. "Yeah, maybe, but he's *really* mad, I can tell. He doesn't usually get so upset about stuff like that." Her hand flew to her mouth. "Oh shit, please tell me you didn't hit on him."

Phil had to laugh. Circe knew his taste in men far too well. "No, Circe, I didn't hit on him." It wasn't really a lie. He *hadn't* hit on Thom just now. Ten days ago didn't count.

Circe's expression said she didn't entirely believe him, but she didn't push it. "He's renting the room upstairs, I hope that's okay. He needed a place, like, right away. You need to sign the lease to make it official."

"Yeah, that's cool." *Bedroom right up the stairs just outside the back door? Hell yeah, I'd say that's pretty fucking cool.*

She gave him a stern look. "I know what you're thinking."

"I'm sure." Phil stuck his hands in his pockets and tried to look unconcerned. "Oh, your dentist called. You need to call back and confirm your appointment."

"Yeah, okay. Don't change the subject." She shook one delicate finger under his nose. "Thom is your employee, Phil. Do *not* try to get into his pants."

*Too late.* Forcing back the memories of James—no, *Thom*—fucking him into sweet oblivion, Phil schooled his face into a reasonable facsimile of innocence. "I swear I'll be good." He planted his left hand over his heart and raised his right. "Scout's honor."

She patted his shoulder and headed for the employee restroom tucked into the corner opposite the office. "Phil, honey, you were never a Boy Scout."

Laughing, Phil sauntered across the room and into his office. Maybe if he buried himself deep enough in the pile of paperwork on his desk he could resist the urge to run to the bar and molest his newest employee.

Maybe. Hopefully.

A sudden image flashed into his mind. Thom, naked and sound asleep in the rumpled hotel bed, giggling in his dreams when Phil's hair brushed the backs of his bare thighs. The memory of that sweet little sound, so beautifully at odds with Thom's tough-guy persona, still had the power to turn Phil's legs to jelly.

Leaning against the wall of his office, he shut his eyes and thought of Thom kneeling at his feet, mouth stretched wide around his cock and eyes blazing up at him. Phil's cock swelled, and he swallowed a moan.

*I am so fucked,* he thought, palming his erection through his cargo shorts. *This is bad. Very, very bad.*

8°

*Fuck, this is bad. Bad, bad, bad. Damn it.*

Thom scrubbed furiously at the sticky spot on the bar. Or, well, what used to be a sticky spot. After twenty minutes of

Thom taking out his frustrations on the bar, all stickiness was long gone and the entire wooden length shone like a mirror.

He didn't care. The fury, the fear and especially the thrice-damned, annoying *desire*, had to be worked out somehow, or he'd end up exploding at a customer. If Phil the Boss was anything like Phil the Insatiable Sex Monster, he'd be reasonable enough to let it go with a warning, but Thom didn't feel like betting his job on that. He still hoped the Rosewood job would come through, but for now he had an income and a temporary home, and he had no intention of risking either just because he was pissed off. Never mind that he had a fucking right to be *royally* pissed off.

*Why? Because the two of you hooked up before either of you knew you were working for him? That's not his fault any more than it is yours. Maybe he's just as shaken up by this as you are. You could at least give him a chance.*

Thom wrinkled his nose. He hated it when his inner voice guilted away his righteous anger.

He turned to look at the clock behind the bar. Another hour until they opened. Plenty of time to go find Phil and apologize for being a gigantic jackass.

With a put-upon sigh, he hung the rag on a hook behind the bar and stomped across the restaurant toward the kitchen. "I'm going to talk to Phil," he said to Mike, the busboy, who'd been watching him with the wary expression of a mouse trapped behind the sofa by a hungry tabby. "Everything's ready to go. I'll be back in a few minutes."

Mike nodded, brown eyes wide and thin shoulders hunched. Thom shook his head as he stalked across the floor. The kid really needed to grow a pair.

In the kitchen, Circe was writing the lunch specials in bright green marker on a couple of dry erase boards. He nodded in response to her smile, but didn't stop to talk. If he didn't say what he had to say to Phil right now, he'd lose his nerve for sure.

Phil's office door was closed. Thom crossed the storeroom and stood in front of it, heart hammering and knees shaking, and tried to summon the courage to knock. He didn't mind apologizing for being a jerk, and he didn't think for a second that Phil would try anything unethical. Phil wasn't the type of person who would use his position as the boss to extort sex from his employees.

No, Thom's biggest fear was much simpler. If Phil touched him again, or gave him that slow, wicked smile, he wouldn't be able to stop himself from having the man right there in the office. The tip of his finger still burned with the lingering warmth of Phil's kiss.

*God, his lips are so fucking soft.*

Grimacing, Thom shook off the haze of desire threatening to overpower him. *Get it together, Thom. Just knock on the door, and when he opens it, say you're sorry, shake his hand and go back to work. You can do this.*

He drew a deep breath, blew it out and lifted his hand. Before his knuckles could make contact with the scarred wood, however, the door opened, and Thom found himself face-to-collarbone with Phil.

Thom looked up to meet Phil's gaze. "Um. Hi."

"Hey." Phil gave him a cautious smile. "What's up, Bu...I mean, Thom?"

"I, uh, I just wanted to say I'm sorry. For how I acted before." Thom wiped his damp palms on his jeans. "So, yeah. Sorry. I was surprised, is all."

Phil's smile widened. "No problem. I was kind of surprised myself."

The mischievous twinkle in Phil's hazel eyes had Thom's head whirling with thoughts completely inappropriate for the workplace. He swallowed, fighting the urge to shove his hand inside those ridiculous black cargo shorts Phil wore and wrap his fingers around the man's impressive prick. "Okay. Well, bye."

Thom turned to go. A big hand clamped onto his arm, stopping him in his tracks. "Where're you going?" Phil voice rumbled behind him, far too close for comfort.

"Back to work." Thom winced at the transparent lust in his voice. "Please let go."

Phil's hand fell away, but the solid warmth of his body pressed to Thom's back, freezing him in place. "You know I won't hold this over you, right?" Phil's breath stirred the hair at Thom's temple when he spoke.

"I know." Thom smiled over his shoulder. "It's just kind of strange working for someone who's had his tongue up your ass, you know?"

A low, needy sound emerged from somewhere deep in Phil's chest. He rested one open palm on Thom's hip. "I want you," he whispered, stray wisps of silky hair brushing Thom's ear. "And I'm not afraid to go after what I want. But I won't ever pressure you. If you want to end it right here, right now, just be friends, I'm cool with that." His head dipped, his lips nuzzling Thom's neck. "You want me, though, you just say the word."

A polite but firm request to end any possibility of more sex between them was on the tip of Thom's tongue. Then Phil's hand slid up and forward, his thumb slipped between the buttons of Thom's shirt to caress bare skin, and that was all Thom could take.

Whipping around, Thom grabbed Phil's head in both hands, craned his neck and captured Phil's lips in a bruising kiss. Phil's mouth opened wide for Thom's tongue. One arm crushed Thom's body to his, the other hand fisting in Thom's hair.

He didn't even seem surprised by Thom's sudden change of heart. Thom thought he ought to find that insulting, but couldn't be bothered to worry about it right then.

"Inside," Thom growled when the kiss finally broke. "Now."

Phil's eyes went dark, his cheeks pinking above his neatly trimmed beard. To Thom's shock—and secret delight—Phil lifted him right off his feet. Thom clamped his legs around Phil's waist and fastened his mouth to Phil's. Groaning, Phil staggered backward into his office, kicked the door shut, turned around and set Thom gently on his feet against the wall.

Before Thom could translate the pornographic pictures in his head into a coherent request, Phil fell to his knees and mouthed Thom's crotch through his jeans. Thom let out an embarrassing whimper. "God..."

Phil grinned up at him, long fingers working his fly open. "Wanna taste you, pretty baby. Okay?"

"Ohmyfucking*God*yes." Thom canted his hips up in a bid to make Phil's hands work faster.

Holding Thom's gaze, Phil yanked Thom's zipper open and shoved his jeans and underwear down around his thighs. Thom moaned, back arching away from the wall. He thought he might die on the spot if he didn't get his prick inside Phil's mouth *right fucking now*.

One hand cupping Thom's balls, Phil leaned forward and drew a deep breath. "Mmmm. You smell so good." He licked a wet stripe up Thom's shaft. "Taste good too."

Thom let out a sharp gasp when Phil's tongue curled around the head of his cock. "Jesus, Phil, *please*!"

Phil's teasing expression vanished in a wave of pure lust. With one last smoldering look up at Thom, Phil opened wide and sucked Thom's cock right down.

"Oh fucking shit, fuck, fuck yeah..." Thom threaded his fingers into Phil's hair, holding on for dear life. He felt like he might come unglued any second. Damned if Phil wasn't even better than Thom remembered. Which was saying a lot, considering how fondly—and how often—he relived those memories. Mental images of his prick buried in Phil's mouth or pumping away at his ass had become Thom's favorite masturbatory fantasy lately.

Even the most vivid memory couldn't compare to the real thing, though, and soon enough Thom was coming down Phil's throat, shuddering from head to toe and moaning like a cheap whore. It wasn't until the aftershocks ebbed away that he realized Phil had not only swallowed, but had swallowed so thoroughly that not one drop of spunk had spilled on either of them. It was pretty impressive.

The second Phil drew back and Thom's softened cock popped from his mouth, Thom dropped to the floor. He grinned at Phil's dazed expression, figuring it probably matched his own pretty well. "Damn, I needed that."

A lazy smile curled Phil's swollen lips. "My pleasure. Believe me."

Thom was glad he was already on the floor, because that filthy I-just-sucked-your-cock smile made his legs shake.

He glanced down between Phil's thighs. His shorts were undone, his erection jutting out. One hand was clamped around the shaft.

Thom's mouth watered. Obeying a sudden, irresistible urge, he bent and slid the wide, leaking head between his lips and deep into his throat.

"Oooooh, yeeeaaaah." Phil's fingers sank into Thom's hair, kneading his scalp. "Yeah, angel. Feels good."

The sultry purr in Phil's voice sent shivers racing along Thom's skin. Closing his eyes, he let Phil's earthy male scent surround him while he sucked for all he was worth. Phil mewled like an overgrown kitten, hips pumping and hands clutching Thom's hair in a nearly painful grip.

Thom would've moaned if he hadn't had his throat full of cock. He loved the feel of Phil holding his head still and fucking his mouth. Not that he would ever tell Phil that. The man already had the capacity to reduce Thom to a quivering puddle of goo with no more than a glance from those sinful bedroom eyes. Thom wasn't about to let Phil know exactly how much power he really had.

Far too soon for Thom's taste, Phil tensed, groaned and spilled in Thom's mouth. Thom gulped as fast as he could, trying to keep up with what seemed like gallons of semen spurting into his throat. His inner safe-sex fanatic frowned at him, but he ignored it. He and Phil had talked enough the last time to reassure Thom that Phil was just as clean as he was. They'd even shared test results, and had a good laugh at the realization that they both carried their results with them to pick-up joints.

When the come finally stopped, well, coming, Thom straightened up, licking his lips. He didn't even have the chance to say a word before Phil dragged him close and kissed him. He opened gladly, his arms winding around Phil's neck.

It wasn't until they drew apart that the enormity of what he'd just done slammed home in Thom's brain. He'd attacked his *boss. During work*, for fuck's sake. They'd sucked each other off, right there on the miniscule square of unoccupied floor in Phil's office.

At work.

That part bore repeating.

Pushing out of Phil's embrace, Thom scrambled to his feet and wrestled his clothes into place. "Jesus, Phil, why'd you let me do that? Why didn't you stop me?"

Phil blinked, the hurt plain as day in his eyes. "You didn't want to suck me?"

Thom gave himself a mental smack. *Good job, asshole, you hurt his feelings. Fix it.*

"No, that's not what I meant. Or, well, it kind of is, but not exactly." Frustrated, Thom ran a hand through his hair. "Look, I wanted to suck you, or I wouldn't have done it. But we shouldn't be doing this sort of shit, especially not at the restaurant."

Understanding dawned in Phil's eyes. Rising to his feet with enviable grace, he tucked his limp cock back into his shorts and zipped up. "You're right. We shouldn't be having sex at work. I'm the boss, I should've stopped it before it started."

"Yeah. Okay." Thom stuck his hands in his pockets, feeling supremely uncomfortable. "So, um, I'm sorry for jumping you like that. It won't happen again."

Phil nodded, but said nothing.

Unable to meet Phil's sharp, penetrating gaze, Thom turned away. He opened the door and walked across the storeroom toward the kitchen door.

"Thanks for the memories, sweet thing."

Thom stopped mid-stride, heat pooling in his belly. God, but it did things to him when Phil called him "sweet thang" in that smoky, molasses-thick accent. Made him want to run straight back into that office, rip Phil's clothes off and bend him over the desk.

*Down, boy. He's your boss, which means he can't be your lover. Get over it.*

Thom half turned and managed what he hoped was a casual smile. He gave Phil a quick nod, but didn't dare meet his gaze. It scared him how little control he apparently had around Phil.

*Damn the sexy bastard to the pit.*

Squaring his shoulders, he marched out of the storeroom, through the kitchen and into the restaurant. He had work to do.

# Chapter Five

Over the next week and a half, Phil and Thom fell into a routine of sorts. Every morning, Phil greeted Thom with a polite hello and his very best fuck-me-across-my-desk-now smile. And every morning, Thom returned Phil's cordial salutation, along with a frustrated glare. He never really lost his temper—a feat whose true enormity Phil was only beginning to appreciate—but the exasperation in his eyes gave him away.

Phil knew he was playing with fire, but he couldn't help it. The rosy flush that suffused Thom's adorable face when he was angry made Phil's heart flutter like an overexcited moth.

August was almost over by the time Tory came back to work after an unexpectedly extended bout with pneumonia. Thom worked alongside her for a couple of days before going back to the evening shift for which he'd been hired. The day Thom stopped working overtime was the longest day of Phil's life. By the time Thom arrived at three o'clock that afternoon, Phil felt about ready to jump out of his skin.

"Hey, Thom," Phil called as Thom sauntered past the open office door. "How's it going?"

Thom shot him a wary glance. "Fine."

He kept walking. Phil stood and followed him. "So. You glad to be off overtime?"

"I guess. The extra money was nice, though."

Thom kept his back to Phil, but Phil sensed his discomfort. Sighing, Phil laid both hands on Thom's shoulders and gently turned him around. "Look, Thom, I'm sorry. You've made it pretty clear that you're not interested in continuing anything between us. I haven't exactly respected that, and I'm sorry. I really didn't mean to push myself on you."

Thom's tight expression softened into a wry smile. "You didn't. I'm just suspicious and defensive. Always have been."

Phil let his mouth curve into the grin that always made Thom's cheeks pink with better things than anger. "Hey, don't apologize for being who you are. I like it, personally. You're sexy when you're mad."

*And here we go*, Phil thought as Thom's eyes narrowed with indignation. Thom stepped closer and glared up at Phil. "I didn't apologize. And I am *not*—" he jabbed Phil's chest with one finger, "sexy." He whirled around, put a hand on the kitchen door, then dropped it and turned to face Phil again, blue eyes snapping. "When I'm mad. I'm not sexy when I'm mad." Pivoting around, he shoved the kitchen door open and stomped through.

Phil waited, grinning. A second later, Thom came through the door again, quivering with fury. "No, you know what? I take that back. I *am* sexy when I'm mad. I'm sexy *all the fucking time!*"

Phil half expected him to say "so there" and stick his tongue out, but he didn't. Instead, he kicked the door open so hard it hit the kitchen wall with a resounding bang, then strode off in high temper.

The second Thom was out of sight, Phil leaned against the wall and tried to calm his racing pulse. Part of him felt horribly guilty about goading Thom like he had. The rest of him liked the results far too much to care. And what the hell was wrong with him anyway, that he felt this irresistible urge to stir up trouble every time Thom seemed to soften toward him?

*Phil, you are so sick. You're going to end up making him hate you. Is it really worth risking that, just because his mad face turns you on like crazy?*

He might not have ever been good at tests, but he knew the answer to that question all right. Hot as it was when Thom's fiery temper got away with him, Phil would rather they remained friends.

Actually, he'd rather they moved on and became lovers. *Real* lovers, with a real relationship, rather than occasional fuck-buddies. But he knew that wasn't likely to happen. If a purely platonic friendship with Thom was the only way to keep him around, Phil wanted it.

Maybe one day Thom would get over this crazy idea that they couldn't be together and give in to the mutual attraction that already went beyond the physical.

*You know what you have to do. Apologize. And this time, don't fuck it up.*

Pushing away from the wall, Phil squared his shoulders and steeled himself to face the livid little blond.

He walked through the bustling kitchen to the far corner, where an archway led to the area behind the bar. Just inside the arch, he stopped short, staring at the drama unfolding a few feet away. A patron had evidently gotten a little too friendly with Thom, and was currently receiving a barrage of aspersions on his masculinity—and his very humanity—in return. It was impressive and frightening, and *fuck*, so hot.

Phil backed away, turned and fled to his office. He leaned against the door, breathing hard. Thom's voice still rang in his ears. If he closed his eyes, he could still see Thom's sweet Cupid's bow mouth forming words sharp enough to draw blood. The mental image was enough to make Phil's prick harder than concrete.

God, if he tried to talk to Thom now, he'd throw the man over his shoulder like a fucking caveman and ruin any miniscule chance he had with him.

"Okay," he muttered, wiping the sweat from his brow. "So I'll apologize to him after he's calmed down some."

He just hoped he hadn't used up his last chance already.

&

As it turned out, Thom didn't calm down enough to be even remotely approachable for two more days. He was reasonably pleasant to the staff and unfailingly nice to the customers— except the ones who wouldn't take no for an answer—but he nevertheless radiated a simmering fury that made Phil's insides twist. Uncertain of his ability to keep from mauling the other man if they got within five feet of each other, Phil limited his interaction with Thom to brief hellos in passing.

Thom was off Sunday. Phil was supposed to be off as well, but he couldn't stand the thought of kicking around his empty house by himself. So here he was, spending his free time helping out with the dinner crowd.

*Could be worse*, he reasoned as he hefted a loaded tray in both hands and headed toward the boisterous party of twelve by the front window. *I could be at Belial's right now, being hit on by Brad.*

The thought gave Phil shudders which were unpleasantly different from the ones Thom gave him.

Business had been steady all day, and they actually had a crowd waiting at the bar for a table at dinnertime. It was one of the busiest Sunday nights Phil could remember having since they'd opened. Patrons arrived in a steady stream, keeping Phil happily occupied and his mind off Thom.

Mostly, anyway.

At ten o'clock, Phil ushered the last late diners out into the summer night and locked the door behind them. Sighing, he pulled down the shades across the glass door and the windows. Swamped as they'd been all night, he wasn't ready to close up. It meant he'd have to go home to an empty bed, which was just depressing.

Of course, he still had to count receipts, close the register and put the day's cash and checks in the safe. He'd be here another hour at least. Maybe he could draw it out to an hour and a half if he moved slowly enough.

"Pathetic, Phil," he muttered, punching the cash register buttons with more force than was strictly necessary. It was irritating as hell to realize how close he was to becoming one of the workaholic type-A jackasses he used to make fun of in college.

*Next thing you know, you'll be driving a Hummer.*

He snorted at the thought of himself behind the wheel of one of those hideous pollution machines.

Mike's head popped around the corner. "What?"

Phil stopped the automatic eye roll before it could start. Mike could hear anything resembling a laugh from a mile away, and he *always* wanted to know what was funny. Though to be fair, it hadn't started irritating Phil until about the thousandth time.

"Nothing, Mike." Phil smiled at the boy. "Why don't you and Tory go ahead and take off? I can finish up here."

Mike's eyes widened. "But you already came in on your day off. We can—"

"Mike." Turning from the register, Phil grasped Mike's shoulders and gave him a gentle shake. "Thank you. Really. But to be honest, I'd kind of like to have a little quality time alone with my HO. Okay?"

Mike grinned. "Okay, sure."

"Great." Phil let go of Mike and started pulling receipts out from under the cash tray. "Tell Tory, will you?"

"'Kay. Thanks, Phil."

"You're welcome."

"I'm off 'til Wednesday, see you then."

"Yeah, see you."

Mike hurried toward the kitchen, pulling his apron off as he went. Phil heard him talking to Tory, then her high-pitched voice thanking him as she and Mike left.

Alone at last, Phil went to the bar and put a Massive Attack CD in the boom box before returning his attention to the day's profits. He called a distracted good night to Helene when she popped her head in to say she was leaving. A glance up at the clock told him it was only ten thirty. He took a deep breath and slowed down his counting.

When he heard the kitchen door squeak open a few minutes later, he didn't even look up. Helene had probably forgotten something. It wouldn't be the first time.

"Phil?"

Phil went still, his heart suddenly thudding like a jackhammer. Plastering what he hoped was a casual smile on his face, he turned to face the unexpected visitor. "Hey, Bub—uh, Thom. What're you doing here? You're off tonight."

If Thom noticed Phil's almost-slip, he didn't let on. One fair eyebrow arched up. "So are you."

Phil shrugged. "I got bored at home."

"Yeah, well, you're entertaining yourself kind of loudly here."

"What?"

Thom gestured toward the bar. "Sound goes right through the floor upstairs."

The light dawned, and Phil winced. "Oh shit. Sorry. I'll turn it down."

He started to brush past Thom in order to lower the volume on the boom box, but Thom's hand on his arm stopped him. The heat of Thom's palm made Phil's stomach flutter. He gulped.

"It's okay," Thom said, his voice soft. "I wasn't asleep or anything. I was just wondering who was still down here, is all. Wanted to make sure everything was all right."

Phil licked his lips. He wished his prick wouldn't react with such adolescent enthusiasm to Thom's touch. "Well. Um. Everything's fine. I'm just finishing things up."

"Oh. Okay." Letting his hand drop, Thom took a step back. He stuck his hands in the back pockets of his threadbare jeans, the ones that hugged every mouthwatering curve and plane of that lithe little body. "Phil, I think I owe you an apology."

Surprised, Phil tore his gaze from Thom's crotch to look him in the eyes. "Huh?"

Thom ducked his head, letting his hair fall down to hide his face. "I shouldn't have gotten so upset the other day. It was uncalled for, and I'm sorry."

Phil stared, shocked. It hadn't even occurred to him that Thom might feel just as bad as he did.

Thom stood there shifting from foot to foot, looking for all the world like a nervous teenager. Something about this unfamiliar, vulnerable Thom made Phil want to pick him up and cuddle him. The certainty that Thom would not appreciate it stopped him.

"It's fine," Phil spoke up before the silence could become seriously uncomfortable. "I'm the one who should be apologizing to you. For real this time."

*That* made Thom look at him. "Are you saying you pissed me off on purpose?"

Those big eyes seemed to see right through Phil's skull and into his innermost thoughts. Phil hunched his shoulders and forced himself to hold Thom's gaze. "Um. Yeah."

"Because I'm sexy when I'm mad."

"Oh yeah."

"You've been doing that all along, haven't you?"

Phil swallowed. "Maybe."

Sighing, Thom ran a hand through his hair. "What the hell's wrong with you?"

*He's not yelling. That's a good sign.* Phil ignored the rebellious parts of him which disagreed and risked a cautious smile. "There's just something about a hot little blond with a temper that turns my crank like nothing else."

Thom eyed him with a calculating look. "Hm. Isn't that interesting?"

The predatory way Thom was looking at him sent goose bumps racing up Phil's arms. "So. Are you mad?" He sounded hopeful. Dammit.

Thom gave him an evil grin. "Do you want me to be?"

*Oh. Mommy.* Phil groped behind him for something to hang onto, since his legs had gone all rubbery. He found the edge of the shelf where the cash register sat and clutched it hard. "Uh. Well, I... Kind of. I mean, wait, *no!* I want..."

"Yes? You were saying?" Slinking forward, Thom stood a

hairsbreadth from Phil's chest and stared up at him with a hungry expression that made Phil's cock sit up and beg. "What do you want?"

*I want to get to know you. I want to know what you dream about. I want to find out what songs you play when you're feeling sad and what you like on your pizza and what you watch on TV when you're home alone with nothing else to do.*

He almost said it, but lost his nerve. Anger, he could handle, even enjoy. If Thom laughed at him and called him a hopeless sap, he thought he'd die.

"I just want you to fuck me," Phil blurted out. "Doesn't matter if you're mad. I want you." It was at least the truth, if not the *whole* truth.

Thom's eyes went dark, the familiar, adorable pink flush coloring his pale cheeks. "We shouldn't. You're my boss. It'll all go bad in the end."

At that point, Phil's need to have Thom inside him was so strong he barely noticed the thread of sadness and regret in Thom's voice. His patience worn to the breaking point, Phil curled one hand around the nape of Thom's neck and kissed him with all the desperate horniness in his soul.

To his delight, Thom responded with typical fierce passion. When they drew apart, Thom looked straight up into Phil's eyes. "Pull your pants down and bend over that stool."

Phil's mouth went bone dry, stopping the triumphant whoop which wanted to emerge. Incapable of making a single sound, Phil undid the button fly on his dark blue Sunday jeans, shoved his pants and underwear down, shuffled around and obediently laid his chest on the three-legged stool in front of the register.

Small, warm hands smoothed over Phil's ass, thumbs dipping into the crease. "Mmmm. Nice."

Phil let out a whimper and pushed back against Thom's palms. If he didn't get Thom's fingers up his butt *right now,* he'd spontaneously combust and burn the restaurant down, and he didn't much want to explain that to the insurance company.

Behind him, Thom chuckled. "Either you're going to have to get that ass lower, or I'm going to have to stand on a box. And I am *not* standing on a box."

Luckily for Phil, he'd had this problem countless times before and knew just what to do. If he'd had to actually *think* right now, he'd have been shit out of luck, as all the blood in his body seemed to have taken up residence in his prick. Toeing his left sneaker off, he tugged his foot free of his tangled clothes and widened his stance as much as he comfortably could.

An appreciative rumble told him Thom approved. "Oh, now *that's* hot." Wisps of silky hair brushed Phil's ass a split second before his shirt was rucked up and soft lips pressed to the skin of his lower back. "You wouldn't happen to have anything slick close by, would you?"

*Crap! Lube. Need lube.* Phil's mind struggled free of the clinging lust and started mentally rifling through the shelves and cabinets of the wait station. There was a small bottle of olive oil for oil-and-vinegar salad dressing...

No. Circe and/or Tory would kill him. Not to mention the health department, if they ever got wind of it.

He was on the verge of telling Thom to just use spit when his gaze lit on the oil burner Circe kept on one of the lower shelves.

*Bingo.*

Stretching out one arm, he snatched up the clear glass vial from its spot beside the burner and handed it behind him. "Essential oil," he explained.

The little bottle was plucked from Phil's hand. "The Big 'O',"

Thom read from the hand-written label. He laughed. "Seriously?"

Phil groaned, partly in frustration and partly at the memory of Circe telling him, in excruciating detail, why she'd christened her special blend of essential oils with that particular name. "Don't ask."

"Duly noted." The mingled scents of mandarin, jasmine, ylang-ylang and eucalyptus suffused the air as Thom opened the bottle. "Mmm. Smells good."

Cool slipperiness drizzled between Phil's ass cheeks, warming fast to the gentle massage of Thom's fingers. Phil moaned. "Oh. Oh yeah."

"Like that, do you?" Thom's fingertip rubbed light circles over Phil's hole, drawing a series of sharp, needy noises from him. "What about that? Do you like that too?"

Phil tried to answer in the affirmative, but no sound came out. He nodded so hard it made him dizzy, then wiggled his ass just in case Thom hadn't gotten the point.

"Fuck, you're gorgeous like this." The finger stopped its feathery caress and penetrated Phil with a single oil-slicked jab. "I can't wait to get my cock inside you."

*You're not the only one.*

Phil nearly came out of his skin when Thom's fingertip hit his prostate. He wished he could make his voice work so he could ask Thom to *stick his dick in already*, pretty please with a cherry on top.

Barring that, he supposed chanting, "Oh, oh yes, oh fuck yes," probably got the point across pretty well.

The finger in Phil's ass withdrew, and returned a second later with a friend beside it. Both digits pumped in and out, in and out, twisting as they went. Every few strokes, a fingertip nudged Phil's gland and made his vision blur.

Phil let out a pleading whine. He appreciated Thom's thoroughness and care, but he needed to be fucked, and he needed it right this second. After all the pounding his hole had taken over the years, it pretty much relaxed out of pure instinct whenever a hard cock approached.

The fingers withdrew once again. Phil almost cried with relief when he heard the purr of a zipper sliding down.

His T-shirt was shoved all the way up to his shoulders. Thom's warmth draped across his back, the head of Thom's cock lodging against Phil's hole. "Ready?" Thom murmured, and nipped at Phil's right shoulder blade.

In answer, Phil pressed backward, forcing Thom's prick inside him. They both gasped.

"Oh. God." Thom pressed his cheek to Phil's back. Both arms slid around Phil's waist, one hand splaying across his stomach while the other curled around his erection. "So fucking good."

Phil expressed his agreement with a ragged moan and another push of his butt against Thom's groin. Thom responded by biting him again—harder this time—and giving his cock a firm squeeze.

Thom stayed there, perfectly still except for his hand lazily caressing Phil's prick, for what felt to Phil like ages. He was concentrating on creating speech, so he could beg Thom to *please God* just fuck him now, when Thom finally began to move.

All thought fled from Phil's brain with the first slow glide of Thom's prick out of his ass and back in again. Phil grasped the stool's rungs in both hands and hung on for dear life while the world spun around him.

He'd expected Thom to pound him fast and rough, but that

wasn't how it went at all. Not that Phil was complaining. There was something intensely fulfilling about being taken with such unhurried tenderness. The rhythm of Thom's hand on Phil's shaft matched the leisurely slip-slide of Thom's cock in and out of his body. Combined with the sexual throb of the music and the heady perfume of the scented oil, the feel of Thom around him and inside him threatened to drown Phil in a tidal wave of sensation.

Drugged as he was with sensory overload, Phil didn't notice the orgasm sneaking up on him until it pounced. He came with a strangled scream, his body writhing out of control. Darkness ate at the edges of his vision, and he fought not to pass out. He'd be damned if he was going to miss the moment of Thom's release.

Thom let out a groan that sounded like it was torn out of him. His hands locked onto Phil's hipbones in a bruising grip. He thrust into Phil in short, hard jabs, once, twice, three times, then went still. Phil felt the frantic thud of Thom's heart against his back.

"Oh fucking shit," Thom breathed, and came, his cock pulsing in Phil's hole.

Phil could have sworn he felt Thom tremble. But it might've been his imagination. The aftershocks spiking through him played hell with his perceptions.

When Thom peeled himself off Phil's back and his cock slipped out, Phil couldn't hold back a groan of loss. The mournful sound morphed into a surprised squeak when he felt hands spread his butt cheeks wide, and Thom's warm, wet tongue lapped at his hole. The tongue stud scraped over the sensitive skin, sending shockwaves up and down Phil's back.

Seized by the urge to watch, Phil twisted his head around as best he could without dislodging Thom's tongue. Thom was kneeling behind him, face buried in Phil's ass crack. His head bobbed with the enthusiastic motion of his mouth as he licked Phil clean.

Phil thought it just might be the sexiest thing he'd ever seen.

He was about to say so, when Thom's lips sealed themselves around his hole and sucked. Hard.

Phil let out a high-pitched, breathy shriek. "Oh, my God. Oh my God. Are you...? Oh. My. *God.*"

He felt Thom's mouth curl into a grin, then warm breath on his now highly sensitive entrance as Thom laughed. "Don't tell me nobody's ever sucked their own come out of your ass."

*Like that's* so *common*, he intended to say. *I'm sure everybody does it. Not.* What actually came out was, once again, "Oh. My God."

He grimaced. *Way to sound like a broken record, stud.*

Snickering, Thom gave Phil's hole a quick swipe of his tongue. "Got a straw?"

The resulting mental image gave Phil a fit of most unmanly giggles. "Gross!"

"Oh, that's gross, but me sucking it straight out of your butt isn't." Thom pushed to his feet and gave Phil's ass a resounding smack. "I can see you need to be educated."

"Yeah, maybe." Phil straightened up, clutching at the stool as a wave of lightheadedness hit him. "I'm ready and willing, Mr. Teacher."

Silence. Phil turned around. Thom was watching him with a strange expression, half wariness and half...longing?

*Wishful thinking, my man. He only fucked you because you begged him, and you promised you'd leave him alone if he did.*

The thing was, Phil knew that wasn't entirely true. Thom

returned his lust, if not his desire for more than that. But Phil had made a promise, both to Thom and to himself, and he was determined to keep it.

Of course, that didn't mean he couldn't tell the truth. He'd always been a terrible liar.

Reaching out, he took Thom's hand and laced their fingers together. The fact that Thom made no move to stop him sent hope soaring inside him.

"I swore I'd leave you alone if you fucked me tonight," he said, watching Thom's face. "I'll keep that promise. But I'd be lying if I said I didn't still want you. I do. And I want it to be more than just sex. I think we could be really good together, and I'd like to give it a shot."

Thom's expression became guarded. "Phil, look—"

"I know. You don't feel the same. I understand, and I respect that. If all we can ever be is friends, then I'll take it and be happy." Phil used his free hand to tuck a lock of hair behind Thom's ear. "I just want you to know that if you ever change your mind, all you have to do is say so. I'm yours, if you want me."

For a long moment, Thom stared up at Phil with an unreadable expression. He opened his mouth, closed it again and shook his head, and Phil knew nothing was going to change tonight.

Tugging his hand from Phil's grip, Thom stepped back, tucked himself into his jeans and zipped up. "I have to go." His eyes cut upward, his gaze meeting Phil's for a heartbeat before he looked away again. "It was good. Um, thanks."

Phil smiled. "Sure."

"I'm off tomorrow too. See you Tuesday?"

"Yeah. Night."

"Night."

With one more inscrutable look, Thom turned and strode away. Only then did Phil realize he was still standing there with one shoe off and his jeans and underwear tangled around one ankle.

Leaning against the wall, he thought about what had just happened while he unwadded his clothes and got dressed. The sex was incredible, but that was hardly a surprise. He and Thom had some powerful chemistry between them.

What surprised him was the sense of hope he felt after the fact. Thom had been pretty clear that he didn't want a relationship with Phil. Didn't even want to fuck him again, in fact. But Phil had always been good at reading people, and what he'd seen in Thom's eyes told him he shouldn't give up just yet.

Things hadn't changed tonight. But change was coming. All Phil had to do was hold on and wait.

Whistling to himself, Phil went in search of a rag and some spray cleaner. Once he'd swabbed all the semen off the floor and the stool, he turned his attention to the work he'd abandoned when Thom showed up.

Thom.

*Thom kneeling behind him, sucking his own spunk right out of Phil's freshly fucked hole.*

The memory made Phil's cock twitch.

He grinned. *I am so trying that next time.*

# Chapter Six

To Thom's surprise, he made it all the way to his one-room-and-a-bath efficiency above the restaurant before collapsing into a mortified heap.

"Oh my fucking God," he groaned, sitting down hard on the green shag carpet in the tiny living area. "You just thanked him for sex. Nice job, idiot."

Even worse, he'd called what was quite possibly the best fuck of his life "good". *Good!* Amazing, stupendous, earth-shattering—those might come close to describing it. "Good" wasn't even in the ballpark, yet he'd said it anyway.

It felt like high school all over again. At least this time, unlike those horrible, awkward years, he'd walked away with his dignity as intact as was possible under the circumstances.

Actually, he thought he'd done well to walk away from Phil at all. Something about the man drew him like gravity. Maybe it was the peace-and-love vibe Phil radiated, or the impish sparkle in those big hazel eyes, or the way Phil always smiled like he was thinking something dirty. Or maybe it was the fact that he really was always thinking something dirty.

Now that Thom thought about it, maybe his way-more-than-sexual attraction to the big hippie was what had fueled his escape. It terrified him beyond all reason to feel this way about anyone at all. The fact that Phil was his *boss* was just the moldy icing on this particular shit cake.

Groaning, Thom flopped onto his back, the heels of both hands pressed to his eyes. "Why do these fucking things always happen to me?"

*Always* was a huge exaggeration and he knew it, but he was in the mood for a little self-pity tonight. He'd allowed himself to be tempted *once again* into a sexual relationship with his employer. After what happened the last time he got involved with a superior at work, he damn well knew better than to do it again. Yet here he was, in an all-too-familiar situation.

He liked The HO. The work was fun, the people there were nice and the majority of the patrons were polite, cheerful and interesting. Having to not only leave work without notice, but leave town in the dead of night with no forwarding address, was not something he ever wanted to do again.

Not that he really thought that would happen this time. Phil was a nice guy. In fact, he was one of the most fundamentally *decent* people Thom had ever met. If they started seeing each other then broke up, he would never react with stalking and death threats the way Rob had.

Funny how much the thought of breaking up with Phil hurt. Especially since they weren't actually together.

Sighing, Thom pushed to his feet and shuffled into the bathroom to get an ibuprofen. Trying to think his way through the maze of his own hopes, fears and desires was giving him a monster headache.

Beneath his feet, the floor still vibrated with the music Phil had never gotten around to turning down. Thom smiled and shook his head. Phil always seemed to play Massive Attack when he needed to think through something. Thom couldn't help wondering what was on Phil's mind this time.

*Probably the same thing that's on your mind, genius.*

Shit.

Leaning both hands on the sink, Thom stared at himself in the mirror. Looking back at him was a grown man with the face of a toddler—*Bubbles!* the demon living in his head gleefully supplied—the body of an undernourished fourteen-year-old and a temper which had been getting him in trouble ever since he'd first yelled at his mother in the grocery store when he was six. What the hell did Phil see to make his face light up like a hundred-watt bulb every time he laid eyes on Thom?

"I don't get it," Thom confessed to his reflection. Phil was a popular guy. Everyone liked him. He could have his pick of men. Why did he want Thom? Not even as a simple fuck-buddy, but as a *boyfriend*?

And why, in his weaker moments, did Thom think just maybe he wanted the same thing?

*I can't think about this anymore. It'll drive me crazy.*

Pushing the tangled thoughts to the back of his mind, he brushed his teeth and splashed cool water on his face, then wandered back into the combination living room/bedroom/kitchenette. He stripped off his clothes and pulled out the sofa bed. Scratching his stomach, he crossed the room to flip the lights off before crawling naked under the sheet. He was exhausted. The combination of fantastic sex and hard thinking—okay, mostly the fantastic sex—had worn him out.

The music still thumped up through the floor from downstairs. For some reason, knowing Phil was down there made Thom feel safe.

He drifted off to the sultry invitation of the singer to "live with me". Thom's last thought before he fell asleep was to wonder if the song was some sort of prophecy.

He didn't know whether to hope it was, or wasn't.

ಬೆ

Disappointingly, sleeping on it didn't untangle Thom's mixed-up emotions any. When the morning sun poured through the gap in the drapes to shine in his eyes and wake him, he didn't know just what the hell he wanted any more than he had the night before. However, the few restless hours of sleep had been good for one thing—he knew now what he had to do.

He had to talk to Phil. Explain why he kept jumping Phil's bones then shoving him away.

More daunting still, the two of them needed to sit down and work out just what they were to each other, and what they were each looking to become.

The thought made Thom's stomach churn. He decided to stop thinking about it, at least until he'd had breakfast.

Yawning, Thom shuffled into the bathroom, flipped up the toilet lid with his toes and peed with his eyes still half shut. He washed his hands and face and brushed his teeth, then headed to the kitchenette to make coffee. No way was he going to face Phil without plenty of caffeine in his system.

While the coffee brewed, he sifted through his clothes, trying to find the perfect wardrobe combination. Casual, but not ratty. Sexy, but not outright seductive. Something that would show his seriousness without making him seem inaccessible.

He snorted. If getting dressed was this damn complicated, he must be even more nervous than he thought.

Eventually, he settled for a short-sleeved silk shirt that matched his eyes and the black jeans which always made Phil stop whatever he was doing to stare at his ass. The pure, bright blue of the shirt made his hair and skin glow, and the ensemble's classic jeans-and-button-down styling kept him from looking like he was just trying to get laid.

Although, he couldn't say he would mind if his little talk with Phil ended that way. Just please God not in the restaurant again.

It was a little after ten a.m. when he left his apartment and headed downstairs to The HO. He tried to tell himself his hands weren't shaking when he unlocked the employee entrance, but it was no use. They definitely were.

So were his knees.

And just to make the whole situation as perfect as possible, his palms were sweating.

All in all, Thom figured he resembled nothing so much as the biggest dork in eighth grade about to ask the prettiest girl in the class to slow dance. At least Phil wasn't likely to sneer, or laugh, or ignore him altogether and run off to giggle with his friends in the corner.

Thom was standing in front of Phil's closed office door, trying to work up the nerve to knock, when Mike came slouching in from the kitchen. "Hey, Thom. Phil's not here."

"Oh." Thom stuck his hands in his pockets, feeling at once relieved and irritated. "I thought he was working today."

"Yeah, he was supposed to, but he decided to take today off since he worked yesterday. He's at home." Mike crossed the floor to the employee restroom and paused in the doorway. "You could call him, though. He said he was gonna do some more work on the house, so he'll be there all day."

"Actually, I kind of need to talk to him in person." Thom tapped his tongue stud against the back of his teeth. "Guess it can wait until tomorrow."

"You could go over there, if you want. He won't mind."

A sudden image of bending Phil over his own kitchen table

popped into Thom's head. It looked good, even though Thom had no idea if Phil even had a kitchen table. In fact, he had no idea where Phil lived.

"What's his address?" Thom's mouth asked before his brain could decide whether or not it was a good idea.

"Fourteen oh one Groverdale Circle, in the Montford district." Mike started to shut the restroom door, then pulled it open again. "You know how to get there?"

"No, but I'll get directions on my phone." Thom gave the boy a genuinely grateful smile. "Thanks, Mike. See you later."

Mike's cheeks went beet red. "Sure. See you." He shut the door. The lock clicked into place.

Thom chuckled as he went back outside. If he didn't know for a solid fact that Mike was straight, he would've sworn the kid had a crush on him. As it was, Thom figured Mike was just scared of him. That seemed to happen to Thom a lot, for reasons he had never understood.

Out in the alley, Thom ran up the outside stairs to his apartment to grab his phone, sunglasses, bike keys, jacket and helmet. He punched Phil's address into Google Maps on his phone as he walked back down the steps. According to the map he pulled up, Phil's house was only a couple of miles away, on a cul-de-sac at the end of a winding side street a couple of turns off of Patton Avenue. He could be there in less than ten minutes, barring any unusually heavy traffic.

Ten minutes. In ten minutes, he'd be with Phil. In his house.

Alone.

A wave of dizziness hit him. He clung to the railing while his heart attempted a flying leap up his throat. Why he should be so scared of having an honest conversation with Phil, he had no idea, but there it was. He was fucking terrified.

*No room for fear.* His first serious boyfriend used to say that all the time, particularly when he wanted Thom to indulge one of his kinkier fantasies. In spite of how he usually used it, it was one of the few nuggets of true wisdom the smug asshole had ever spewed forth.

It certainly fit now. There was no room for Thom's doubts and fears right now. No place for them. If he wanted to keep his sanity, he and Phil were going to have to clear the air. Phil had left it up to Thom to decide what, if anything, happened next between them. Therefore, it was up to Thom to take the initiative.

For the first time in his life, he very much wished that wasn't the case.

*Suck it up and just do it, boy.*

Squaring his shoulders, he descended the last few stairs and walked over to his Harley.

Nine minutes later, Thom pulled into Phil's driveway at the apex of the cul-de-sac in one of the city's most historic neighborhoods. He sat there for a second, staring at the house and trying to decide whether it was charmingly offbeat or merely appalling.

The Victorian-style structure sat well back from the road, on a spacious lot shaded by gnarled oaks and graceful elms. Like many urban homes from that era, the deep, narrow house boasted a covered porch, intricate woodwork, a gabled roof and plenty of tall bay windows. However, the resemblance to anything old-fashioned or quaint ended with the architecture. The clapboard walls were painted bright cornflower blue, while rich purple adorned the gingerbread woodwork, the window trim and the porch railings. In contrast, the front door was done in the same retina-searing yellow as the anthropomorphic onion which welcomed patrons to The HO.

It was bright, eye-catching, unique. It stood out among its more sedate neighbors like a belly dancer in a monastery, flaunting its one-of-a-kind appeal with unabashed joy.

It was, in other words, unmistakably *Phil*.

For some reason, Thom found that fact endearing rather than scary.

Drawing a deep breath, Thom swung himself off his Harley, pocketed the keys and strode up the flower-lined flagstone path to the porch steps before he could change his mind. The steps were painted the same pale spring green as the porch floorboards. Black footprints formed a barefoot trail up the steps and across the porch to the door. Thom followed them, a grin tugging at his mouth. The prints looked suspiciously similar in size and shape to Phil's feet.

And wasn't it just beyond disturbing that Thom remembered Phil's bare feet well enough to notice?

As he approached the door, Thom heard music thudding from inside. He listened for a moment, trying to get a sense of Phil's current mood. The music he played nearly always reflected how he felt. Thom let out a relieved sigh when he recognized a track from Beck's *Midnite Vultures*. Phil only played that one when he was feeling upbeat.

Gathering his courage, Thom lifted his hand and gave three firm raps on the sturdy wooden door. A few seconds later, the door swung open, blasting "Sexx Laws" to the neighborhood at the ear-splitting volume Phil seemed to prefer.

Phil stood in the open doorway wearing a pair of ripped, faded and paint-splattered jeans and nothing else. Sweat threaded tiny rivers through the thick fur on his chest and plastered curling tendrils of golden brown hair to his flushed face.

He looked positively edible. Thom gulped.

The slow, sexy grin that always turned Thom into a slack-jawed idiot spread over Phil's face. "Hey, Bubbles. What brings you here?"

*We need to talk. We need to figure out where whatever we have between us is going. After that, if we decide to pursue a relationship, we will need to set boundaries and limits. Then, and only then, you may take me to bed.*

Not one word of Thom's carefully rehearsed speech emerged from his dry mouth. *Sex!* his overactive libido screamed instead. *Sex now! Sexsexsex!*

He licked his lips. "Uh... I..."

Phil frowned. "Thom? You okay?"

Thom breathed deep in a desperate bid to calm himself. Bad idea. The ripe smell of sweat-soaked, overheated male skin flooded his brain, and he was lost.

He heard the growl rumble up from inside him, felt his palms plant themselves on Phil's warm, damp chest, but he couldn't stop himself any more than he could stop the sun from rising in the morning.

Phil stumbled backward when Thom shoved him into the foyer. "Hey! What the hell?"

Thom followed him inside and kicked the door shut. He tore off his jacket. It fell to the floor with a muffled thump.

Phil eyed him with a curious mix of arousal and trepidation. "Uh, Thom? What's up, man?"

*My dick. And it's all your fault, you fucking sexy damn granola-head.*

God, it made him angry to lose control like this. Stupid Phil, standing there all flushed and gorgeous, making Thom hard with nothing but his naked chest and his raw masculine scent and the growing fire in his eyes.

Stalking forward, Thom ripped Phil's jeans open with a couple of swift, practiced movements. He fell to his knees, yanking the jeans and orange polka-dotted briefs down as he went.

Phil let out a yelp as his clothes dragged over his privates, but Thom ignored it. He felt if he couldn't wrap his lips around that fat prick *right this minute,* he would surely die. Even the hideous underwear couldn't distract him from his goal. Circling his thumb and forefinger around the base of Phil's half-erect cock, Thom opened wide and gulped a mouthful of hot, salty dick.

"Oh fuck," Phil gasped. His hips jerked, shoving his rapidly stiffening cock so deep into Thom's throat his pubes got up Thom's nose. Long fingers dug into Thom's hair, pulling hard enough to hurt. "That's it, pretty baby. Just like that. Shit."

Thom hummed around the head of Phil's cock, causing Phil's words to degenerate into low, rough moans. Fuck, that was sexy.

Fumbling his jeans open with his free hand, Thom wrapped his fingers around his shaft and started stroking himself. His rhythm was irregular, clumsy, but he didn't care. As long as Phil kept fucking his mouth and making those sweet, needy sounds, Thom was in heaven. Jerking himself off probably wasn't even necessary. He could almost come just from the feel of Phil's prick stretching his jaw wide.

Phil's body tightened, his shaft swelling in Thom's throat. "Oh, oh, oh God, baby, gonna come, ooooh, oh *fuck*!"

*Yeah, that's the stuff.* Thom shut his eyes and swallowed the warm, slick fluid spurting down his throat. Phil's semen tasted just a little sweet, like it always did, and Thom didn't want to miss a drop.

Phil sighed, fingers raking through Thom's hair. "Damn,

Bubbles. So fucking beautiful."

Surprised by the reverent tone of Phil's voice, Thom opened his eyes and looked up. Phil's gaze locked with his, full of heat and tenderness. Phil's lips curved into *that* smile, the one that made Thom's insides quiver, and it sent him tumbling over the edge. He came all over Phil's gleaming hardwood floor, his cries muffled by Phil's cock filling his mouth.

His body was still twitching with the aftershocks when Phil tugged his prick free of Thom's mouth, reached down and hauled him up by the armpits. Thom couldn't even find the energy to be indignant about such handling, which he figured said a lot about his state of mind right then.

Chuckling, Phil leaned down and licked the remains of come off Thom's lips. "Don't think I'm complaining, angel face, but what the hell was *that*?"

Heat crept into Thom's cheeks. He scowled at the floor, feeling uncomfortable as hell all of a sudden. How, he wondered, was he supposed to say what he'd come here to say with spunk all over his jeans and his breath smelling of sweaty cock?

"Hey. Thom." Phil's hand cupped his chin, forcing him to meet Phil's gaze. Phil's smile remained in place, but concern shone in his eyes. "Awesome as it was, I know you didn't come all the way out here just to suck me off."

Thom shook his head. "No."

Nodding, Phil slid an arm around Thom's waist. The other palm covered his cheek. "So why are you here?"

Thom stared up into Phil's calm, waiting face, and had no idea what to say. Half an hour ago, he'd known the answer to that question. Now, he wasn't so sure. As usual, Phil had thrown him completely off track without even trying.

Hardly surprising from a guy who could stand there and

conduct a serious conversation with his pants around his ankles and saliva drying on his dick.

"I want to try this," Thom blurted. "With you. Us seeing each other, I mean."

Phil blinked. Thom bit his lip and forced himself to keep quiet. It wasn't quite what he'd meant to say, but what the hell. It was true, even if he hadn't realized it until just now.

Just when Thom began to think he'd fucked up royally, Phil's shocked expression relaxed into a catlike grin. He rubbed his thumb over Thom's lower lip. "You're off tonight?"

Not exactly what Thom had expected. He frowned. "Yeah."

"Stay."

*Didn't expect that either.* "What?"

"Stay with me." The grin widened. Phil raked a slow look down Thom's body and back up again. "We can spend the rest of the day in bed talking about us."

Thom's eyes narrowed. "If you're making fun of me, I swear to *God* I'll kick you in the balls and walk right out that fucking door, you asshole."

For once, his flare of temper didn't bring the familiar lustful glow to Phil's eyes. Instead, Phil pulled him closer, bent and kissed the end of his nose. "Calm down, Bubbles. I'm not making fun of you. I was serious."

"You want to 'talk about us'?" Thom snorted. "Right."

"Okay, so maybe I was being kind of a smartass."

"Kind of?"

"A total smartass," Phil amended, his face the picture of solemnity. "I was being a total smartass. I'm sorry."

"Huh."

"I am. You know I want to be with you, sweet baby. I'm a

tease, I can't help it." That damned sexy smile came back, making Thom's pulse race. "Forgive me?"

He'd already been forgiven, but Thom figured he didn't need to know that. "I guess."

"Come to bed with me."

Thom grinned with a sudden giddy rush of joy. "Might as well, since we're already half-undressed."

Phil's smile widened. His legs moved as he shuffled from foot to foot. For a second, Thom thought he was doing some weird kind of happy dance. He only realized Phil was stepping out of his jeans when the big ape swooped Thom into his arms and started climbing the stairs.

"Phil," Thom said, with what he felt was remarkable restraint, considering. "What are you doing?"

"Carrying you to bed." With a laugh that probably wasn't supposed to sound sultry but did, Phil shifted one hand enough to squeeze Thom's ass. "C'mon, Bubbles, relax. Enjoy it."

Thom thought about that. Somewhat to his surprise, he didn't find being hauled around like a fairy-tale princess nearly as humiliating as he thought he should have.

*What the hell. How often do you get to be carried to bed by a gorgeous naked man?*

Winding his arms around Phil's neck, Thom laid his head on Phil's shoulder. The resulting contented rumble from Phil made him smile.

It wasn't until Phil tossed him onto the king-sized bed and they were caught up in a deep, searching kiss that Thom realized Phil had called him Bubbles at least twice. Possibly more.

Phil's tongue curled around Thom's, and he decided he didn't care. There would be plenty of time for lectures later.

Right now, he had an afternoon in bed with a hot guy ahead of him. He had no intention of wasting it.

# Chapter Seven

Something was tickling Phil's nose. Fine, silky threads that smelled like new hay and sex.

He scrunched his face up. The tickle intensified.

He tried to lift his hand to brush the whatever-it-was away. His hand wouldn't move. Something was wound around his arm, holding it down.

No, he realized with a surge of delight. Not some*thing.* Some*one.*

Thom. It was Thom spooned naked in his embrace, trapping one of Phil's arms beneath his body and cuddling the other across his chest. Phil's hand was trapped in the hollow of Thom's throat.

Smiling with his eyes still shut, Phil buried his face deeper in Thom's soft, fragrant hair. Thom mumbled something about pancakes and wriggled his backside snug against Phil's groin before lying still again with a sigh. Phil stifled a laugh in the curve of Thom's neck. It was so cute how Thom turned into such a snuggler when he slept.

Opening his eyes, Phil pushed up on his elbow—as far as he could manage with Thom on top of his lower arm—and peered into Thom's face. His eyes were closed, long golden brown lashes brushing his sleep-flushed cheeks. The plump pink lips were parted just a little. He looked even younger than

Ally Blue

usual, his delicate features as sweet and innocent as a child's.

Luckily for Phil, looks could be deceptive. Extremely so, in this case.

Speaking of which, Phil wondered if Thom would be up for some morning sex. Or evening sex, he mentally amended after a glance at the clock told him they had in fact only slept a couple of hours and it was now dinnertime.

The thought of dinner made Phil's stomach rumble. *Okay. Sex first, then food.*

His plans set, he leaned down and brushed his lips against Thom's ear. "Bubbles," he whispered. "Wake up."

Thom curled up tighter. "Nn-uh."

Grinning, Phil tickled Thom's chin with one finger. "C'mon, pretty baby. Rise and shine."

Thom's brows drew together. "Go 'way," he grumbled, rendering his own request impossible by tugging Phil's arm even tighter across his chest. "Wanna sleep."

"You've been sleeping for the last two hours. I want you to fuck me again." Phil thrust his swelling prick against Thom's rear. "Please, sweet thing? I'll bring you dinner in bed."

Blue eyes cracked open. "Say that again."

"What? Please?"

"Not that."

Phil raised his eyebrows. "Dinner? You hungry?"

"No. Well, yeah, actually, but that's not what I meant."

The light dawned. Phil grinned. "Sweet thing?"

"That's it." Thom's mouth curved into a sleepy smile. "I like how you say that. It's fucking hot."

"It is?"

"Mm-hm. You have a sexy accent."

86

"Really?"

"Yeah." Thom pushed Phil's hand downward until the palm rubbed against his crotch. He was every bit as hard as Phil, and he moaned when Phil curled his fingers around the shaft. "It turns me on when you call me that."

"Hmm." Phil traced the edge of Thom's ear with his tongue, chuckling when Thom squealed and tried to squirm away. "Well then, sweet thaaang," he purred, deliberately accentuating the drawl in his voice. "Since we're both evidently up for it, how about you fucking me before dinner?"

Thom turned his head to capture Phil's mouth with his. The kiss was brief, but sizzling. Phil moaned, fingers tightening around Thom's shaft.

"I have a better idea," Thom murmured, and nipped Phil's bottom lip.

"Oh, yeah?"

"Yeah."

"Tell me."

To Phil's shock, a rosy blush crept into Thom's cheeks. "Iwantyoutofuckmethistime," he mumbled, the words rushed and uncharacteristically self-conscious.

"Sorry, what?" Phil wasn't about to take it on faith that he'd actually just heard what he'd thought he heard. If he acted on it and it turned out he was wrong, Thom would probably cut his balls off with a butter knife.

A crease appeared between Thom's eyes. "I. Want. You. To. Fuck. Me." He glared at Phil, as if daring him to be his usual teasing self right then.

Phil flirted with the idea of deliberately pissing Thom off, but let the urge pass without acting on it. Hot as it was when Angry Thom fucked him so hard he walked bowlegged for a week, he wasn't about to pass up what he suspected was a rare opportunity. Not because he was dying to fuck Thom. He was perfectly happy to let Thom top him every single time. No, he wanted this because Thom did, and as far as Phil was concerned, what Thom wanted, Thom got. Besides, Phil couldn't deny that he wanted to experience every possible facet of sex with Thom.

He knew himself well enough to know what that meant. It made him happy, even knowing Thom might not feel the same.

Letting go of Thom's prick, Phil slid his hand between their bodies and dragged one fingertip up the length of Thom's crease. Thom moaned, and Phil smiled.

"Where's the lube?" Phil murmured in Thom's ear.

Thom's head came up, flicking the hair out of his eyes. Flashing a smile that made Phil's heart thud painfully against his sternum, Thom reached beneath his pillow and drew out the three-quarters-empty bottle of gel they'd been using earlier. He handed it to Phil without a word.

"Thanks." Phil pressed the pad of his thumb against Thom's anus for a second before worming his other arm out from beneath Thom's body. He sat up, the lube clutched in one hand and the other palm splayed against the curve of Thom's hip. "Roll on your stomach for me."

Somewhat to Phil's surprise, Thom did as he was told. Kicking the bedspread aside and shoving the pillow out of the way, he turned onto his front, slender legs parted slightly and both hands curled near his shoulders. His cheek rested on the sheet, heavy-lidded eyes watching Phil with unveiled desire. His skin glowed nearly pure white against the emerald green sheets.

Phil's throat tightened. He ran a hand down the length of Thom's spine to cup one firm ass cheek in his palm. Part of him longed to wax poetic about the man's almost-ethereal beauty.

But a larger part of him didn't want to ruin the moment by turning into a girl, so he decided to keep his inner Keats to himself for the time being.

Rising to his knees, Phil shuffled across Thom's legs, pushing those fucking gorgeous thighs apart so he could kneel between them. He bent and pressed a kiss just above the swell of Thom's ass. Thom hummed, hips lifting toward Phil's mouth like the potted cactus in Phil's bathroom seeking the sunlight.

Phil smiled against Thom's skin. "You want me to eat your ass, pretty baby?"

The violent shudder that ran through Thom's body answered *that* question well enough. Thom's breathless "hell yeah" simply confirmed it.

Raising his head, Phil spread Thom's cheeks and stared down at that sweet little hole. His mouth watered. He'd had wet dreams about rimming Thom. The way Thom had writhed and moaned when he came with Phil's tongue up his ass that first morning was permanently burned into Phil's brain. He'd been dying to relive it ever since.

He lowered his face and drew a deep breath. Thom smelled like sweat and come, ripe and dirty and *God*, so fucking sexy. Fingers holding Thom open, Phil dragged the flat of his tongue across the tightly furled opening. The salty-bitter taste went straight to Phil's crotch. He groaned, Thom echoed the sound, and Phil wondered if a guy could possibly come just from that sexy little noise.

"Damn, Bubbles." Phil darted his tongue out for one more taste before sitting back on his heels. "Sorry, man, but it's got to be either my tongue or my cock. I can't handle both right now."

Thom twisted his head around to meet Phil's gaze. "After all that fucking earlier, you're telling me you're about to shoot just from rimming me?" Phil shrugged, and Thom sighed. "Sad, Phil. Really sad."

Thom's tone was light and teasing, matching the sparkle in his eyes. Phil grinned at him. "What can I say? You make me incredibly horny."

Snickering, Thom pulled his knees beneath him, lifted his hips and wriggled his backside. "All right, horn dog. Get your cock in me before you come in your pants."

"I'm not wearing pants."

The growl Thom let out sent a brain-scrambling wave of lust through Phil's body. "Just shut up and fuck me, before I change my mind."

Phil bit his lip and kept quiet. Pointing out that he knew damn well Thom wasn't about to change his mind would only piss him off, and not in a good way.

Flipping open the cap on the lube, Phil squeezed a generous amount onto his fingers, shut the plastic bottle and tossed it aside. He laid his unlubed hand on Thom's raised ass and slid a single slick finger into his hole.

"Oooooh, yes," Thom moaned, hands fisting in the covers. "More."

Happy to oblige, Phil pumped his finger in and out a couple of times before pulling it out altogether and shoving two in. He was rewarded with another low, rough moan. Thom shifted, propping himself on one elbow, and a heartbeat later a slender hand appeared between his legs. His fingers curled around his shaft and started stroking.

Phil swallowed. "Wait for me, pretty baby. I'd kind of like you to come with my dick up your butt."

A tremor ran down Thom's back. "Me too. So get it in there."

Phil liked being ordered around by Thom under any circumstance, and since that particular order suited his current plans perfectly, he wasted no time in obeying. Holding Thom open with his thumbs, he positioned the head of his cock at that sweet hole and pushed.

It was kind of like having his cock snared in a padded, heated and velvet-lined bear trap. Phil went still, fingers kneading Thom's butt cheeks. He was dying to move, but he was half-afraid if he did, his prick would be ripped right off. *Damn*, but Thom was tight.

With a frustrated sound, Thom pressed his ass back against Phil's groin. The movement forced Phil's cock in a couple more inches. Pleasure jolted up Phil's spine, and he gasped.

"Move." Thom rocked his hips again, taking Phil's cock to the root and tearing a ragged cry from Phil's throat. "Fuck me."

The growled command shattered the last of Phil's hesitation. He grabbed Thom's hipbones and pounded into him as hard as he could.

Any fear Phil might've had of hurting Thom was quickly wiped away by his very vocal—if incoherent—approval. Thom panted and moaned, the muscles of his back tensing with each thrust. His whole torso jerked with the frantic movement of his right hand on his cock.

In other words, he was clearly enjoying himself. Which was a good thing, because Phil didn't think he could stop at that point.

When he felt the orgasm coiling in his belly, Phil draped himself across Thom's back, holding his weight on his left hand and curling his right around Thom's shaft. Thom's own hand was shoved out of the way, but he didn't seem to care. In fact, he didn't even seem to notice. His head hung down so that his face was half-hidden behind a veil of hair, but his openmouthed cries and the swell of his prick in Phil's hand said it all. He was as close to coming as Phil.

"Come on, sweet thing," Phil breathed, angling his thrusts to nail Thom's gland and pull more of those wonderful cries from him. He pressed his thumb to Thom's slit, which caused Thom's hole to contract around his shaft and made both of them gasp. "Come on. Come on."

Even though he'd half expected it, Phil was still surprised when Thom came at his command. Thom's insides clamped down on Phil's cock as he keened and shot all over Phil's sheets. Warm semen spilled over Phil's hand, and it was one sensation too much for him. He came with his cock balls-deep in Thom's ass and his face buried in Thom's tangled hair, and it was the most fucking perfect moment of his life.

He managed to pull out and tilt himself sideways before his strength gave out, so that he collapsed onto his back beside Thom rather than on top of him. Crushing him right after such fantastic sex would be unforgivably rude.

Phil got another surprise when Thom scooted over and draped himself over Phil's chest. One hand on Phil's cheek, Thom leaned down for a slow, lingering kiss. Winding his arms around Thom's waist, Phil closed his eyes and sank into the kiss. He let one hand slide down to caress Thom's pert little ass. It felt so peaceful to lie there like that, naked and sticky and sated, kissing in a beam of early evening summer sunlight.

When the kiss eventually broke, Thom sighed and curled up in Phil's arms, his head tucked beneath Phil's chin. "Wow."

Chuckling, Phil gave Thom a squeeze. "Is that a good wow or an 'oh shit I can't believe how mind-bogglingly awful that was' wow?"

"The first one, Einstein."

"Good."

"I can't believe you even had to ask."

"Well, how else was I supposed to know?"

"Oh, I don't know. Maybe by the way I came so hard my ass almost yanked your dick off?" Thom gave Phil's nipple a pinch, making him yelp. "Don't pretend to be stupid. It's unbecoming."

Phil grinned, twirling a lock of Thom's hair between his fingers. "Yessir, Miss Manners."

Lifting his head, Thom aimed an amused look at Phil. "Your nicknames are getting worse."

"Hey, a guy's got to have a hobby, right?"

Thom raised one eyebrow. Phil widened his eyes and gave Thom his very best guileless look. At that, Thom burst into laughter. "You're such a fucking smartass." He pushed away and sat up in spite of Phil's protests. "Didn't you say something about dinner earlier?"

"Yeah. Dinner in bed." Phil grabbed for Thom, pouting when he laughed and scooted out of reach. "Aw, pretty baby, don't get up yet."

Shaking his head, Thom slid to the edge of the bed and stood. "Come on, you hedonist. Let's go shower, then you can feed me."

"I can feed you something right now," Phil said with a leer.

"Phil, even he-man sex machines like you need a little recovery time." Taking Phil's hand, Thom gave it a tug. "Up, big boy. Let's get clean."

Phil allowed himself to be coaxed to his feet. "Can we get dirty again later?"

Thom shot him an indulgent look. "If you can get it up again, then yeah."

"If *I* can?"

"Well, I *know* I can."

"Now who's a smartass?" Phil swatted Thom's tempting rear end, dancing out of reach of the return blow. He snagged Thom's wrists, pulled him close and stared down into those laughing blue eyes. "I'm glad you came over, Thom. I really am."

Thom smiled. "Me too."

The uncharacteristically tender expression on Thom's face made Phil's heart swell. Afraid to say anything else for fear he'd start spilling truths Thom wouldn't welcome right now, Phil laced their fingers together and led him to the bathroom without a word.

Phil wanted to tell Thom how he felt, but it could wait. Things were perfect between them right now, and Phil wasn't about to ruin it by telling Thom he loved him.

∞

As it turned out, neither of them could get it up again, though they spent the better part of their shower trying. Phil didn't much care. They'd already fucked enough that day to satisfy even the randiest person. He was content simply to run his soapy hands all over Thom's lithe little body, stealing soft, slow kisses now and then.

After they got out of the shower, Phil put on clean shorts and an old Ozomatli T-shirt, then went back down to the foyer to fetch Thom's clothes for him. While Thom dressed, Phil returned downstairs, thinking maybe he could whip up a couple of his famous grilled tomato and asparagus sandwiches for dinner. He still had a few vegan banana-maple-walnut cookies from Sugar Momma's too. They would make an awesome dessert.

Passing through the foyer on his way to the kitchen, he noticed Thom's jacket still lying in the middle of the floor where it had fallen. He picked it up. As he reached to hang it on the coat tree beside the door, he heard the sound of a vaguely familiar tune coming from one of the pockets.

"Thom!" he yelled toward the stairs. "Your cell's ringing."

"Answer it, would you?" came the muffled reply. "I'll be down in a sec."

"'Kay." Reaching into the pocket, Phil pulled out Thom's cell phone, flipped it open and pressed it to his ear. "Bubbles' office, this is his love slave, how may I direct your call?"

Silence. Phil grinned. He could almost see the confusion on the caller's face, never mind that he had no idea who it was.

"Excuse me," said a prim-sounding female voice. "I believe I have the wrong number. My apologies for having disturbed you."

"No, wait. Are you looking for Thom?" Footsteps sounded above. Phil glanced toward the stairs. He hoped Thom wouldn't be too angry with him for having a little fun with whoever it was calling.

"I'm calling for Thomas Stone, yes. Is he available?"

Phil stifled a laugh at the unspoken "who the hell are *you?*" in the woman's voice. "Yeah, hang on a sec."

He turned around just in time to see Thom bounding down the stairs. He held out the phone. "Here. I don't know who it is."

"Okay, thanks." Thom took the phone and glanced at the screen. His eyes widened. Darting a swift glance at Phil, he pressed the phone to his ear and walked toward the front parlor to the left of the foyer. "This is Thom."

Phil bit his lip. He knew it was wrong to listen in, but he *really* wanted to know who the caller was, and what she and

Thom were discussing. Something in the way Thom had just looked at him made him think Thom might be reluctant to tell him after the fact. Besides, he reasoned, he'd only be able to hear Thom's end of the conversation anyway.

Moving as slowly as he could, Phil sauntered around the end of the stairs and past the parlor door. He had to pass it to reach the kitchen, which was at the end of the narrow hallway running the length of the house. It wasn't eavesdropping if he had to go that way anyhow.

"Love slave?" Thom shot Phil his patented death glare as he passed the door. Phil grabbed at the doorframe for support when his knees went rubbery. "Ignore my friend. He's just being a pain, as usual." Scowling, Thom made a shooing motion with one hand. *Asshole*, he mouthed.

Phil gave him a shrug and a sheepish grin. *Sorry*, he mouthed back. Thom's lips curved into a wry smile, and Phil knew he was forgiven. He blew Thom a kiss, then pushed away from the doorframe and started down the hall to the kitchen.

He was slicing tomatoes when Thom joined him a few minutes later. The curiosity must've been clear as day on his face, because Thom just shook his head and answered the question Phil hadn't asked.

"That was Leta Duncan, with Bradford & Lehrer." Thom pulled a chair out from the kitchen table and sat. He let out a snorting laugh as he ran his fingers over the battered but sturdy old farmhouse table. "So what's for dinner?"

"Grilled tomato and asparagus sandwiches on panini." Laying the knife down, Phil turned to lean against the counter so he could face Thom. "Bradford & Lehrer, the developers?"

"Yeah."

"Why are they calling you?" Phil frowned at the strangely lustful way Thom was eyeing the table. "And why are you groping my table? Is there something I ought to know here?"

Thom grinned. "Just thinking about all the things you could use this for other than eating."

The wicked gleam in Thom's eyes made Phil's cock stir in spite of its exhausted state. He ignored it. Finding out what interest the world's most evil developers had in *his* Bubbles took precedence even over sex.

Crossing his arms over his stomach, Phil put on his serious face. "Thom, why are Bradford & Lehrer calling you?"

Thom blinked, obviously surprised by Phil's reaction. "To let me know their funds have been unfrozen, and I can come to work for them now."

Phil gaped. He felt like he'd been sucker-punched. "What?"

"They're why I was in town in the first place. They hired me a while back to manage the on-site nightclub at Rosewood. I moved from Santa Fe to work there. Then when I got here, I found out they couldn't pay me or anything until this dispute over land rights was ironed out and their funds released. That's how I ended up working for you. I needed a job right away." Thom frowned. "What the hell's wrong with you, Phil? Are you worried I'm going to cut out on The Happy Onion? I mean, yeah, I'm taking the Rosewood job, but I'm not going to just leave you in the lurch. I'll work both jobs until you find somebody else."

Phil laughed. It sounded strangled and a little hysterical. "Dispute? Is that what they told you?"

"Yes, it is." Thom jumped up and stalked over to stand toe-to-toe with Phil. "What the fuck's the matter with you? I already told you I wouldn't leave you short."

"I know that."

"Then what the hell are you so upset about?"

Phil eyed the man standing in front of him, brow furrowed

with confusion and frustration. Could he possibly not know?

Sighing, Phil shuffled over to the chair Thom had abandoned and plopped into it. "It's more than a simple land-rights dispute. Part of the land Rosewood is being built on was actually given to the city of Asheville around fifty years ago, to be used as a public park. It's not supposed to be developed."

"Well, maybe they decided the condos were needed more than the park."

Phil raised his eyebrows. "Needed how? For all those poor rich people moving in from all over? You do realize those condos are gonna be by far the most expensive real estate in this part of the state, right?"

Thom stared at the floor. "Well, yeah, I knew they were high-end. But so what? Won't it bring in more money to the area?"

"Oh, sure. More money. More chain stores crowding out the locally owned businesses. More gentrification, less common ground." Sitting forward, Phil rested his elbows on his knees and gazed into Thom's thoughtful face. "That's bad enough. But it's a distinct possibility that Bradford & Lehrer got that piece of land not through the city council's apparent ignorance of where the property lines are, but through greasing the right palms."

Thom's head shot up, his shocked gaze fixing on Phil's face. "Bribery? Do you really think that's true?"

He did, but he had nothing other than rumor and speculation on which to base his opinion, and he couldn't very well lie about that. "I do, but there's no proof."

"So it's nothing but rumors."

Phil shrugged. "So far."

Shaking his head, Thom stuck his hands in his jeans pockets and stared at Phil with transparent irritation. "Okay, let me get this straight. You're giving me attitude because of a few unfounded rumors about the company I'm going to work for. No proof, just hearsay. Is that what you're telling me?"

"Well, I don't think it's all unfounded."

"You don't think. Nothing concrete, though." Thom let out a deep sigh. "Christ on a crutch, Phil."

"This isn't the first time they've been involved in potentially illegal stuff. I'm telling you, they're trouble." Phil tapped his fingers against the table, watching Thom thoughtfully. "Are you just taking this job because you don't want to date your boss?"

Thom's eyes narrowed. A muscle in his jaw twitched. "No. I am taking the job because it's the sort of opportunity I've been looking for for *years*. Strange as it might seem, I don't actually want to be a fucking *bartender* for the rest of my life. I'd kind of like to move up in the world."

*Ouch.* Phil winced. "Look, Thom—"

Thom wasn't done yet. "I did my homework when Bradford & Lehrer first offered me the job. I know there's been talk before, mostly from people who opposed whatever it was they were building. But nothing has *ever* been proven, and their reputation in the business is still one of the best." He crossed his arms, blue eyes shooting sparks. "I think you don't like me working for them because you have some kind of weird thing against rich people. That's it, isn't it?"

Annoyed, Phil rose to his feet and glowered down at the smaller man. "No, I don't. Listen, I know you think I'm just some dumbass hippie, but I fucking well believe in doing what's right for this community. And as far as I'm concerned, that does *not* include stealing land from the people to build another ivory tower for the super rich just so they can come waltzing in and try to change everything that makes this town what it is."

Shock and anger held a brief but furious war in Thom's

eyes. Predictably, anger won. Thom stuck his chin out and held Phil's glare with one of his own. "First of all, I agree with you about what's right. All I'm saying is that you shouldn't judge the company until you have the facts, and you *damn* well shouldn't assume the people moving into the Rosewood condos are going to try to change anything. You don't know anything about those people, so how can you say that? Secondly, I do *not* think you're a dumbass hippie, and how dare you assume I do. And lastly..." Thom smacked both palms into Phil's chest hard enough to send him stumbling backward. "Do *not* try to intimidate me with your size. I've been little forever, and I've been threatened by scarier guys than you. I wasn't afraid of them, and I'm sure as fuck not afraid of someone who I know damn well won't hurt me. Got it?"

Phil stared, caught in a whirlwind of conflicting emotion. On the one hand, he knew in his bones that Bradford & Lehrer were involved in some seriously shady business, even if he couldn't prove it, and he hated the thought of Thom being caught up in that. On the other hand, it made him *so fucking hot* when Thom got all up in his face like that.

Torn between aggravation and arousal, Phil reached out, fisted a hand in Thom's hair and dragged him into a fierce kiss.

For a few seconds, Thom responded. His mouth opened beneath Phil's, his body arching forward and his hands coming up to clutch Phil's shirt. Then he turned his head away and broke out of Phil's embrace. He stepped back, breathing hard.

*Shit, I fucked up.* Phil brushed his fingers across Thom's arm. "Hey, Thom, I'm sorry."

Thom shook his head. "Don't be. It's fine. We'll just have to agree to disagree." He bit his lip, looking more uncertain than Phil had ever seen him. "I'm sorry I got so mad. You know how my temper is."

"Yeah. It's okay. I shouldn't have gone off on you either."
Phil scratched nervously at a mosquito bite on his arm. "So.
How much notice do I get before you leave The HO?"

"They wanted me to start right away, but I told them they'd
have to wait 'til next week."

"Next week. Wow."

"I know it's soon. But don't worry. I already told you, I'll
work both jobs until you find someone else." Stepping forward,
Thom took Phil's hands in his and squeezed. "This could be a
good thing for us, you know. We can see each other without
that whole boss/employee thing hanging over us."

"Yeah. You're right about that."

"I know." Thom closed the remaining distance between
them, wound his arms around Phil's waist and smiled up at
him. "So. What about those sandwiches? I'm starved."

"Mm-hm. Me too." Phil laid a hand on Thom's upturned
face, thumb caressing the corner of his mouth. "Sit down, angel
face. Dinner'll be ready in a few."

Nodding, Thom raised up on tiptoe to brush a kiss across
Phil's lips before going back to the chair he'd been sitting in
earlier. Phil turned his attention back to the food. His pulse was
racing, and it wasn't just from Thom's kiss.

He knew he couldn't very well stop Thom from taking that
job, but the idea of Thom being involved in the Rosewood
project made him feel queasy. Bradford & Lehrer were neck-
deep in shit with Rosewood. When their dirty dealings came to
light—and Phil had no doubt they would, in time—Thom could
easily be caught in the fallout. Phil wanted to protect him from
that, if he could.

The problem was, he couldn't think of any way to do it
without alienating Thom, and he *really* didn't want that.

He glanced over his shoulder. Thom smiled at him, eyes shining, and he smiled back.

*I'll think of something*, he promised himself. *Just need a little time, that's all.*

Feeling some of his normal good cheer returning, Phil opened the cabinet and reached for the panini bread. He had a hungry lover to feed. After that, maybe a nice little romp around the kitchen. Maybe Thom could bend him over the kitchen table and fuck him until he needed a pillow just to sit down.

He grinned at the cardinal on the feeder outside the kitchen window. Life was good.

Once he'd sweet-talked Thom out of working for the devil, it would be better still.

# Chapter Eight

"And this will be your office." Leta Duncan swept into the bright, spacious room on the second floor of the Rosewood complex. "As you can see, it holds a prime location in this building."

Thom looked around the room, trying to play it cool and not show how impressed he was. It wasn't easy. The place screamed wealth. A bank of windows overlooking Pack Square took up one entire wall. Built-in bookshelves covered the opposite wall, framing the door through which he and Ms. Duncan had just entered. A tremendous desk of what looked like cherry wood sat in front of the window, a brand-new flat-screen computer in sleek black on one side and a matching black phone on the other. The plush dove gray carpet felt soft and springy under his feet.

It was easily the most luxurious office Thom had ever seen, even though it still smelled like paint and new carpet. It was intimidating as hell, frankly.

Not that he'd ever admit to being intimidated by a *room*. Phil would never let him live it down. A week after Thom had accepted the job at Rosewood, Phil still gave him shit about it in ways both subtle and not so much. Thom wasn't about to give the sneaky bastard any more ammunition than he already had.

At least Phil had managed to hire another bartender in the

allotted week. Thom thought he might just lose it if he had to listen to Phil's "Bradford & Lehrer are Satan and Rosewood is hell" spiel any more than he already did.

Turning to Ms. Duncan, Thom nodded with his blank face on. "Nice."

"It is, yes." Ms. Duncan gave him an irritatingly smug smile. "Well. You've seen all the finished areas of the building. Do you have any questions?"

"When will my staff and I be able to start getting the club ready?" Thom paced across the thick carpet toward the window. "It opens in five days. We need to stock the place and learn the layout."

"Actually, everything's ready for you to begin today. Most of the waitstaff are meeting at another location to learn the menu today, but the head waiter and head bartender are here and are ready to help set up Midnight Rose for the grand opening."

Thom pursed his lips, thinking. He and Phil had plans to catch a special showing of *An American Werewolf in London* at the college after dinner, then meet some of Phil's friends for drinks later. He glanced at his watch. It wasn't even noon yet. Still plenty of time to get quite a lot done before he had to pick up Phil at The HO.

"Okay, great. Thanks." Thom turned to meet Ms. Duncan's beady-eyed gaze. "For the record, I still think you should've let me do the hiring. If I'm going to be the boss, I'd rather hire my own staff."

Ms. Duncan's expression soured. "You hired the head bartender. You know as well as I do that there wasn't time for you to hire the entire staff before the opening this weekend."

"The opening should've been delayed." He held up a hand before she could start getting defensive. "I know. Announcements have already gone out, people were already hired before you called me. The future residents of Rosewood are expecting Midnight Rose to be up and running Saturday night. There's nothing I can do about it now. I just wanted you to know that I don't agree with how you handled this."

A red stain crept up Ms. Duncan's thin throat. "You'd best remember, Mr. Stone, that *I* am *your* boss."

"Oh, I know that. I don't mean any disrespect," he lied. "And I would never undermine you by saying any of these things in front of the other employees. But if I think there's a better way of handling something—a way that's better for Rosewood and the people who are going to be living and visiting here—I *will* say so." Thom widened his eyes. "I was under the impression that employees were encouraged to speak up with any ideas or concerns. Was I wrong?"

Her lips thinned so much they nearly disappeared. Thom fought back a grin. He had her, and she knew it.

Phil must be rubbing off on him. He was enjoying this way too much.

And why the hell did he have to think of Phil "rubbing off" on him *now* of all times?

*Save it for later, when you can do something constructive with it.* Stifling a grimace, Thom adjusted his stance and willed his cock to stay the fuck down.

"Of course you should speak up. But, as you say, what's done is done." Ms. Duncan's words sounded tight and forced. She smiled as if she'd rather snarl and throw something. "Now if you'll excuse me, I do have other duties to perform. You already have keys to all Midnight Rose entrances. Please feel free to stay as late as you like."

"I appreciate that. But I won't be staying late today." Thom shot her a grin that made her take a wary step backward. "I have a date."

She blinked rapidly a few times, fingers twisting together. "Oh. Very well. Please do bring your young lady to the club once it's open. You're allowed one guest pass per month."

He considered telling her his "young lady" was a tall, bearded, well-hung man who would rather remove all his body hair with tweezers than ever grace Midnight Rose with his ultraliberal vegan presence. But Ms. Duncan's face was already dangerously red, and Thom didn't want her to have a stroke right there in his new office.

"I remember." He rubbed his tongue stud against the back of his teeth, wishing the woman would just go ahead and leave. "Okay. Well. I'll get started on my work, and let you get back to yours. Thanks very much for showing me around and updating me on the construction schedule for the rest of the complex."

She bobbed her head in a curt nod, spun on one sensible navy blue heel and hurried out the door. Once she was gone, Thom fell into the black leather chair behind the desk, snickering under his breath. God, he'd never seen anyone who needed to get laid as badly as she did. He'd fix her up, if he could think of any man he disliked that much.

*Or maybe she's into girls.* He laughed out loud, one hand over his mouth to stifle the sound. There were *definitely* no women he hated enough to inflict Leta Duncan on.

Planting both palms on his new desk, he ran his hands over the smooth, cool wood. The thing probably cost more than he'd made in a month at The Happy Onion. Phil would no doubt dub it an "overpriced yuppie status symbol" and turn his nose up.

*And I could show him my opinion by bending him over it and fucking him into next week.*

The thought made Thom's prick strain at his underwear. Dammit. He was really going to have to get control of his sex drive.

Forcing the mental images of what he wanted to do to Phil to the back of his mind, he pushed to his feet again. He had a nightclub to run. He could tell Phil about his fucking-on-the-desk fantasy later.

Maybe they could even find a desk and act it out.

Grinning, Thom headed out the door and down the hallway to the club.

∞

Phil was standing in the doorway of The Happy Onion talking to Circe when Thom roared up on his Harley ten minutes late that evening. Thom cut the engine and waved. With an answering wave and a smile, Circe patted Phil's shoulder and went back inside. Phil sauntered over to Thom, flashing the devilish grin that always made Thom's heart stutter and his balls pull up.

"Sorry I'm late," Thom said as Phil strapped on his helmet and straddled the passenger seat. "Some dumbass tried to go the wrong way down Walnut Street and caused a major pileup. It's got traffic backed up in all directions. It took me a while to go around it."

"No problem, we have time." Phil leaned down and kissed the curve of Thom's shoulder. "Everything go okay at the hellhole?"

Thom sighed. "Phil..."

"Sorry, Bubbles." Snaking both arms around Thom's waist, Phil gave his crotch a quick squeeze before clasping his hands around Thom's belly. "Seriously, how was your first day?"

"Fine. Everything's a little hectic right now, but that's to be expected. Midnight Rose is opening Saturday night, and most everyone who's bought a Rosewood condo is coming. Gonna be a hell of a party."

Phil didn't say anything, but that was okay. Thom preferred tactful silence to pontificating any day of the week. At least Phil was trying to be supportive, in his own weird way. It was sweet, really.

Cranking the bike, Thom glanced behind him to make sure the narrow road was clear of oncoming traffic and pulled away from the curb. He and Phil maneuvered the city streets in a comfortable silence. Thom smiled behind the face shield of his helmet. The two of them looked ridiculous, with the elevated passenger seat emphasizing the already considerable difference in their sizes, but Thom didn't care. He loved riding his Fat Boy through the warm summer evening, with Phil's arms around him and Phil's knees pressed against his thighs. Cuddly, silent Phil was his favorite lately.

They arrived at the UNC-A movie theater just in time to take the last two seats in the back before the lights went down and the film started. For a while, Thom forgot all about the fact that the man beside him—the man he was beginning to fall rather hard for, if he were honest with himself—despised his current career choice. He laughed, gasped and cringed along with the rest of the audience. Sharing the experience with Phil gave the whole thing an extra shine.

Afterward, they went back to The HO to ditch the bike, then walked the three blocks to meet a group of Phil's friends at Bar None, a dark little pub wedged between a vintage clothing store and a tattoo shop in the heart of downtown. Phil's buddies were a great deal like him—smart, optimistic and incorrigible mischief-makers. Thom had liked them immediately when he'd met them the previous month at The HO.

A few drinks later, the entire bunch was starting to get loud and rowdy. Fortunately, so was everyone else in the bar, so they didn't attract any particular attention. Thom lounged against the back of the padded faux leather seat, listening with half an ear while he sipped his third 7 & 7. He'd reached the pleasantly buzzed phase and was content to hang out there for a while, letting the conversation wash over him.

He was drifting in an almost-trance when Phil's elbow dug into his ribs. Rubbing his side, he gave Phil a sheepish grin. "What is it?"

"Greta was trying to get your attention, but you were off on another planet somewhere." Phil grinned, hazel eyes sparkling. "What's the matter, Bubbles? Can't hold your liquor?"

Ignoring the laughter around the table, Thom pinched Phil's arm. "You must really want me to spank you pretty bad."

The laughter turned into howls and catcalls. "Oh, man," Rollin chuckled, shaking his head. "He's got your number, Phil."

"Uh-huh," Phil mumbled in distracted acknowledgement. He licked his lips, staring at Thom like he was the lone chocolate bar in a bowl full of sugar-free hard candy.

Thom grinned. He loved putting that lust-crazed look in Phil's eyes.

Leaning his elbows on the scarred wooden table, Thom smiled at Greta, who was still snickering at Phil. "So, Greta. What was it you asked me? I was kind of dozing off, sorry."

She waved a dainty brown hand in a dismissive gesture. "'S okay. I was just wondering if you wanted in on our protest."

Phil's head whipped around so fast his braid hit Thom's arm. "He's not into that sort of thing, Greta, leave him alone."

The sharpness in Phil's voice made Thom frown at him. "I

think I can decide for myself whether or not I want to protest something."

"I know, but—"

"Phil. Let the lady talk." Clamping a hand over Phil's mouth to stop any further arguments, Thom turned back to Greta. "You were saying?"

Greta eyed them both as if wondering which course of action would cause the least trouble. "Well, we're planning a protest against The Evil Empire. We don't have any concrete plans yet, but we're thinking of a sit-in type deal."

"I still think we oughta egg the building," Greta's boyfriend Andy spoke up, oblivious as usual to the sudden tension around the table. "That would *rock*."

Nodding, Thom ran his tongue stud over the back of his teeth while Greta reminded her meat-eating partner that vegans don't throw eggs and chided him for being childish. *If this is going where I think it is, Phil and I are going to have to have a serious talk.* "I see. And what, exactly, is The Evil Empire?"

"Bradford & Lehrer. We're protesting the Rosewood complex." Rollin glanced between Thom and Phil. "Uh, guys? What the hell's going on?"

*Fuck. I knew it. He kept this from me, on purpose. So what's that say about how he sees me?*

Moving with a calmness he didn't feel, Thom took his hand away from Phil's mouth and rose to his feet. "I'll let Phil explain that. Guys, it was great to see you. I'm calling it a night."

Phil reached out to brush his fingers across Thom's elbow. "Hey, it's not—"

Thom managed to smile and squeeze Phil's hand instead of screaming like he wanted to. "I'm just tired, Phil. It's been a long day, and I'm beat."

"I'll walk you home." The borderline desperation in Phil's eyes said he knew Thom was mad, and knew *why* he was mad.

"No, it's okay. Stay and visit." Leaning down, Thom pressed a quick kiss to Phil's lips. Some of the tightness in his chest eased with the soft touch. "I'll call you tomorrow, okay?"

He turned to walk away, but Phil jumped up and grabbed his arm before he got more than a few feet. "Let go, Phil." He managed to keep his voice calm, but it wasn't easy.

"Bubbles, please," Phil whispered, too close for comfort. "Just let me explain."

Thom closed his eyes and took a couple of deep breaths. He could *not* talk to Phil right now. He was too angry, and too hurt. If they tried to talk it out now, Thom knew as surely as he knew his own name that he'd end up saying something awful. Something he couldn't take back. And even as furious as he was, he didn't want to lose Phil now.

"Not now," Thom said, opening his eyes and staring at the exit. "Later. Please."

For a second, he thought Phil wasn't going to let him go. Starting to panic, he tried to tug his arm loose of Phil's grip. To his relief, Phil's hand opened and Thom was free.

"We'll talk later," Phil murmured, still far too close.

Nodding, Thom walked away without looking back.

He pushed through the crowd, yanked the front door open and strode out into the humid summer night. Passersby gave him wary looks as he slouched along the sidewalk muttering to himself, but he didn't care. He hadn't been this furious in years, but at the same time he felt absolutely gutted. The fact that Phil hadn't told his friends Thom worked at Rosewood was a little irritating, but understandable. What cut Thom to the core was that Phil had kept the protest from him.

The protest itself wasn't the problem. Phil and his friends were standing up for what they believed in. Thom respected that. What he didn't respect, or understand at all, was the fact that Phil obviously didn't think enough of him to tell him the truth. He was surprised by how much that hurt.

Thom made it to The Happy Onion and up the back stairs to his apartment without seeing anyone he knew, for which he was grateful. His composure hung by a very thin thread, and he didn't think he could hold himself together if anyone asked him what was wrong. Inside, he kicked the door shut so hard the frame rattled, flung himself into the closest of the two dinette chairs and dropped his head onto the table. His forehead hit the hideous yellow Formica with an audible crack.

His anger dissolved completely with the sharp pain in his skull, leaving him wrung out and exhausted. A hollow ache lodged itself deep in his chest. Lifting his head, he squeezed his eyes shut and pressed both palms to his brow.

*Why couldn't he just tell me? Why did he feel like he couldn't trust me with this?*

*You're no better*, his guilty conscience prodded. *He still doesn't know why you were so skittish about dating him in the first place, because you never told him.*

"I meant to," he whispered, cradling his head in both hands. He *had* meant to. He'd gone to Phil's place for the express purpose of explaining to him about Rob and the death threats and the fear which had driven him from Minneapolis to Santa Fe. Then Phil had distracted him with sex, and after that Ms. Duncan had called with the news about the Rosewood job being back on and it hadn't seemed important anymore.

*He didn't distract you, dumbass. You let yourself be distracted and blamed it on your incurable case of the hots for him, because you didn't want to tell him about your past.*

That was it in a nutshell. Thom knew it was true, even though he had no clue *why*. After all, Phil could hardly blame Thom because his former lover was a total whackjob. If anything, Phil would be sympathetic. He would be horrified by some of the threats Rob had made. Most likely he'd pull Thom into his lap, cuddle him and pet him and swear to him that no one would ever hurt him again.

And that, Thom suspected, was exactly the problem. He despised being seen as weak or helpless, or in need of any sort of protection. People had always been inclined to think of him that way, and Thom had spent a great deal of time and energy in his life making damn sure no one held onto that particular misconception for long. It made him cringe to think of Phil seeing him as vulnerable. Therefore, he'd kept a massive chunk of his history secret.

Which, just possibly, made him a hypocrite.

*Fuck.*

Sighing, Thom opened his eyes and stared at the Florida-shaped rust stain on the ancient white refrigerator. He had no idea what to do now. Part of him wanted to find Phil, apologize for being so damn sensitive in the bar and tell him all the things he still didn't know about Thom's life. Another—admittedly larger—part of him thought Phil should be the one apologizing to him. It stung that Phil clearly didn't think Thom was mature enough to know about the protest.

Before Thom could embark on another journey around the circular argument in his head, someone pounded on the door. He groaned. There was only one person it could possibly be, and Thom wasn't at all sure he was ready to face him.

"Thom? Let me in, okay?"

Hearing Phil's voice made Thom's stomach clench painfully. He ran both hands through his hair. Maybe if he didn't answer,

Phil would think he was already asleep and go away.

"Come on, Thom, open the door." The doorknob rattled. "I'm sorry, okay? Please let me in."

Thom smiled in spite of himself. *Should've known he wouldn't give up that easily.*

"Bubbles, I just want to talk to you. *Please*, pretty baby. Please."

Thom sighed. Why did Phil have to sound so fucking lost? He had to know there was no way Thom could leave him standing out there like a damn stray puppy.

Steeling himself, Thom stood, crossed the few feet to the door and flung it open. "Okay. Talk."

True to his rebellious nature, Phil did no such thing. Instead, he crushed Thom against his chest, raining kisses on his hair. "God, baby, I'm so sorry. I'm an ass, I know it, I'm sorry, please forgive me."

It took every ounce of Thom's strength to resist melting into Phil's embrace. It should be illegal how easily the man dissolved Thom's righteous anger.

Forcing back the urge to pull Phil's shirt off and run his hands all over that beautiful chest, Thom extricated himself from Phil's arms and took a step backward. To his relief, Phil didn't try to pull him back. He couldn't think with Phil so close, and he desperately needed to keep his wits about him right now.

"Why didn't you tell me about the protest?" Thom asked, watching Phil's eyes.

Phil chewed his bottom lip for a moment. "I thought you'd be mad."

Thom couldn't resist. "I thought it turned you on when I get mad."

Phil's eyes flashed. "You know damn well this is different."

"Yeah, I do. Sorry." Dropping into the chair he'd been sitting in before, Thom rubbed both hands over his face. "You didn't trust me with this, Phil. You felt like you had to keep it from me, for whatever reason. What am I supposed to think about that?"

"That I'm an idiot?" Scowling, Phil pulled the second chair from the table and sat. "I've never had a relationship with anyone who didn't share my politics before. I don't want to fuck it up, but it seems like I'm doing that anyway."

"Naw. I guess we're both going to make mistakes here." Thom leaned both forearms on the table. "How do you know I don't share your politics? We never talked about that before." He scraped a bit of some unidentified white substance from the tabletop. "Hell, we've never talked about much of anything, really."

Phil arched an eyebrow at him. "Thom, you're working for Bradford & Lehrer. I think it's a safe bet that you're not politically opposed to them or what they stand for."

"What they stand for? You mean building upscale housing that brings more money and business into downtown? No, I can't say I'm opposed to that."

"Even if they got the land illegally?"

"You have no proof of that. Rumors mean nothing."

Phil pursed his lips. "Even if the land purchase was on the up-and-up—which I still don't think it was, but you're right, I have no proof—even if that was the case, this complex is going to do irreparable damage to downtown."

"How so? The bottom floor is housing lots of new businesses—"

"None of which are locally owned," Phil interjected.

"There are also condos for rent in addition to the ones that are going to be permanent residences. More tourists means more spending, especially when those tourists have lots of money. Everyone benefits from that."

"More money isn't necessarily better." Clasping his hands together, Phil leaned over the table, a pleading expression on his face. "People come to Asheville because of what we are, Thom. They come because this place is special. Rosewood is going to kill that."

"You can't possibly know that," Thom retorted. He was starting to get seriously irritated with Phil's blind opposition to a place he knew *nothing* about.

"I think the fact that they're already petitioning to stop the drum circle is a pretty damn good indication of what's going to happen."

Thom frowned. The drum circle, which was a Friday night tradition in Asheville, took place halfway across town from Rosewood. Even the most enthusiastic drummers couldn't make enough noise to disturb anyone in the new complex. "Where'd you hear that?"

"A friend who works at the paper."

"And where'd *they* hear it?"

Phil made an impatient noise. "I don't know. But—"

"But nothing. The fact is, it's another rumor, and not one that even makes sense. Why would they want to do away with something so well-known and popular?"

"Because they're trying to sanitize this town. Turn it into another playground for rich people."

Maybe Phil didn't intend to sound snobbish, but that's what Thom was hearing. He gritted his teeth. "You don't know any of these people. Why are you assuming the worst about them?"

"I don't assume things about anyone." Reaching across the table, Phil touched Thom's hand. "Bradford & Lehrer has a *history*, Thom. They've pulled this shit before. They've never been prosecuted for anything, that's true, but you don't get people saying these kinds of things about you for no reason. There must be something behind it. Even if their land purchases have all been perfectly legal, they've still caused increased rent everywhere they've built, and they've crowded out plenty of small businesses. I don't want that for Asheville. I don't think you do either."

"Of course I don't. And if you had any kind of proof of any wrongdoing, I'd be protesting right along with you and your friends. But you don't have anything other than rumor and speculation. You can't blame everything on the rich people just because you don't like them."

"That's *not* what I'm doing, dammit."

"I think it is. I think you're obsessed with the idea that anyone with money is evil. Unless they're local small-business owners, of course. Like you."

Phil's expression turned hard. "Better than being a corporate whore."

Thom gaped. "What?"

"You heard me."

"Yeah, I heard you. I just can't believe you fucking *said* that to me."

"Oh, I get it. You can dish it out, but you can't take it." Phil stood and leaned over the table, his eyes blazing. "Fuck you. I'm not gonna sit here and listen to you cut me down at every turn."

"Fine with me." Jumping to his feet, Thom stomped over to the door and flung it open. "Get the fuck out."

Phil's face turned red. "It's *my* apartment, asshole."

Shocked, Thom stared. He considered pointing out that he had a lease, signed all nice and legal by Mr. Holier-Than-Thou himself, but there was no point. Phil already knew that, and dammit if Thom would ever be able to sleep here again anyway.

"Fine," he spat. Pivoting on his heel, he crossed to the closet, fished his giant duffle bag out of the top and started throwing things into it.

"What're you doing?" Phil asked after several silent minutes. He sounded both irritated and wary.

"Leaving." Slinging his bag over his shoulder, Thom snatched his keys and bike helmet from the coffee table and stormed over to the door.

Phil moved in front of him. "I didn't mean you had to leave, Thom. You have a lease."

"Get. Out. Of. My. Way," Thom ground out.

"You're overreacting."

"Move."

"Just fucking typical." Phil shook his head. "You're acting like a child, Bubbles."

The sound of that annoying, irritating, sweet nickname uttered in contempt instead of gentle teasing snapped Thom's tenuous control. Planting his free hand on Phil's chest, he shoved as hard as he could. Phil stumbled backward. Thom pushed past him.

"Keys are on the counter by the fridge." Thom shot a glare at Phil before slamming the door shut behind him. The flash of apprehension in Phil's eyes gave him a surge of savage satisfaction.

Taking the stairs two at a time, Thom crossed the parking lot to his Harley, secured his bag on the passenger seat and strapped on his helmet. Seconds later, he was roaring down the road, on his way to Rosewood to sleep in his office.

It felt wrong to ride the night streets without Phil behind him. When had the stubborn fuck become so damned important to him? When had he gotten to be such an integral part of Thom's life?

*Probably about the time you fell in love with him.*

Startled, he pulled to the side of the road and planted his foot on the curb. Was it true? Did he really love Phil?

He thought about it and realized he did.

Defeated, he hung his head. "Well, isn't that just fucking great."

# Chapter Nine

"I'm sorry, sir," said the silky-voiced young man on the other end of the phone. "But Mr. Stone is in a meeting and can't be disturbed."

*Big fucking surprise.* If all the people he'd talked to at Rosewood could be believed, Thom was in meetings pretty much all the time.

Phil didn't believe them. He knew Thom was avoiding him.

He cleared his throat. "Can you tell him to call me?"

"Of course, sir. And you are...?"

"Phil Sorrells. Tell him to call my cell, he has the number."

"Very well, sir, I'll make sure he gets the message. Will there be anything else?"

Phil could practically hear the smirk in the smarmy bastard's voice. He scowled. "No, just...make sure he calls me. Tell him it's important. Thanks."

He slammed the phone into the cradle and dropped his head into his hands. Thom wouldn't call him back. He'd been trying to get hold of the man for three days. Cell phone, office phone, even Rosewood's general information number. He'd left dozens of messages on voice mail and dozens more with various underlings. No luck. Thom wasn't talking to him.

Raising his head, Phil glanced at the clock on the wall of

his office. Six thirty. Only an hour before he had to meet Greta, Andy and Rollin. He swore under his breath. There wouldn't be time to try calling Thom again.

To be honest, he wasn't sure why he was even trying to warn Thom about the plan to hold a sit-in at Midnight Rose tonight. He didn't owe Thom anything. In a way, it would serve the little terror right to be taken by surprise, after the things he'd accused Phil of Monday night.

*Yeah, because you didn't say anything ugly and horrible at all, did you? It's not like you called him a whore or anything.*

Phil let out a soft laugh. "Guilty much?"

In fact, "guilty" was the understatement of the century. It had taken two whole days before Phil's anger had faded, but once it did he'd been overcome with a nearly crippling remorse. He'd been trying to apologize ever since. This morning, he'd realized that while Thom now knew they'd been planning a protest, he had no idea that they'd settled on a firm plan at last, and that said plan was to take place tonight, at Midnight Rose's grand opening. Phil had added "warn Thom" to his mental list of things he needed to say if he ever got hold of the man and had started dialing with a surge of renewed purpose.

He'd called twenty times since nine o'clock this morning, with no better results than he'd had the previous two days. The thought of facing Thom at the club made him wonder if he should stay at home and leave the sit-in to the rest of the group. He hated to do it, because the Rosewood issue was one he felt passionately about, but if he stayed out of it maybe Thom would recognize what Phil had sacrificed for him and take him back.

His cell phone rang while he was still mulling over the dilemma. Fishing the cell out of the pocket of his cargo pants, he checked the display and nearly had a heart attack when he

121

saw Thom's office number.

He flipped the phone open and pressed it to his ear. "Thom?"

"Yeah. Um. Hi."

The sound of Thom's voice set Phil's insides churning. "Hi. I've been trying to get hold of you."

An awkward, thankfully short silence followed before Thom answered. "I know. Sorry I haven't called you back before. I guess I needed time to cool down."

Phil slumped in his chair. "I hear you. I'm sorry, Thom. I was way out of line Monday night."

There was a heartbeat of quiet on the other end. "I'm sorry too. I shouldn't have said that about you being prejudiced against rich people. I know you better than that."

Phil swallowed around the lump in his throat. "And I shouldn't have called you a corporate whore. I didn't mean it."

A soft laugh floated through the line. "Yeah, you did. You've just thought about it and realized it's not true, that's all."

"I guess so." Switching his phone to his left ear, Phil picked up a pen and drew a lopsided heart on the notepad he kept on his desk. "So where are you staying now?"

"At Rosewood. I slept in my office the first night, but they'd already offered me one of the condos, so I took them up on it and I'm living there now." Thom snorted. "It's kind of ridiculous, really. The place is three times the size I need."

"You could come back to the apartment. Your lease isn't up for a while yet."

The tension coming through the phone line was palpable, and Phil knew what the answer would be. *Oh well. It was worth a try. At least he's talking to me now.*

"I appreciate it," Thom said eventually. "But I don't think

it's a good idea. I'll sign the papers and pay the penalty for breaking the lease early, then you can rent it out to someone else."

"I'm not charging you a penalty, don't worry about that." Phil drew an arrow through the heart on his notepad. "So are we okay now?"

"Fuck, I hope so. I've missed you."

The absolute sincerity in Thom's voice made Phil's eyes well up. Smiling, he doodled a flower next to the heart. "I've missed you too, Bubbles. Wanna go out?"

More laughter. This time it sounded like Thom's normal wholehearted, infectious laugh. "Sure. How about driving up to the Parkway Sunday afternoon for a picnic? I'm kind of busy tonight."

*And there's your perfect segue.* "It's a date. Hey, Thom?"

"Yeah?"

"I have to tell you something."

"Wait, can you hang on a minute? I have a call waiting from the club, it's probably important."

"All right."

"Thanks. Be right back."

A click sounded, and harp music lilted through the line. Phil waited. It made him nervous to put off telling Thom about the sit-in, but at the same time it was a relief. More time to think about how best to say what he had to say was a very good thing, even if it was only a few seconds.

As it turned out, it was nearly two minutes before Thom came back on the line. Phil knew, because he'd counted it out on the wall clock's second hand. "Sorry about that," Thom apologized. "That was the head waiter. One of the registers is acting up. I need to go try and fix it."

"Wait a minute, just let me tell you—"

"I'm sorry, but I really have to go. I'll call you tomorrow, okay?"

"But—"

"Phil. We're fine. I promise."

"Bubbles, just listen for one sec—"

"*Tomorrow*, Phil. Bye."

The line went dead. Irritated, Phil snapped his phone shut and plonked it onto the desk harder than was probably good for it.

"Why the fuck can't he just shut up and *listen*?" he inquired of the papers piled on his desk. "Little shit."

He thought about calling and leaving a voice mail on Thom's cell about the protest, but decided not to. If Thom wasn't going to listen, he could damn well suffer the consequences. A part of Phil knew that was a childish attitude for him to have, but he couldn't help it. He'd tried to warn Thom, and Thom had brushed him off. Maybe next time he'd pay attention.

A knock sounded on the door. Phil sighed. "Come in."

The door opened, and Circe's smiling face popped through the gap. "Hey, Phil. It's just about time for you to go, right?"

"Yeah. I'm heading out in a few minutes, I guess."

"'Kay. I just wanted to say good luck. And call me if you get arrested, yeah? I'll bail you out."

"Sure." Phil gave her a fond smile. "Thanks for holding the fort tonight and tomorrow, Circe. I appreciate it."

"No problem." With a quick glance behind her, she eased herself into the office and shut the door behind her. "Did you get hold of Thom?"

"Yeah. He finally called me back."

"Did you tell him?"

He chuckled at the disapproval in her voice. After he told her what had happened between him and Thom, she hadn't been too happy about his intention to warn Thom of the upcoming sit-in. She thought Thom deserved the slap in the face of seeing Phil at Midnight Rose tonight. Actually, she'd expressed the desire to punish Thom for his sins in rather more physically painful ways, but since she was far too sensible to act on those fantasies she'd figured public humiliation would have to do.

"I didn't get a chance to tell him," Phil answered.

She grinned. "Didn't get a chance. Right, I get you."

"It's true. We made a date for Sunday, then he got called away before I could tell him about the protest tonight."

"Good. He doesn't deserve a warning."

Shaking his head, Phil pushed his chair back and stood. He didn't have time to explain himself, or try to rationalize Thom's behavior to Circe. Especially not when he sort of agreed with her. "Okay, I'm heading out now. I'll call you later, either to tell you how it went or to get you to come bail me out of jail."

"All right." She preceded him out the office door. After he locked the door, she laid a hand on his arm and peered up at him with dark, sorrowful eyes. "I'm sorry about all this mess between you and Thom. I'm still mad at him, but I know how you feel about him. I hope y'all are still okay after tonight."

"Yeah. Me too." Leaning down, he kissed her cheek. "Wish me luck."

"Luck." She smiled at him as he took his bike helmet from the wooden peg by the office door and strapped it on. "Talk to you later."

A few minutes later, he was peddling through the Saturday afternoon traffic to the planned rendezvous in Pack Square. Between the four of them, he and his friends had managed to gather twenty-three people to participate in the sit-in. One of the protesters had promised to talk to a reporter friend of hers, so they would most likely have local news coverage.

That, as far as Phil was concerned, was the main reason for him to attend the protest as planned. If he was there, he could at least warn Thom in time to keep him off camera and out of the news reports. No one else would do it. Greta, Rollin and Andy considered Thom the embodiment of evil right now, and the rest of the group would only see him as a member of the enemy camp. Hell, even the Midnight Rose staff wouldn't be any help. They'd be looking to Thom to protect *them*. If any of the senior management were there, they'd surely disappear at the first sign of trouble, leaving Thom to face it alone.

At the moment, Phil was Thom's only ally.

He just hoped Thom would see it that way.

⊱⊰

Thom whistled a Muse tune to himself as he strolled down the hallway from his office to the kitchen entrance into Midnight Rose. In fifteen minutes, the grand-opening party would begin. For the first time all week, Thom actually felt ready for it.

The last five days had been pure torture, and not just because of the stress of getting the club ready for its debut. His fight with Phil, followed by the realization that he was *in love* with the big goof, had thrown his mind and emotions into turmoil. All week, he'd vacillated between depression and indignation, snapping at employees and generally turning

126

everyone else's life into the same hell his had been up until just a little while ago. He didn't know why he'd chosen to return Phil's call this evening, when he'd been ignoring all the other calls for the past three days, but something had compelled him.

*Probably the fact that you missed the guy like crazy. Or maybe you just didn't see any point in making either of you suffer any longer.*

Whatever the reason, Thom was glad he'd called. They were back together now. Phil was still his, and everything was once again right with the world.

Pushing through the swinging doors into the kitchen, Thom spread his arms and grinned at the black-and-white-clad people rushing frantically around with last-minute preparations. "It's party time, boys and girls. Everybody ready?"

All the noise and chatter halted at once as every single person in the room stopped what they were doing and gaped at him. He laughed. They'd only ever seen him scowling, had only ever experienced his harsher side. Right now, they probably all thought he'd finally lost it.

One of the waitstaff edged toward him, her expression full of wary curiosity. "Mr. Stone? Are...are you okay?"

"Karen, I am more than okay. I am *stupendous.*" He clapped her on the shoulder. "Okay, everybody out in the club. I want to talk to all of you before we open."

The staff scurried out into the spacious, crimson and cherrywood club room. Karen ran over to the bar and said something Thom couldn't hear to the bartenders. They all stared at Thom for a second before following Karen out to the dance floor, where the rest of the workers were gathering.

"All right, people," Thom called, loudly enough for everyone to hear. "I just wanted to say a couple of things before we open. First of all, I'm sorry for how rough I've been on you these past few days. I've been under a lot of personal stress. I took it out on you guys, and that was wrong. It won't happen again."

There were a few nods and murmurs in the crowd, but they mostly watched him in expectant silence. He took a deep breath and continued.

"Secondly, I want to tell you all what a fantastic job you've done this week. We didn't have long to get this place ready for tonight, but you people have done a phenomenal job of it. I'm proud to be working with such a great group of professionals, and I think Rosewood's residents are going to be thrilled with this club." He planted both hands on his hips and beamed at his crew. "Now. The head honchos'll be giving us the signal any minute. Everybody put your party face on."

As the group broke up and went to man the bar and wait stations, Thom strolled through the dimly lit room to the vestibule. A curved half-wall topped with a planter full of ferns set the area apart from the rest of the club. Through the round windows in the padded red double doors, Thom could see the crowd milling around Rosewood's large, richly decorated lobby. Sounds of laughter and conversation drifted in.

Don Bradford wandered into view, a glass of champagne in one hand and an alarmingly skinny redheaded woman hanging off the opposite arm. Catching Thom's eye through the glass, he excused himself to his companion, pushed the door open and slipped into the vestibule. "It's about that time. You ready?"

Thom gave him a confident smile. "We're ready any time you are, Mr. Bradford."

Mr. Bradford's ruggedly handsome face broke into a big grin, creasing his health-club tan. "Thom, how many times do I have to tell you to call me Don? You make me feel like an old man with this 'Mr. Bradford' shit."

Thom remembered the sixty-eighth birthday card they'd all

had to sign for the man on Tuesday and wisely kept his smartass remarks to himself. "Sure thing, Don."

"That's better." Giving Thom a hard clap on the shoulder, Don laid a hand on the door. "Keith and I are going to make the official announcement, then let in the hordes."

Thom nodded, then hurried back to the main part of the club as Don slipped back into the lobby to join his business partner, Keith Lehrer, in front of the doors. "All right, folks," Thom called. "Mr. Bradford and Mr. Lehrer are getting ready to open the club. Let's show those people that Midnight Rose is the best nightspot in the city."

To his surprise, everyone clapped. A few people called out "hell yeah!" and other such sentiments. Frankly, it was more enthusiasm than he'd dared hope for, considering how little they all knew each other and how stressful the last few days had been.

Grinning, Thom strode back to the vestibule and took up his spot beside the host's stand. This was what he'd been waiting for ever since Don Bradford had made that first drunken job offer back in Santa Fe—the chance to prove his skills and abilities outside of the bar. It was his moment to shine, and he was determined to make the most of it.

Irritatingly, part of him longed to share this night with Phil.

*Uh-huh. Like that would ever happen. He wouldn't be caught dead here.*

The double doors swung wide. Locking them open with two rubber stoppers, Don and Keith stood on either side to greet the tenants as they entered the club.

That was Thom's cue. Shaking off the nagging sense of disappointment that he couldn't share this with the man he loved, he put on his brightest smile and stretched his hand toward his first customer.

An hour later, Midnight Rose was packed and the party was in full swing. Thom moved from table to table, introducing himself and making sure people were enjoying themselves. Everything seemed to be moving with impressive smoothness. Thom knew from experience that there was no such thing as a glitch-free opening night, but so far they'd had nothing more than minor difficulties. The register which had been acting up before was working fine now, and the customers had done nothing but gush about the understated elegance of the club and how absolutely *wonderful* the staff was.

Personally, Thom was having the time of his life. It surprised him a bit to discover how much he truly enjoyed talking to patrons and solving the little problems that cropped up here and there behind the scenes. Evidently he'd been right in thinking this job would be a terrific fit for him.

Once again, he wished he could share this with Phil. *Maybe he'll let me tell him about it tomorrow.* In spite of Phil's strong opposition to Rosewood and everything to do with it, Thom had a feeling Phil would listen and be happy for him anyway.

A commotion drew Thom's gaze toward the vestibule. From his current position at the wait station in the back of the room, he squinted through the crowd. A group of people appeared to be cutting a wedge through the invited guests, heading for the bar. He heard cries of "stop!" and "you can't come in here", mingled with a rising agitated murmur.

An ugly feeling settled in the pit of Thom's stomach. If this was the protest he and Phil had argued about, he was going to murder a certain hippie he knew.

Hoping to God he was wrong, he wormed his way through the crush of expensively dressed partygoers toward the disturbance. A rather large group of young men and women had handcuffed themselves to the brass railing running the length of the bar. They all wore white T-shirts with the slogan "Bradford & Lehrer: Bribers & Leeches" written on the front in black marker.

A few of the interlopers were quite familiar to him. He caught Greta's eye. She lifted her chin and glared at him.

He groaned. Of all the times and places the damned idealistic idiots could've held a protest, didn't it just *have* to be here and now. At least he didn't see—

"Thom! Over here!"

He froze. *Dammit, dammit, dammit.* Moving with careful precision, he turned toward the familiar voice. Wide hazel eyes stared into his.

Phil.

Fucking hell.

# Chapter Ten

Thom stalked over to where Phil sat cross-legged on the floor, one wrist cuffed to the bar's railing. "What the fuck, Phil? This is your fucking *protest*?"

"I tried to tell you on the phone, but you wouldn't let me." Phil glanced at something behind Thom. "The reporters are here, you'd better go."

"Why, are you embarrassed to be seen with the enemy?" Thom stared into Phil's eyes, shaking with a combination of fury and hurt. "I can't believe you'd do this to me."

Phil's eyes widened even more. "No, you don't understand."

"The hell I don't." Somewhere to Thom's left, a bright light switched on. The cool, detached voice of one of the weekend reporters on the local news station floated from that direction, explaining to the viewers what was happening. Thom leaned closer to Phil, knowing his out-of-control emotions were plain in his eyes and not caring. "You. Complete. *Fuck*."

"Thom, come on." Phil reached a hand toward him. He stepped backward, and Phil let out an impatient huff. "If you'd just let me explain—"

"Fuck you."

Turning his back on Phil's anguished face, Thom stalked across the room. Thankfully, Don Bradford was already talking to the reporter, meaning Thom wouldn't have to. He was profoundly relieved by that. If he tried to speak to anyone else right now, he'd lose his cool for sure.

The scary part was, right now he was more likely to sob like a teenage girl than to rip anybody a new one.

Stupid Phil and his stupid friends and their stupid *fucking* protest.

Thom shoved open the double doors and walked out into the lobby. It was nearly empty. A few partygoers hovered nervously between the Midnight Rose entrance and the big glass doors leading outside. Near the exit, a group of security guards stood with their hands resting on their holstered weapons, glaring around the lobby. Outside the glass doors, red lights flashed and sirens screamed as a whole row of patrol cars raced toward Rosewood from the police station a couple of blocks away.

Leaning against the wall, Thom drew a few deep, slow breaths, trying to get himself under control. He felt like he'd been kicked in the chest. A few hours ago, everything had been fine, or so he'd thought. What a hell of a way to find out how wrong he'd been.

*Why the fuck did Phil have to come here tonight? Why couldn't he have stayed out of it?* That was the question plaguing Thom more than any other. The protest itself was a shock, for sure. A nasty one. But he could see now that Phil had been trying to tell him about it earlier, on the phone. What absolutely tore him up inside was the fact that Phil was here, chained to the bar along with his cohorts. Why would he be here, unless his political convictions were more important than the relationship he claimed to want so much?

Thom knew he had no right to expect anything else, really, but it still hurt like hell. Especially when he'd let himself hope he could have something permanent with Phil.

"Stupid, stupid, stupid." Running both hands through his hair, he blinked several times until the sting in his eyes went away.

Across the lobby, at least a dozen cops burst through the outside doors and trotted across the polished marble floor toward the club. Thom pushed away from the wall and stepped back so he wouldn't be in the way. One officer turned a cold, assessing gaze to Thom as she passed, but he may as well have been invisible for all the notice any of the others gave him. That was just fine, as far as he was concerned. What he really wanted was to curl up in a dark corner someplace where no one could see just how destroyed he felt. Barring that, being ignored would do.

It took nearly twenty minutes before the cops emerged again, escorting the protesters out of the building in police custody. Thom tried to tell himself he hadn't stood there against the wall all that time waiting for Phil to be brought out before he went back in himself, but it didn't work. He knew damn well that was exactly what he was doing.

Phil was the second to last person removed from Midnight Rose. Thom's heart turned over hard when Phil's roving gaze caught his and held it.

"Thom." Phil dug his heels in and stopped, making the blue-clad mass of muscle beside him frown and tug on his arm. "I never meant it to be like this. Please, you have to believe me. I didn't do this to hurt you."

He *seemed* sincere. But then again, he'd seemed sincere on the phone that evening too. Thom shook his head. What was he supposed to think? And just what the *hell* was he supposed to say?

Before he could come up with anything, the cop grunted

and dragged Phil across the floor. Phil stumbled behind, his body twisting so he could hold Thom's gaze. Those beautiful hazel eyes were bright with desperation.

"Thom, just let me talk to you, let me explain." Phil tried to jerk loose of the police officer's grip, and let out a frustrated noise when the big hand held on tight. "Come on, man, let go for a second."

"Sir," the cop ground out. "If you do not calm down *right now* and come along quietly, I'll charge you with resisting arrest."

*Oh, shit.* Thom sighed. "Phil, settle down. You're going to get yourself in serious trouble."

Phil bit his lip. "Baby, please," he whispered. "Don't let it end like this. Please."

Thom's cheeks heated under the sharp gaze of the officer and the curious glances of the few people still standing around. "We'll talk later, okay? Just go."

Phil stared into Thom's eyes. Whatever he saw there must not have been very reassuring. His shoulders slumped. He followed the cop without further argument. Right before exiting the building, he glanced behind him. The sadness in his face dug into Thom's gut like a knife.

Groaning, Thom covered his face with both hands. How the hell was he supposed to sleep that night with Phil's sorrowful expression haunting him?

When he thought he had himself under control, he dropped his hands, squared his shoulders and marched back into the club. He and his staff had plenty of loose ends to tie up. They'd probably be here for at least a couple more hours. With any luck, by the time he got back to his condo he'd be too tired to miss Phil.

He ignored the nagging little voice in the back of his head

telling him that was wishful thinking.

ŏ⊃

Rosewood wasn't Phil's first protest. It was, however, his first arrest. By the time he was released on his own recognizance a couple of hours before dawn, he had long ago made up his mind that this arrest would also be his last.

Yawning, Phil shuffled out of the bland brightness of the booking room into the cramped hallway with its peeling paint and old-building smell. He was so tired even the tight pain in his chest from the confrontation with Thom felt dull and far away. If he could just make things right with Thom, maybe he'd actually be able to sleep once he got home.

*Speaking of getting home...* He'd promised to call Circe, but it was an absolutely ridiculous hour to call. His bike was still chained to one of the public racks around Pack Square. He could ride home and call her later. Right now, he'd rather be alone anyway.

Okay, so that wasn't exactly true. Only a few blocks away was a certain pretty little blond who Phil ached to hold through the rest of the night and the entire coming day. Too bad he'd screwed up with said blond so badly he'd be lucky to ever be allowed to speak to him again, never mind cuddle him while he slept.

Turning the corner to the hallway leading outside, Phil stopped and blinked. Fuck, he must be going crazy. He wanted Thom so badly he was hallucinating him now.

Frowning, he crossed to the white plastic chair where the figment of his imagination sat with one foot tucked beneath him and his head resting against the wall. His eyes were closed, that sweet mouth open and slack with sleep.

It was, overall, an impressively vivid and detailed hallucination. So perfect Phil couldn't resist the urge to touch. Moving with great care so as not to spoil the illusion, he reached out and brushed his fingertips over one soft porcelain cheek.

The smooth brow furrowed. Delicate eyelids fluttered open and sky blue eyes focused on Phil's face. "Phil. Hi."

Phil's mouth fell open. He wasn't seeing things at all. Thom was actually here.

The corners of Thom's mouth quirked up in a halfhearted smile as Phil took a single reeling step backward. "I take it you didn't expect me to be here."

"Not exactly, no." Phil stuck his hands in his back pockets and stared hard at Thom's left earlobe. He didn't think he could look Thom in the eye right then. "Um. So. What... I mean, are you... Uhhh..."

He'd never felt so stupid and tongue-tied in his life. Fortunately, Thom seemed to know what he was trying to say.

"You want to know what I'm doing here, and if I'm still mad." Rising to his feet, Thom touched Phil's elbow. "Look at me, would you?"

Reluctantly, Phil shifted his gaze to meet Thom's. Thom's eyes were as bloodshot as Phil's felt, making the blue seem brighter than ever.

"I'm here because we seriously need to talk. Am I still mad?" Thom shrugged. "I reserve judgment on that until after the talking part."

Phil had a feeling he knew what *that* meant. He sighed. God, he was tired. "I already explained why we were protesting, Thom. You can't expect me to change my views on Rosewood just because you work there."

"Of course not. I would *never* expect that of you. I just want to know..." Thom looked away, chewing his lower lip. "Why'd you have to go tonight, Phil?"

Listening to all the unspoken questions in Thom's voice, Phil wished he could go back and redo the past half a day. He reached out to brush a stray lock of hair from Thom's eyes. "I was honestly just trying to protect you, Bubbles. When I didn't get to warn you about the protest on the phone—"

Thom winced. "God, I'm sorry about that. One of these days I'll learn to shut up and listen."

Phil smiled. "Why do I think maybe you won't?"

"Because you're smarter than you look, I guess." Thom laid a finger across Phil's lips to stifle his protest. "I'm listening now. Go on."

Taking Thom's hand, Phil kissed his fingertips, then laced their fingers together. "Anyway, when I couldn't tell you then, I almost didn't go. But we all knew there were gonna be reporters, because Lisa's friends with the reporter who came tonight so of course she'd tipped her off about it. I just thought if I went, I could warn you about the news being involved, and then you wouldn't get caught up in all the crap. Everybody else was kind of pissed off at you after our fight, so I didn't trust any of them to protect you." He hunched his shoulders and looked at the floor. "I didn't even think of how you might take it if you saw me there, especially since you didn't even know the protest was going to be tonight. I'm sorry."

For a moment Thom was silent. Phil glanced up. Thom was staring at him with an indefinable expression. Phil's breath caught. He had no clue what was going on in Thom's head, but something about the look in those enormous eyes made Phil's crotch tingle.

"Phil," Thom eventually said, "you are a very strange person."

"Um. Okay." Phil scratched his chin. "So does that mean you're still mad, or you're not? 'Cause I have to tell you, I'm way too fucking tired to try and guess."

Chuckling, Thom shook his head. "No, I'm not mad anymore."

Phil sagged with relief. "Good. I don't think I'd survive it a second time."

To Phil's shocked delight, Thom laughed out loud and flung himself into Phil's embrace. His arms locked around Phil's waist, his cheek pressing to Phil's chest. Phil's throat went tight. Winding one arm around Thom's waist and burying the opposite hand in Thom's fine, sleek hair, Phil kissed the top of Thom's head. He was so exhausted his ears were buzzing, but he wouldn't have moved right then for the world. For the first time in days, he felt whole. No way was he breaking the spell of this perfect moment.

Thom finally stirred, shaking Phil out of the contented half-doze into which he'd fallen. Drawing back, Thom grinned up at Phil. "Come on, let's get you home. You're asleep on your feet."

"Mm-hm." Phil yawned so hard his eyes watered. "Should I call Circe? I was just gonna ride my bike, but I'm sure she'd be glad to come get us both."

"No need. I'll take you home on my Harley."

Phil frowned, trying to remember why that wouldn't work. "I don't have that extra helmet."

A rosy blush colored Thom's cheeks. "I brought it with me. Just in case you'd let me take you home."

"In that case, hell yeah, I'll let you." Cupping Thom's chin in one palm, Phil tilted his head up and planted a soft kiss on his lips. "Will you stay with me?"

This close, Phil clearly felt the hitch in Thom's breath. Thom's hands slid up to caress Phil's cheeks. "Sure, why not? Could be fun." His tongue came out, the tip tracing the line of Phil's bottom lip. "I really have missed you."

Phil's chest went tight. He kissed Thom again, deeper this time. Thom groaned into his mouth, and the sound went straight to Phil's groin. With great effort, he drew away, keeping one hand clasped with Thom's. "Let's go, yeah? I'm wiped out, and I bet you are too."

"You got that right." Thom smiled, the wonderful, unguarded smile Phil had been afraid he'd never see again. "I can't wait to get you in bed."

"Me too, pretty baby. Me too. Maybe we'll even have enough energy left for a quickie when we get home."

Grinning, Phil followed Thom out into the still night.

# Chapter Eleven

As it turned out, neither of them lasted longer than it took to brush their teeth, undress and crawl between the sheets. Thom planted a sweet kiss on Phil's lips, then snuggled against his chest. Phil fell asleep clutching Thom to him like an oversized teddy bear.

Phil drifted back to consciousness an indeterminate amount of time later to the pounding of rain on the roof. A flash of light and a deafening boom from outside told him what must have woken him. Smiling, he drew the covers up to his chin and watched the storm unleash a deluge of windblown water and leaves on his bedroom window.

He couldn't help noticing that Thom no longer lay draped over him. Pushing himself to a sitting position, he rubbed the sleep out of his eyes and squinted around the room. "Thom?"

"In here," Thom called from the half-closed bathroom door. The toilet flushed, the water ran for a while, then the door swung open and Thom sauntered out, still gloriously naked, yawning and scratching his belly. "Hey. Didn't mean to wake you, but I had to pee really bad."

"Naw, you didn't wake me up. It was the thunder."

"Me too. It's damn loud."

"Yeah." Phil snagged Thom's wrist the second he got close enough and pulled him to the bed for a quick kiss and a rather

141

more leisurely grope. "Mmmm. Nice."

Laughing, Thom wiggled his ass in Phil's two-handed grip. "Nice for you, maybe. But you've got morning breath."

"And here you are all minty fresh."

"I borrowed your toothbrush."

"Presumptuous of you."

"Hey, I already used it last night." Thom leaned down, blatantly disregarding Phil's morning breath to kiss him again. "Besides, I think we pretty much have all of each other's germs by now."

Weirdly enough, the thought made Phil feel warm right to his toes. Grinning, he raked Thom's tousled hair away from his face. "I'd sure like to stay in bed and swap germs all day, what about it?"

Thom's lips curved into a wicked smile. "I like that plan." Snaking a hand beneath the covers, he cupped Phil's right butt cheek in his palm. "If you need to get up for anything, you better do it now, because I have plans for this ass."

*Oh* hell *yeah.* "Let me go take a piss, pretty baby, and my ass is all yours."

Heat flared in Thom's eyes. Without a word, he rolled off Phil's chest. Phil scooted to the edge of the bed, stood and shuffled into the bathroom, trying not to think of Thom's bare body stretched out on the rumpled sheets. If he got a hard-on right now, it would take him forever to pee, and he wanted to get back to bed as soon as possible.

*You two need to be talking instead of fucking*, he told himself as he flipped the toilet seat up. The whole Rosewood thing would stay right there between them like the damn Berlin Wall until they talked out their differences and managed to find some sort of common ground. He knew that, and he was sure there must actually be some common ground somewhere in the whole mess for them to stand on.

The thing was, it was bound to take them a while to find it, and they'd never get there without more yelling and hurt feelings. He just couldn't deal with it right now.

*Get the sex out of your system first. Then when you're both feeling all warm and fuzzy, you can have that conversation.*

Thus decided, Phil shoved his worry over the future to the back of his mind. Serious ideological conversations were so *not* sexy, and he didn't want anything not sexy intruding on his sex time.

After relieving himself, Phil took the time to splash cold water on his face and brush his teeth. He cast a critical eye over his reflection as he scrubbed. There were faint bluish shadows under his eyes, but other than that he thought he looked pretty damn good.

He spit, rinsed and grinned at himself in the mirror. He looked every bit as deliriously happy as he felt. Funny how the anticipation of sex with Thom was more exciting than most of the actual sex Phil had had with anyone else.

"You're lucky he's even here," he informed his twin in the glass. "Don't fuck up like that again."

"Phil?" Thom's voice floated from the bedroom. "Are you talking to yourself?"

"Kind of." Phil pulled the rubber band from the bottom of his braid and started unwinding his tangled hair.

"Well, stop it and get in here. I haven't had any sex in *days*."

Phil laughed. "I hear you, angel face. On my way." Still untwisting his hair, he left the bathroom and strolled across his wide-plank pine floor to the bed.

Smiling, Thom held his arms out. "Come here."

Phil took a flying leap onto the bed, making the springs squeak, and scooped Thom into his arms. Thom met him in a deep, openmouthed kiss.

The metal stud in Thom's tongue clacked across the back of Phil's teeth, and Phil felt like whooping for sheer joy. Last night, waiting his turn to be processed and angsting over the evening's events, he'd decided that if Thom left him for good he'd never date anyone with a tongue piercing again, because tongue studs would forever remind him of Thom. His perfect man, the one who'd gotten away. His relief at having Thom and his pierced tongue back again was so huge his body felt inadequate to contain it.

Part of Phil wanted to take it slow, savor every second. After nearly a week of celibacy, however, slow and sensual didn't stand a chance. One of Thom's slender legs wound around Phil's hips, rocking their groins together. The feel of Thom's erection rubbing against his made Phil's skin spark like a blown transformer. Moaning, Phil slid the hand not buried in Thom's hair up the firm thigh draped across his hipbone. He got a good handful of Thom's sweet little ass and squeezed, tearing a ragged groan from Thom's throat.

"I want to fuck you," Thom growled, breathing out the scent of all-natural organic peppermint-oil toothpaste. "Get the lube."

A delicious shudder raced up Phil's spine. "Goddamn, Bubbles. I *love* it when you get bossy."

"Oh yeah?"

"Yeah."

"I see." Thom gave Phil's rear a sound smack, grinning when Phil's cock twitched and jerked in response. "Well, then, I'll get bossy again." Pushing up onto one elbow, he leaned over until his lips brushed the shell of Phil's ear. "Get." He licked

144

Phil's earlobe. "The." Another lick. "Lube." The tip of his tongue darted into Phil's ear, making him squeal. "Now."

Phil nodded. Not wanting to let go of Thom long enough to retrieve the lube from the drawer of the bedside table, Phil tightened an arm around Thom's waist and rolled onto his back with Thom on top of him. He stretched his arm out, yanked the drawer open and groped through the contents.

Thom, meanwhile, shimmied down Phil's body to play with his left nipple. Phil's vision blurred when Thom's teeth dug into the sensitive little nub. Staring down at the wicked mouth attached to his chest, Phil had to wonder how Thom managed to smirk like that while simultaneously applying such mind-blowing suction.

Thom's head lifted, leaving Phil's nipple wet and pebbling in the relative cool of the air. "Got that lube yet?"

"Uh-huh," Phil said, hoping he wasn't about to make a liar out of himself. *Dammit, I know it's here.* He dug frantically through the pens, bookmarks, scraps of paper and half-used plant-based lip balms, wishing he could see what he was doing. Finally, his fingers curled around the familiar round bottle of vegan-friendly gel, and he held it up with a crow of triumph. "There. Lube."

Thom snatched it from him with one hand and nudged his thigh with the other. "Spread."

Phil obeyed so fast Thom bounced when he hit the mattress between Phil's splayed legs. He laughed. "You're not anxious to get my cock up your ass or anything, are you?"

"Only a lot." Reaching underneath himself, Phil pulled his cheeks apart to display his twitching hole. "Hurry up."

Thom's gaze zeroed in on Phil's anus, staring so hard Phil could almost feel the heat of it. "Jesus, Phil."

"Too slutty?"

145

"Do you do that for anyone else?"

"Never."

"Then no. Not slutty. Just incredibly fucking hot."

Bending down, Thom sucked up a purple mark on the inside of Phil's thigh. When he straightened again, he was already squeezing gel into his hand. Two slippery fingers pressed into Phil's hole, searched out his gland and rubbed it.

Phil gasped, back arching and hands clutching the covers in a death grip. "Ohmygodyes! Yes. Do that again."

Thom complied, sending pure pleasure pulsing through Phil's body. "God, you're so..." He trailed off, leaving the thought unfinished. His fingers twisted and scissored in Phil's loosening hole. His wide eyes were focused with unnerving intensity on Phil's face. "I can't wait any longer. Please tell me you're ready."

Unable to speak, Phil nodded so hard it made him dizzy. He drew both legs up to his chest, spreading himself in blatant invitation.

Thom's fingers withdrew. Biting his lip, he took hold of his cock with one hand and rested the other on Phil's thigh. The blunt head of his prick nudged Phil's hole.

Their gazes locked. A single sharp thrust, a brief burn and a lube-slicked slide, and Thom was inside and all was right with Phil's world.

"Oh." Thom fell forward, catching his weight on his hands. His eyes were half-closed, his mouth open. He rocked his hips, eliciting a whimper from Phil. "God, you feel so good. So fucking good."

Phil agreed, but he still couldn't get his voice to work, so he expressed his concurrence by draping his legs over Thom's shoulders and lifting his butt to meet Thom's next thrust. They groaned in stereo, the soft sound nearly drowned out by a clap of thunder that shook the house.

Phil reached up, tangled a hand into Thom's hair and tugged. Taking the hint, Thom stretched forward—folding Phil in half in the process—and took Phil's mouth in a surprisingly gentle kiss. Phil shut his eyes and let it carry him away. His hip joints would bitch at him later for the abuse he was heaping on them now, but at the moment he didn't care. With Thom's metal-studded tongue in his mouth and his ass full of his favorite cock in the world, Phil was in heaven.

Not so long ago, going five days—six? Maybe it was six now, he couldn't remember—without sex would've been no big deal. Before Thom came along, Phil had regularly gone up to two weeks without a fuck, and once he'd had a dry spell lasting almost three months. Since he and Thom had decided to start seeing each other, however, he'd become accustomed to sex at least once—and sometimes twice—a day. Their relationship had only been official for a week before the whole protest debacle caused that hellish temporary breakup, but it was enough.

Phil was spoiled, and six days was now *way* too long to do without. Which was probably why he felt his orgasm building inside him after an embarrassingly short time.

Judging by Thom's litany of broken moans and the way his smooth thrusts devolved into furious, mindless pounding, he was having the same problem as Phil. It made Phil feel better to know he wasn't the only one.

"Oh my God," Thom panted against Phil's lips. "Phil. Oh."

Phil framed Thom's face in his hands, separating them enough to let him stare into Thom's eyes. "I know. Let go, sweet baby, come on. Come on."

"Fuck, yeah," Thom groaned, and came, his shaft pulsing deep in Phil's ass.

Phil didn't even have time to mentally congratulate himself

Ally Blue

for lasting the longest before his own release overpowered him. He let out a hoarse cry, his toes curling hard as his untouched cock splattered them both with almost a week's worth of semen.

Dipping his head, Thom collected a quick kiss from Phil before shrugging Phil's legs off his shoulders and collapsing onto Phil's chest. His softened cock slipped from Phil's hole. Phil squeaked, and Thom laughed. "Man, I seriously needed that."

"Me too." Phil wrapped both arms around Thom. He raked his fingers through the fine tresses, gently working through the tangles. "I'm glad you're back, Bubbles. I like having you in my bed."

Thom lay still, his cheek resting in a puddle of spunk just below Phil's collarbone. "Just your bed?"

His voice was quiet and calm, but Phil heard the uncertainty behind the question he'd just posed, and the one he hadn't quite asked.

Tucking a finger beneath Thom's chin, Phil lifted his face and peered into his eyes. "No. Not just my bed."

It didn't seem like very many words to convey all the things Phil was feeling at the moment. It sure as hell didn't get across his desire to see Thom at his best and his worst every single day for the rest of their lives.

Thom, however, seemed to get the gist of it, if not the full depth of what Phil felt for him. He smiled, and a whole flock of butterflies swooped through Phil's chest.

Pushing himself up, Thom planted a kiss on Phil's lips before curling into his embrace again. Phil rested his chin on Thom's head, one hand cupping Thom's ass and the other tracing patterns up and down his spine. With his lover in his arms and the rain falling outside, Phil felt lazy and content. He wished they could lie here forever, boneless with post-coital bliss, listening to the storm and not talking. Specifically, not

148

talking about Rosewood and the protest and how in the nine hells they were supposed to get over this particular ideological hurdle and come to an understanding that would let them stay together.

"We're going to have to talk eventually, you know," Thom murmured.

Phil grimaced. "I was just thinking that, actually."

"I kind of figured."

They fell silent. Thunder rolled in the distance as the storm moved on.

"I don't want to talk right now," Thom declared after a few minutes. "Do you?"

"Nope." Phil tightened his grip on Thom. "Cuddle now. Talk later."

Thom chuckled. "Good plan."

It was. A few minutes later, Thom was fast asleep and drooling on Phil's chest. Phil was drifting in a half-doze when he realized with a shock that he had no idea if Thom had to be at work tonight. He thought about waking Thom to ask, but decided not to. If there was one thing he'd learned about Thom over these last few weeks, it was that the man took his responsibilities very seriously. If he was supposed to work, he would've made damn sure he was up and ready in plenty of time. Phil had already scheduled himself off for the next few days, just in case he'd had to spend time in jail. Circe had come up with that idea, because she'd had a friend once who'd spent two days in jail after a protest.

*Circe. Oh shit, I still have to call her. She's going to be frantic.*

Thom shifted, burrowing his face into Phil's throat. A faint snore escaped his open mouth. Smiling, Phil caressed Thom's soft cheek. Circe could wait a few more minutes.

# Chapter Twelve

They needed to talk. Thom knew it, and he knew Phil knew it. But four and a half weeks after the event which had nearly broken them up for good, they still hadn't discussed it. In fact, they'd avoided the subject like the plague, letting themselves fall into a comfortable routine of sex and small talk.

Well, mostly sex, if Thom were honest with himself. Anytime it seemed like one of them might start the conversation neither of them wanted to have, they ended up fucking instead. It was great fun, even though Thom had started to worry about developing calluses on his dick, but they couldn't ignore their potentially relationship-destroying differences forever. One day, they were going to have to sit down and get everything out in the open.

Thom dreaded it. Obviously, Phil dreaded it too. Thus the current unprogressive—if sexually rewarding—situation.

The quiet burr of the telephone jarred Thom out of his thoughts, reminding him that it was the middle of the afternoon on a Thursday and he had work to do. He picked up the receiver and pressed it to his ear. "This is Thomas Stone."

"Mmmm. You sound sooooo sexy, Mr. Stone. What are you wearing?"

The voice was a low, teasing, very familiar purr. Thom laughed. "Hi, Phil."

"Hey, pretty baby. Want to go out to dinner?"

"I can't. We're one short tonight, I have to stay and help out."

He neglected to mention that the reason they were short-staffed was because Ms. Shit-For-Brains Duncan had taken it upon herself to fire Karen Edwards, one of his best waitresses. Over the phone. Just after lunchtime on a day she was scheduled to work. The worst part was, this was the second time in as many weeks Leta Duncan had pulled this shit. The remaining staff were understandably nervous, and not looking at Thom with any particular favor right now. Not that he could blame them. Having his superior go behind his back like that made him look weak, and no one liked a spineless boss.

Scowling, Thom hit the space key to wake his computer, which had decided to have a nap while he was daydreaming. *I swear to God, if that stupid old bag undermines my authority like that one more time, I'll go postal on her saggy ass.*

"Thom? You still there?"

Thom scowled harder when he realized he'd zoned out again. "Yeah. Sorry. I was just thinking."

If Phil wanted to know what he was thinking about, he didn't say so. "Do you want me to bring you something to eat? Helene just made some tofu pizza with a new recipe she invented. It's really good."

Thom suppressed a shudder. There were lots of good things about dating a vegan—the relative sweetness of his semen being Thom's personal favorite—but the ever-present threat of tofu was *not* one of them. "No thanks. I'll just run upstairs to my place and grab something."

"Okay. So, I guess if you're that busy tonight, you won't have time to come over after work."

Phil sounded positively mournful. Thom knew how he felt.

He hated those days when he and Phil didn't get to see each other. "I'm off tomorrow. You want to get together then?"

"You know I do, pretty baby. Come over to The HO for lunch. I'll cook for you."

Thom considered. Phil was almost as good in the kitchen as he was in bed, which was saying something. With any luck, a couple of well-placed suggestions would keep him from cooking tofu.

"Okay, sounds good." Thom looked up as one of the waitstaff appeared in the doorway, gesturing at him. "I have to go. I'll see you tomorrow."

"Looking forward to it, Bubbles. Bye."

"Bye."

Thom hung up the phone, plastered a smile on his face and beckoned to the young man hovering in the doorway. "What's up, Jimmy?"

Jimmy glanced around the hallway before shuffling inside. He looked nervous, as if he wasn't supposed to be here. Which was ridiculous. All the Midnight Rose staff knew they were welcome in Thom's office at any time. Well, unless he was fucking Phil across the desk, and since that probably wouldn't happen anytime soon—or, more likely, ever—it wasn't really a concern.

Edging over to the desk, Jimmy leaned both palms on the polished wood. "Dave was here," he declared in a conspiratorial whisper. "Just a few minutes ago."

Thom frowned. Dave Griffin was the first employee Ms. Duncan had fired, last week. While Thom didn't agree with her decision, he hadn't exactly advertised that fact, since it would make him look even more powerless than he already did. And since Dave had no idea that Thom hadn't condoned his firing, Thom had to wonder why he'd come here.

"What was he doing here? Ms. Duncan should have already given him his final paycheck."

"She did. But..." Jimmy broke off, glanced behind him and leaned closer. "He wants to talk to you," the boy continued in a voice so low Thom had trouble hearing him. "Him and Karen both do."

"Why didn't either of them just call me, then? Why did Dave get you to come tell me?" Thom made an exasperated noise when Jimmy shot another hunted glance over his shoulder at the open door. "And for God's sake, what's with all the cloak-and-dagger stuff?"

A flush crept into Jimmy's cheeks. "He told me because we're *friends*. He *trusts* me. And he didn't call because he was afraid Duncan would find out."

It made sense, especially considering that Dave was every bit as given to melodrama as his *friend* Jimmy. Of course that still didn't explain why Karen hadn't called. Thom had always thought her to be more levelheaded than the other two combined.

"All right." Thom fixed the young man with a curious look. "I'm happy to talk to them. But how do I get in touch with them?"

A sly grin spread over Jimmy's face. With another furtive glance behind him, he reached into his pocket, pulled out a crumpled piece of paper and pressed it into Thom's hand. That task accomplished, he straightened up and cleared his throat. "Okay. Well. Thanks, Mr. Stone. I'll get back to work now."

With a swift nod in Thom's direction, Jimmy hurried out of the office and fled down the hall. Amused, Thom shook his head. The kid watched *way* too many spy movies.

He examined the scrap of paper in his palm. It was a sheet from one of the Midnight Rose order pads. Unfolding it, he scanned the brief message. *We have information you need to know. Meet us at ten o'clock tomorrow night at the bottom of the stairs between Battery Park and Wall Street. Come alone, and don't tell anyone.*

The note was unsigned, but Thom recognized Dave's cramped, angular handwriting. He snorted. If Dave and Karen expected him to show up for a secret meeting alone and with no one knowing where he was, they clearly knew nothing about him. The question was, who could he tell? It was pretty obvious that the two believed they were under some sort of threat. Thom had no idea what sort of danger they could possibly be in, but if there was even a remote possibility that they were, he didn't want to make matters worse by blabbing to the wrong person.

*Tell Phil*, his inner voice whispered. *He'll keep it quiet, plus he'll watch your back.*

The part of Thom that had been avoiding the subject of Rosewood for over a month quailed at the prospect of telling Phil. The more sensible parts of him, however, realized there was no one else he could trust to handle this the way he wanted.

It looked like the time had finally come to open the whole Rosewood can of worms again.

Sighing, Thom dropped his head into his hands. He was *so* not ready for this.

&#8452;

At eleven fifteen Friday morning, Thom stood in the October sunshine outside The Happy Onion, trying to work up the nerve to go in. Things had been good between him and Phil lately. He hated to disturb their comfortable, relatively peaceful pattern.

Sure, Phil had a habit of irritating him until he lost his temper, but that was just Phil's "Angry Thom" fetish rearing its horned head. Thom would yell something scathing, Phil's eyes would blaze with pure lust and they'd end up with Phil bent over the nearest convenient piece of sturdy furniture and Thom fucking him clear into next month.

Those incidents were no threat to their relationship, and they both knew it. They hadn't had a single real fight since the protest at Midnight Rose. Thom was terrified that bringing up Rosewood, even obliquely in the form of two disgruntled former employees, would tear them apart again.

"I won't tell him," Thom decided out loud, drawing a few strange looks from people passing on the sidewalk. "I'll either go by myself tonight, or I won't go."

A pair of arms slid around him from behind, making him squeak in surprise. Phil's husky laugh sounded in his ear. "Hey, sweet thing."

"Phil." Turning in Phil's embrace, Thom hooked both arms around Phil's waist and smiled up at him. "You scared me half to death."

Phil grinned. "Sorry."

He didn't sound sorry. Thom shook his head. "Kiss me, you big goofball."

Chuckling, Phil cupped Thom's cheek in one hand, bent and covered Thom's mouth with his.

For a few moments, Thom let himself get lost in the feel of Phil's lips on his, the surprisingly soft beard rasping against his face. Phil smelled like apples and cinnamon, with a hint of underlying musk. When the kiss broke, Thom rested his head on Phil's shoulder and relaxed against the big, warm, solid body. It amazed him how Phil could make him feel so peaceful just by holding him like this.

Eventually Phil drew back and tilted Thom's face up with a finger beneath his chin. "So. Bubbles. What sort of adventure are you off on tonight, and why weren't you going to tell me?"

Thom winced. "I sort of hoped you hadn't heard that."

"I guess I'm just too stealthy for you." With a quick peck to the tip of Thom's nose, Phil took Thom's hand and led him toward the restaurant door. "So it *was* me you weren't going to tell whatever you weren't going to tell, huh? I wasn't sure."

"Dammit," Thom grumbled, following Phil inside The HO. For some unfathomable reason, a ska-flavored cover of "Secret Agent Man" was playing on the boom box behind the bar. "I *knew* I should've denied it."

Phil laughed. "Don't beat yourself up. I would've gotten it out of you one way or another. Speaking of which." Pulling a chair away from an empty table near the window, he pushed Thom into it and plopped into the chair across from him. "What's up that you didn't want to tell me?"

Thom traced a fingertip around one of the triangular purple tiles embedded in the tabletop. Now that it came to it, he wasn't sure how to start.

"Thom?" Phil leaned over the table, a worried crease between his eyes. "You're not in some kind of trouble, are you?"

"No. Nothing like that."

"Then what?" Phil took Thom's hands in his. "You're starting to freak me out here."

"It's nothing to worry about. I'm just not sure how to explain it without taking all day."

"Just start at the beginning, and take your time. I don't think either of us is in any rush."

"Yeah, I guess you're right." Thom rubbed his tongue stud

along the roof of his mouth, thinking hard. Maybe if he showed Phil the note and went from there? Retrieving his hands, he reached into his pocket, pulled out the slip of paper and set it on the table. "Read that."

With a curious glance at Thom, Phil picked up the note, unfolded it and read it. His eyebrows shot up. "Okay, that's...something."

"It's from a Midnight Rose employee who was fired last week. He and an employee who was fired just yesterday want to talk to me for some reason."

"Yeah, they want to talk to you alone, with no one knowing where you are. I'd say it's pretty obvious why they're calling this little meeting."

Thom stared, surprised by the venom in Phil's voice and the fire in his eyes. "Well, it's not obvious to me."

Phil looked at him as if he'd just grown tentacles. "You don't think they're looking to get some kind of sick revenge on you for firing them?"

The light dawned, finally, and Thom shook his head. "No, I didn't fire them. My stone-age, piece-of-shit boss Leta Duncan did. Without even consulting me, I might add." He scowled. Thinking of what the old bat had done still made him see red.

"Oh." Phil frowned. "Then what the fuck are they after?"

"Exactly what I'm wondering."

"You don't have any idea?"

"No, not a clue." Thom ran both hands through his hair. "But I have to say, I'm dying to find out."

"So you're going to this meeting?"

"Yeah. I think I am."

Phil regarded him with uncharacteristic solemnity. "I don't think you should go alone."

"I agree with you. I know both of these people, and I don't believe they'd hurt me or anything, but still. You never know."

Nodding, Phil took Thom's hand again and intertwined their fingers. "I'm coming with you."

Thom smiled. "I kind of hoped you would."

"Damn right I am. There's no *way* I'm letting you walk into something like this by yourself. If anybody so much as looks at you cross-eyed, I want to be there to clean their fucking clock."

The hard shine in Phil's eyes and the determined set of his jaw shouldn't have set Thom's pulse racing, but it did. Ignoring the buzz of conversation all around him, Thom stood, leaned across the table and captured Phil's lips in a needy kiss. Phil's mouth opened, his hands coming up to frame Thom's face.

"Damn, baby," Phil murmured when they drew apart who-knew-how-many minutes later. "What brought that on?"

Shrugging, Thom rubbed his cheek against Phil's palm. "I've never seen you look all protective like that. It's really hot."

"Yeah?"

"Yeah. Definitely."

"Hm. I'll have to remember that." Phil swiped a thumb across Thom's bottom lip. "Wanna go to my office and polish the desk before lunch?"

By way of an answer, Thom snagged the stroking thumb between his teeth and dragged his tongue stud across the pad. Phil's eyes went dark, his lips parting on a soft gasp. Closing his lips around the calloused digit, Thom sucked it from base to tip in a graphic simulation of what he hoped to do to other parts of Phil's anatomy once they were alone. Phil let out a groan that made the couple at the next table halt their own pubic display of affection to gape at him.

Phil's wet thumb pulled free of Thom's mouth with an

audible pop. "Let's go," Thom ordered, straightening up and giving Phil's hand a tug.

"Hell yeah."

Phil rose and followed Thom like a big horny puppy. Thom breathed a silent thanks to whoever might be listening that this discussion had gone so well. He'd half believed they'd end up not speaking again. A midday quickie in Phil's office was, in Thom's opinion, highly preferable to another fight.

Of course, they hadn't exactly engaged in a deep, heartfelt discussion of their philosophical and political differences. Thom had mentioned the note and the meeting—which was, as far as Thom knew, only related to Rosewood because the note-writer had worked there—Phil had displayed his devastatingly sexy inner caveman, and now, once again, they were about to "polish Phil's desk" instead of talking.

When Phil pushed Thom into his office and bent to give him a mind-melting kiss, Thom decided he didn't care. Kicking the door shut, he fell to his knees and yanked Phil's jeans open. The talking could wait a while longer.

৪৩

At nine forty-five that night, Thom and Phil stood just inside the bottom-level door of the Wall Street parking garage, staring out the small square window at the spot where Thom was about to meet his two former employees. Two couples strolled past, but no one else was in sight. Wall Street tended to be quiet at night, devoid as it was of clubs and bars. Looking out at the nearly deserted road, Thom was glad of the streetlight shedding a puddle of illumination on the sidewalk, and even more glad of Phil's comforting presence at his side.

Looping his arms around Thom's neck, Phil turned away from the window to look down at Thom. "Okay, Bubbles. Let's go over the plan."

Thom let out a sharp, somewhat nervous laugh. "We have a plan?"

"Come on, babe. Humor me."

"Okay." Thom glanced out the window. The sidewalk remained empty. Turning back to Phil, he slid both hands around Phil's waist to grope his ass. "You'll stay here, hiding behind the door. I'll keep them out there under the light, where you can see us, and we'll keep this door propped open so you can hear."

"And?"

"And what?"

"The *signal*, Thom. What's the signal in case you need my help?"

"I yell 'come help me'?"

Phil gave him a long-suffering look. Thom countered with his best innocent expression. Phil sighed. "Scratch your ass, okay? If you need help but you can't say so, scratch your ass."

"Why do I have to scratch my ass?" Thom shot Phil a pleading look. "Can't I just scratch my head or something?"

"No."

"But—"

"Listen, angel face, we already talked about this. We agreed the signal should be something you don't normally do, so you wouldn't do it by accident. You're a fidgety little thing, but I don't believe I've ever seen you scratch your butt in public."

"Yeah, well, there's a reason for that," Thom grumbled. Next time, he wouldn't agree to any of Phil's plans until after the blood siphoned out of his prick and back into his brain. He

161

sighed. "Okay, I'm going out now. I want to be waiting for them when they get here."

"'Kay." Sliding a hand into Thom's hair, Phil bent and gave him a toe-curling kiss. "Be careful, sweet thing. I'll be right here if you need me. And I *will* come charging to your rescue if I think you need me, whether you signal me or not."

"You know, I actually kind of like that." Thom smiled, caressing Phil's cheek with one hand. "Thank you for coming with me. I feel a lot safer knowing you're here."

"There's no place I'd rather be right now." Phil kissed Thom's nose before pushing him gently away. "Go on."

Taking a deep breath, Thom squared his shoulders, shoved the door open and walked out into the chilly fall night. Behind him, stone scraped against metal as Phil propped the door open with the rock they'd found in the alley behind The HO.

For several endless minutes, he stood there alone under the harsh white light, feeling like a complete idiot. The occasional groups of people hurrying along the sidewalk all gave him a wide berth and identical wary looks as they passed. He stuck his hands in his jacket pockets, hunched his shoulders and scowled at the tuft of withered grass sticking up through a crack in the sidewalk. His posture probably made him look *more* like an ax murderer, not less, but he couldn't be bothered to care. He wished Dave and Karen would come on already so he could get this over with. The night had turned cold, and all he really wanted to do was climb into bed with Phil and fuck until they both collapsed from exhaustion.

At eight minutes after ten, just as Thom was about to say "fuck it" and leave, Dave and Karen emerged from the shadow of the stairs. "It's about time," Thom complained as they approached him. "I was about to give up."

"Sorry we're late." Dave darted a furtive glance around the

nearly deserted street. "Thanks for meeting us."

"No problem." Thom looked from Dave's nervous expression to Karen's. "So. What did you two want to talk with me about?"

"We know you're gay," Karen blurted out.

Thom blinked at her. "Um. It wasn't exactly a state secret, but okay. Is that all?"

He couldn't decide if he hoped it was, or it wasn't. If "we know you're gay" was in fact their big announcement, he could go on his way and that would be that. On the other hand, he would *not* be happy if he found they'd dragged him out here just to announce that they knew something he hadn't even tried to hide in the first place.

Dave shot his companion an irritated look. "What she's trying to say is that since you're gay, you might end up in the same boat we're in. That's why we wanted to talk to you. To warn you."

"Warn me of what, exactly?" Thom asked, though he had a pretty good idea. Just because he himself hadn't run into any anti-gay discrimination since his teenage years didn't mean he was stupid enough to believe it never happened.

Karen glanced at Dave, who shrugged. Clearing her throat, she met Thom's gaze. "I was fired because I'm a practicing Wiccan."

Thom's mouth fell open. "What? But...but that's..." He bit his lip before he could embarrass himself by pointing out the painfully obvious fact that religious discrimination was *highly* illegal. "Are you sure?"

"Yes." Sighing, she ran a hand through her hair. "I don't have any hard evidence. But she fired me the day after she found out. She fed me some line about unacceptable job performance, but that was bullshit. I'm an excellent waitress, and I know you would've said something to me if you thought I

163

wasn't doing a good job."

"Damn right I would've. But that was never the case. You were one of the best we had." Feeling shell-shocked, Thom turned to Dave. "Did she give you that same shit?"

"No. I was fired because I've been way too visible in the city council meetings." Dave let out a harsh laugh. "At least she was halfway honest with me about why she was giving me the boot. She said it reflected poorly on Midnight Rose and the whole Rosewood project to have an employee constantly speaking out at the public meetings and getting himself on the news. She also said my attending the meetings was affecting my job performance."

"But you don't think that's the whole story." It wasn't a question. Thom couldn't imagine what else there might be to it, but Dave's expression clearly said he believed Leta Duncan had other reasons for firing him.

"No, I don't." Dave fell silent as a group of young women scurried past, all talking at once. When they'd gotten out of earshot, he moved closer and lowered his voice. "I don't know if you're aware of this, Thom, but Bradford & Lehrer are the backers for a gated community being built out in West Asheville. They're in it officially as silent partners, but they're the ones pulling the strings. A lot of us who live out that way are concerned about possible environmental violations on the construction site. We've been trying to bring that to the attention of the city council. Everything's been very non-confrontational, the council's listening and they're working with the company to get things straightened out, but it seems Ms. Duncan took offense to my speaking out."

"You're sure that's why she fired you?" *I sound like a broken record*, Thom thought irritably.

"Pretty sure, yeah. I mean, I've always gone to the council

meetings when they're open to the public, that's nothing new. It's never been a problem before. But all of a sudden it *is* a problem, right after I say something at one meeting against a project that happens to involve the company which happens to own Rosewood?" Dave shook his head. "It's too much of a coincidence. That has to be why I was fired."

"Oh, my fucking *God*." Thom shot a brief, glowering look toward the open doorway where Phil lurked. *I bet he's just fucking loving this shit.* "Thanks for the heads-up, guys. I can't imagine that there's anyone at work who doesn't know or hasn't at least guessed I'm gay, but I'll be careful."

"I know you're not trying to hide your sexuality, Thom, but it isn't exactly obvious, and I'm pretty sure your boss has no idea. Maybe it wouldn't matter, but after what happened to Dave and me, I don't trust any of the powers that be at Rosewood to have any sense of what's right or wrong." Karen laid a hand on his arm, her expression serious. "Dave and I are both looking into legal representation. We're fighting this. Neither of us wants you to get caught in the crossfire, but we can't ignore what happened."

"Of course not." Taking her hand, Thom gave it a squeeze and let her go. "Good luck, to both of you."

"Thanks." Dave held his hand out. Thom took it and they shook. "If you hear about any other instances of discrimination, will you call me?"

Thom managed a nod and a shaky smile. Linking arms, Dave and Karen hurried back up the steps and vanished into the crowd at the top.

Phil's head poked out from around the edge of the parking-garage door. "Are they gone?"

"Yeah." Thom walked toward Phil, who had emerged from the garage and was standing just outside the door. "I guess you heard."

"Yeah, I did."

Thom waited for the inevitable "I told you so". It didn't come. Relieved but curious about Phil's silence, Thom frowned up at him. "This is gonna sound weird coming from me, but why aren't you gloating?"

Phil gave him an inscrutable look. "Thom, look, I..." He trailed off, worrying his bottom lip between his teeth. His brow creased. "Okay. I have a confession to make."

Dread pooled in Thom's gut. "What?"

Taking both of Thom's hands in his, Phil gazed down at him with a strange flinching in his eyes. "You know all that they were saying? About discriminatory firings and environmental violations and all?"

"Yeah. What about it?"

Phil licked his lips, and in a flash of insight Thom knew what he was going to say. His stomach dropped into his shoes. "Phil—"

"I knew, Bubbles," Phil interrupted, confirming Thom's suspicions. "I knew it all."

# Chapter Thirteen

Phil wasn't surprised when Thom's adorable rosebud mouth hardened into a thin line, or when he pulled his hands from Phil's grip. It still hurt, though. Sighing, Phil steeled himself for the onslaught of Thom's temper.

"How long have you known this?" Thom asked, his voice shaking with the anger Phil knew he was trying to suppress.

"Um. Ever since Bradford & Lehrer first came to the city council with the proposal for Rosewood. There's all sorts of stories out there about people claiming they'd been fired on religious grounds and stuff like that. There was even one woman who filed a sexual harassment suit against them a few years ago, but they settled out of court and she sort of faded from view. There's a whole message board online for people who've been victimized by the company."

"I see." Thom glared at him, blue eyes hot with fury. "Why the hell didn't you tell me this before?"

Phil scratched his beard, trying to think of some way to answer that wouldn't result in Thom ripping him a new asshole. Nothing came to mind, so he decided to just lay it out there and let the proverbial chips fall where they may. "I didn't think you'd listen. I could show you loads of personal testimony from at least a hundred different people, but none of them have any hard evidence of wrongdoing. So I figured you wouldn't want to hear it."

"Well, if all you have is more rumors, then I wouldn't have just taken it all at face value, no. But I *would* want to hear it."

"I don't believe the people who have been fired would call them rumors," Phil ground out. He didn't bother to express his opinion about whether or not Thom would actually have paid any attention to what he'd learned about Bradford & Lehrer.

Thom swore under his breath. "Okay, so what are these people saying?"

Phil shivered in a sudden gust of chill wind. "Maybe we could go inside someplace and talk about this?"

"Just *tell* me, Phil!"

"If you want me to talk to you, don't fucking yell at me like I'm five," Phil shot back, his anger bubbling over in spite of himself. "This is exactly why I don't tell you these things."

Thom gave him an incredulous look. "Because you're afraid I'll yell at you?"

"No, goddammit, it's because you don't *listen*. You'd rather get mad and scream at me than actually pay attention to what I have to say."

Thom stared at him with eyes full of shock. "That's not true."

"Yeah, sweetheart, it is." Frustrated, Phil rubbed his face with both hands. "For some reason, you'd rather argue with me than talk things out." He thought about it. "Except for the times you'd rather fuck me than talk. And I haven't been any better, really, because I've avoided uncomfortable subjects too."

"Like the subject of all these supposed problems with Bradford & Lehrer."

Thom's voice was soft and uncertain, so Phil let the "supposed" slide. "You wouldn't have believed me because I had no real proof to show you. You would've scolded me like a fucking child for repeating rumors, and never once considered that I might actually be right." He dropped his gaze to the concrete beneath his feet and studied a blob of dirt-crusted gum. "If you want to know the truth, I was scared to death that if we had another serious fight like before, you'd leave me again, and this time you wouldn't come back."

For a second Thom stood still and silent. Phil waited, staring at the toes of Thom's well-worn leather boots and wondering if he'd just blown everything to hell. Dread sat like a stone in the pit of his stomach. When Thom finally moved toward him instead of walking away, he could've cried in sheer relief.

Thom wound both arms around Phil's waist, pressing their bodies together. Phil wrapped him in a tight embrace and nuzzled his silky hair.

"We're as bad as each other, aren't we?" Thom observed, one hand stroking Phil's back and the other resting on the curve of his butt.

Phil smiled. "Yeah, I guess we are."

"I'm sorry I'm such a prick."

"And I'm sorry I didn't tell you this stuff before. I should've, even though I knew you'd be upset."

"We have to talk. I mean *really* talk. No fighting, no fucking, just talking. We have to get everything out in the open once and for all if we're going to make this work." Thom raised his head, gazing up at Phil with undisguised fear in his eyes. "Please tell me you still want that as much as I do."

A giant fist seemed to close around Phil's heart and squeeze. Cupping the back of Thom's head in one palm, Phil bent and kissed those pretty pink lips. Thom opened to him with a needy little sigh.

"Of course I want it," Phil murmured when they pulled apart. He swiped a thumb across the corner of Thom's mouth. "Nobody's perfect, Bubbles. We just have to work a little harder on that whole communication thing."

Thom let out a breathless laugh. "You got that right."

"So. We're going back to my place?" Stepping out of Thom's embrace, Phil took his hand and wove their fingers together.

"Yes. No sex, though. Not until we clear the air. Agreed?"

Phil winced, even though he'd been thinking the same thing himself. "No sex?"

"No sex. As you so cleverly pointed out, we've been substituting fucking for talking pretty much all the time. So all the bits stay inside the pants until we've both told each other everything we've been keeping to ourselves." Thom gave Phil a stern look as they headed up the sidewalk to The HO, where Thom's bike was parked. "You know I'm right, don't you?"

"Yeah." Phil heaved an exaggerated sigh. "Okay. No sex until we're all talked out."

Thom beamed, and Phil decided he could deal with a long, difficult and sex-free conversation if it meant keeping this man in his life.

❧

In hindsight, Phil figured they both should've known they wouldn't be able to keep their "no sex until we talk" bargain. But lying spent and panting across his bed an hour and a half later, sweat streaming down his sides and spunk leaking out of his ass, he couldn't bring himself to give a flying fuck. Maybe the vigorous romp would settle them both enough to have a rational discussion. Most things seemed easier in the mellow haze of post-sex afterglow, so why should talking be any different?

Thom stirred from his position sprawled across Phil's chest and propped his chin on his folded hands. "You know what?"

"What?" Phil kissed Thom's nose. He looked adorable with his pale cheeks flushed pink and his flaxen hair stuck to his face in damp clumps.

Thom flashed a loopy grin which made Phil's insides clench. "I looove your ass."

Laughing, Phil slid both hands down to squeeze Thom's naked butt. "The feeling's mutual, angel face."

Thom's smile faded into a solemn expression. "I guess we didn't do so well with our promise to talk before fucking, though." He wriggled his backside in Phil's grip.

"You got that right." Phil dug his fingers deeper into Thom's firm rear. "And if you don't hold still, we're probably gonna end up fucking again."

"Tempting." Thom shimmied his hips again.

Phil squeaked when Thom's balls scraped over the sensitive head of his prick. "Oh no, you don't. We're not avoiding this talking thing any longer."

"Fine," Thom sighed. "Okay, what should we talk about first?"

"Do you want to hear all I know about Bradford & Lehrer?" Phil wasn't sure he wanted to discuss that just yet, but if Thom wanted him to, he'd give it his best shot.

To his relief, Thom shook his head. "I can't do that naked. Let's start smaller."

"Fine by me. Anything in particular you want to know?"

Pushing up onto his forearms, Thom tilted his head sideways and studied Phil's face. "We've been seeing each other for over a month, but I feel like I don't know anything about you. Tell me something I don't know."

"Okay. Let's see." Phil brought one hand up to swipe a trickle of sweat from his eyes. The other hand idly caressed the curve of Thom's lower back. "I can play the accordion."

Thom's eyebrows shot up. "Really?"

"Yeah. My mom used to play professionally. She taught me, hoping I'd follow in her footsteps I guess."

"That's cool." Thom's lips curved into the smile that always made Phil's heartbeat stumble. "Will you play for me?"

"Oh my God, you don't want me to do that. I suck really bad."

The grin widened, Thom's eyes sparkling with mischief. "Actually you suck really well."

"Thank you." Chuckling, Phil touched Thom's flushed cheek. "It's your turn. Tell me something I don't know about you."

Thom dipped his head and peered at Phil through a veil of damp hair. "When I was growing up, my family used to watch *The Sound of Music* every year at Christmas, and, um...I still do it."

Phil burst out laughing. "Are you serious?"

"Yes." Thom pinched Phil's nipple hard. "Stop laughing, you prick, I'm sharing a private thing with you here."

"Sorry, babe." Choking back the cackles that still wanted to come out, Phil raked the hair from Thom's eyes. "I bet you look adorable all curled up on the sofa in your pajamas watching that movie."

"Shut up," Thom mumbled, blushing. "All right, it's your turn again."

"Hm." Phil rubbed his beard. "I'm afraid of snails."

Thom snickered. "Snails?"

"Oh, I guess you're not afraid of anything."

"Uh. No?"

Phil smacked Thom's ass, making him yelp. "Try again."

"Okay, okay." With a halfhearted glare at Phil, Thom twisted around to rub his butt cheek where Phil had slapped him. "I'm afraid of bridges."

Phil gaped. "Seriously?"

"Yeah."

"How in the hell did you manage to drive halfway across the country on a motorcycle without going over any bridges?"

"It's not *all* bridges. Just the suspension kind." Thom wrinkled his nose. "All that crap hanging over me freaks me out." Squirming farther up Phil's body, Thom leaned in and kissed him. "Tell me about your first time."

"My first time doing what?"

"Stop being a smartass, you know what I'm talking about."

"Okay." Phil chewed on his bottom lip. "My first time was in tenth grade. With a girl."

"A girl?" Thom hooted. "Really? You were a closet case?"

"Not for long." Grinning, Phil dipped a single fingertip into the crease of Thom's ass. "I was only with Jocelyn once before I realized I'd much rather have her brother's cock in me than my cock in her."

"I bet she was just thrilled with *that.*"

"Oh, like I was gonna tell her. I don't think so. She was a total hellcat. Even her big brother was scared of her." Phil looped an arm around Thom's waist. "All right, now you tell me about your first time."

"I lost my cherry to my mom's best friend's son. I was

fifteen, he was nineteen and home visiting from college. He fucked me in the storage shed in their backyard." Thom shrugged. "Not much of a story, really."

"I guess you'll just have to tell me a better story, then, won't you?"

He was pretty sure Thom knew he was teasing, which was why the sudden seriousness in Thom's eyes was such a surprise. Worried, Phil laid his hand on Thom's cheek. "What's wrong, pretty baby?"

A faint smile curved Thom's lips. "Nothing's wrong. You just gave me the perfect opening for something I've been meaning to tell you for a long time, and now I'm nervous about telling you."

Something in Thom's voice made Phil's pulse speed up. He tightened his arm around Thom. "It's okay. You know I'll listen."

"Yeah. I know." Rolling off Phil's chest, Thom curled against Phil's side, head pillowed on his chest and one arm tucked around his middle. "I've been wanting to explain why I was so dead set against getting involved with you when you were still my boss."

Phil stroked a hand down Thom's arm. "It was frustrating, but I never really thought anything of it. Most people would probably agree with you."

"Maybe so." Thom slung a leg across Phil's thighs. "The thing is, I had kind of a bad experience a few years ago with a man I was working for. He was the manager at the restaurant where I was working. The whole thing kind of biased me against dating an employer."

Phil couldn't see Thom's face, but he heard the echo of old heartache in Thom's voice loud and clear. He sifted his fingers through Thom's hair. "What happened, sweet thing?"

Thom sighed, his breath stirring the hairs on Phil's chest. "It was great, at first. We had fun together. I didn't love him, but

174

I liked him a lot. I thought he felt the same way. Then he started getting possessive and jealous. He'd get really angry with me if I went out with my friends and he wasn't invited, or if I wanted to stay home one night by myself instead of being with him. I was in school part-time, working toward a business degree, and he didn't even like me going to class. When he tried to talk me into quitting school, quitting work and moving in with him, it was just too fucking much. I broke up with him."

Thom fell silent, and the tension melted from Phil's shoulders. He'd expected to hear something much more traumatic. Clearly, the relationship had been a bad one, but it seemed that Thom had handled it with the decisiveness which had drawn Phil to him from the first.

"He sounds like a real asshole," Phil said. "I can totally see where you wouldn't want to get involved with another boss after that."

Thom laughed, the sound sharp and bitter. "If that's all it was, it wouldn't have been a big deal. But he couldn't let it go."

An ugly feeling settled in Phil's chest. His arms tightened around Thom in a protective reflex. "What'd he do?"

"For a while he just kept calling me, no matter how often I told him to lay off. He wouldn't leave me alone. He started following me around, sending me presents and stuff. I'd leave my apartment, and he'd be sitting in his car across the street waiting for me."

Thom trailed off into silence again. Phil held him and waited.

"I quit my job at the restaurant," Thom continued eventually, his voice soft but calm. "But I couldn't get another job anywhere. No one would hire me. I eventually found out Rob had been telling people I was unreliable, that I showed up drunk, shit like that. He even started a rumor that he

175

suspected me of stealing from the register."

"Jesus."

"Yeah. I tried to ignore it, but after the tenth place I applied for work told me no thanks, I was fed up. I called him and told him to lay the fuck off."

"I'm guessing he didn't."

"You're guessing right. He started leaving messages on my cell and notes on my front door, telling me how much he loved me and how he wasn't going to let me go. I took out a restraining order on him. He stopped following me, but he kept calling. I eventually ran out of money and lost my apartment. Things were even worse at the homeless shelter. Rob started coming around while I wasn't there and leaving messages for me saying I could take out all the restraining orders I wanted, but no piece of paper was going to keep him from taking what was his."

"Shit, Thom. What'd you do?"

"I wanted to have him arrested. But he never got physically near enough to break the restraining order, so the cops said they couldn't do anything. One night, he sent me a bouquet of roses with a note telling me he was coming for me the next morning and I could either come back to him or die. So I left. Just grabbed what little belongings I had left and hitchhiked from Minneapolis to Santa Fe."

Shaken, Phil nuzzled the top of Thom's head. "That bastard. That fucking bastard. Please tell me that fucking psycho went to jail and was repeatedly ass raped."

Thom snuggled closer. "Not for me, no. I didn't really care to wait and see if he was going to make good on his threat. But I heard he was arrested for breaking into another ex's house about a year after I left. Hopefully he did some time for that. All I know is, he hasn't found me yet, and I hope he never does."

"He better fucking *not* come around here trying to get his filthy paws on you again," Phil growled, his fingers digging possessively into Thom's back. "I'll rip his dick off and strangle him with it."

Thom lifted his head to level a heated stare at Phil. "God, it's hot when you go all alpha on me like that."

"Me Tarzan, you Bubbles." Phil pulled a fierce face, which dissolved into a grin when Thom started laughing. "C'mere, pretty baby."

Still smiling, Thom stretched forward to meet Phil's mouth with his. Phil brought both hands up to card through Thom's hair as the kiss went deep.

There wasn't much talking after that, but Phil didn't mind. They had all the time in the world to learn about each other. This time, he knew they would both listen.

ॐ

"So what you're telling me," Thom said, brow furrowed, "is that there have been allegations of discrimination and/or environmental violations on practically every Bradford & Lehrer project."

Phil nodded. "Yeah, pretty much."

"And I've never heard about it before now because...?"

"Because they have a whole team of crackerjack lawyers and lots of friends in strategic places. Hell, Keith Lehrer's brother-in-law is a California congressman, and Don Bradford's good friends with two of the Illinois Supreme Court justices. Plus they're smart, and sneaky. They know when to throw money at someone to shut them up, and how much money to throw."

Thom shook his head, but remained silent, gazing into his coffee mug with a pensive expression. Phil took a sip of his own coffee while Thom processed all the things Phil had been telling him over breakfast. Tales of people fired or passed over for promotions because of their religion, where they lived, who they were related to, organizations with which they were involved. Hushed-up accounts of environmental violations and buildings not up to code. Way too much information for even a skeptic like Thom to dismiss as mere rumors.

It was a lot to come to terms with. Phil was just happy that Thom was trying to understand instead of holding on to the fantasy of it not being real.

"I don't want to quit."

Phil looked up at Thom's outburst. Thom was frowning at Phil's kitchen table. "I hope you know I wouldn't ask you to do that," Phil said, watching Thom's face.

"I know. But I almost feel like I should, after what happened to Dave and Karen and what all you just told me. And on a purely selfish note, I sure as hell don't want to get pulled down with them if they get caught and prosecuted for anything." Thom raised his head to meet Phil's gaze. "I don't *want* to quit, though. I like it there. I like the club, I like the Rosewood residents, I even like the people I work with. Well, except that bitch Leta Duncan." With a deep sigh, Thom planted an elbow on the table and rested his chin in his hand. "Dammit, this sucks. I finally get my dream job, and it turns out to be with a company that's possibly up to their eyeballs in illegal fucking *crap*. Not that I'm totally sold on that yet, but still."

The forlorn expression in Thom's eyes hurt Phil's heart. Setting his mug on the table, Phil scooted his chair next to Thom's and wound an arm around Thom's shoulders. "I'm sorry, Bubbles."

Thom laid his head on Phil's shoulder. "What do I do now, Phil? I can't just ignore the possibility that this is all true."

"I don't know. I wish I did." Phil tilted Thom's chin up to kiss his lips. "Whatever you decide, though, I'm behind you one hundred percent."

Thom stared into Phil's eyes. "Even if I decide to keep working there?"

"Yes," Phil answered without hesitation, even though a large part of him wanted to scream *no*. "Whatever you need, baby."

The smile Phil got in return was worth ignoring his values just this once. Sliding a hand around the back of Phil's head, Thom pulled his face down and kissed him.

"I have an idea," Thom declared when they drew apart a few long, glorious minutes later.

Phil blinked, trying to clear the fuzz of lust from his brain. "Huh?"

Grinning, Thom patted Phil's cheek and sat back in his chair. "You have a one-track mind."

"Oh, like you don't."

"Touché."

Phil turned sideways, one bare foot tucked beneath him, took Thom's hand and linked their fingers. "Okay, tell me this idea of yours."

"I can keep working there, and see if I can gather any evidence of wrongdoing by the company."

Phil's jaw dropped open. "What? No! That's...that's *dangerous*. You can't."

The second the words were out, Phil cringed. No way would Thom let *that* go without giving Phil several very large pieces of his mind. *When, oh when, will you learn when to keep your big*

179

*mouth shut?*

To Phil's surprise, the anger he'd expected didn't materialize. Instead, Thom leaned forward and laid his free hand on Phil's knee. "Think about it, Phil. I'm in a perfect position to collect information. If I don't find anything, I can rethink whether or not I want to keep on working there based on what I already know. If I *do* find anything incriminating, we can take it to the police."

It was tempting. Torn, Phil chewed his thumbnail. "I don't know, Thom. I see what you're saying, but I don't like the idea of you putting yourself in the crosshairs like that."

"I don't think there *are* any crosshairs. Even if there were, I won't be in them. I'll just keep my eyes and ears open, and find out what I can when I can."

Phil stared hard into Thom's eyes. The determined expression there was one Phil knew very well, and knew better than to try and fight. He sighed. "Promise me you'll be careful?"

"I will. I really don't think I'm going to be in any danger, though." Thom's thumb stroked the edge of Phil's kneecap. "I'm sorry I was such a jackass before, when you tried to tell me they were crooked. I'm not saying I necessarily believe it all. Not yet, not without any real proof. But I'm going to at least listen with an open mind from now on. And if they're really involved in some shady shit, I want to do what I can to stop them."

*Well, you wanted it, Phil, you got it.* Phil had to laugh at the irony of it.

"What?" Thom demanded. "What's so funny?"

Phil shook his head. "Nothing. Just thinking next time I ought to be more careful what I ask for."

Comprehension lit Thom's eyes. Rising from his chair, he straddled Phil's lap, framed Phil's face between his hands and kissed him. "It'll be fine. They're just businessmen.

Unscrupulous businessmen, maybe, but this isn't the mob we're talking about here. The worst that can possibly happen is I'll get fired."

Phil wasn't so sure about that. However, since he suspected his trepidation was based on his protective instincts rather than reality, he elected to keep his thoughts to himself.

"You're probably right," Phil said, looping both arms around Thom's waist. "I want to help you, though."

Thom laughed. "If by 'help' you mean keeping me up to date on the latest news from the underground, then I'm counting on it."

"Actually, I thought I could dig into the other project, the one out in West Asheville. See if I can find out if there's anything to what Dave said last night about environmental violations on the construction site."

"That's a good idea. I'll call Dave and ask if he'll talk to you."

"Great." Grinning, Phil gave Thom's butt a squeeze. "This playing detective thing could be fun."

"Absolutely." Thom ground his crotch against Phil's lower belly, tearing a low moan from Phil. "We can pretend we're hard-boiled P.I.s, like what's his name. Jack Hammer?"

"*Mike* Hammer," Phil corrected, chuckling. "But I think the two of us are more like Nancy Drew."

Thom wrinkled his nose. "Are you sure you're gay? You keep trying to make me into a girl."

"Don't know what you're talking about, Bubbles."

"Exactly my point. First Bubbles—who isn't even an *adult* girl, you pervert—and now Nancy Drew?"

"Well, you *are* little and cute—" Phil's words ended in a yelp when Thom leaned in and bit his neck. "But no one would ever mistake you for a woman. Especially not with that thing hanging between your legs."

"Better damn well believe it." Thom leaned back with a smirk. "You know, I just realized something."

"What's that, pretty baby?" Phil slid a hand up the back of Thom's T-shirt to rub circles on his warm, satin-soft skin.

"I haven't fucked you yet today. And now you've got me feeling the need to prove my manliness." Thom's smirk turned into a wide smile. "What say we put this table to good use?"

The feral shine in Thom's eyes was all it took to make up Phil's mind for him. He grinned. "Bubbles, you have the best ideas."

# Chapter Fourteen

"You shouldn't have come here, Mr. Mo—"

"Don't use my name," the deep, silky voice insisted. "Refer to me as C.M."

Thom, eavesdropping outside the door of Leta Duncan's office, rolled his eyes. As if anyone who saw the man would fail to recognize Cassidy Morton, chair of the city council's Housing and Community Development Committee. His flair for the dramatic—especially during council meetings—tended to land him in the news a lot in the year since he'd been elected to the council. Every Asheville citizen not currently living in a cave knew the man's face.

"C.M., then," Ms. Duncan continued, sounding as if she were forcing the words out through clenched teeth. Which, Thom figured, she probably was. She *hated* being interrupted. "As I was saying, you should not have come here. People have already begun to speculate about the nature of your involvement in Rosewood. If anyone should see you here..."

"Ms. Duncan, everyone here is far too busy to pay the slightest attention to one more businessman entering this building. Besides, I made certain to disguise myself. No one noticed me, I assure you."

*Except me, dumbass.* Thom stifled a snicker. The man might look like an evil villain, with his slicked-back black hair and gray-streaked goatee, but he wasn't nearly as sneaky as he believed himself to be. And if he thought sunglasses and a Fedora constituted a disguise, he was sadly mistaken.

"Yes, well. I hope you're correct, for all our sakes." Papers shuffled. A chair wheel squeaked. "If you have something to discuss with Mr. Bradford or Mr. Lehrer, I suggest you call one of their private lines. I am under strict instructions not to discuss the terms of their agreement with you in such a public place as this."

"Your office is a public place?"

"Many people work in this building, Mr. Mo— C.M. Anyone might happen by. It is hardly a secure place to have this discussion. You did not even close the door properly."

*Oh shit.* Thom sidestepped away from the cracked-open door, ready to slip around the corner into the other hallway if anyone should decide the door needed to be shut now.

"It doesn't matter," Mr. Morton declared. Breathing a sigh of relief, Thom inched back to his previous position. The man inside swept on, oblivious to Thom's presence. "I didn't come here to talk to your bosses. I just want you to give them a message for me."

"Mr. Bradford is on the Rolling Hills construction site in West Asheville today. You have his private cell number. I suggest you use it." Ms. Duncan's voice had turned frostier than ever, which was saying something.

"Madam, when the police confiscate that phone, I do *not* want them to find my number on it."

Thom held his breath. Maybe this would be it, maybe the idiot would finally admit to taking bribes from Bradford & Lehrer in exchange for creating the confusion about property lines. Over the past two and a half weeks since that oh-so-revealing conversation with Phil, Thom had seen and heard enough to convince him that bribery was indeed how his employers had finagled the council's approval of the Rosewood project. Little things, snippets of conversation here and there mostly, but it was enough. He couldn't believe he'd been so blind before.

Of course, he still didn't have anything in the way of real evidence. Even if good old C.M. spilled the beans right here and now, it wouldn't be anything but hearsay. No one would listen. No one who could actually do anything about it, anyhow.

Thom scowled. It sucked being on the other side of the fence.

"There will be no police confiscations," Ms. Duncan insisted. "Mr. Bradford and Mr. Lehrer have dealt with situations such as these many times in the past. They know how to stay on the right side of the law."

*Yeah, greasing the right palms. Not the best way to keep the law off your back in the long term.* Thom got the distinct feeling that Cassidy Morton agreed with him.

"You'll excuse me if I decline to stake my future on that assumption."

A deep sigh. "Very well. What is your message?"

Mr. Morton's voice dropped so low Thom could barely hear him. Edging closer, Thom leaned in so that his ear brushed the doorframe.

"Tell them I won't be their whipping boy any longer," the city councilman growled. "If they truly have the evidence they say they do against me, they can damn well bring it forward. Having that come to light wouldn't be half as damaging to me as having my involvement with them become public knowledge."

Thom's pulse sped up. Cassidy Morton was infamous for his innate ability to offend everyone from retirees to the homeless—at least he was an equal-opportunity bigot—but

185

there had never even been the faintest rumors of him being involved in anything illegal. What sort of information did Bradford & Lehrer have on him? More to the point, was this a case not of bribery, but of blackmail?

"I can assure you that will not happen," Leta Duncan stated in her crispest voice.

"And I can assure *you*, Ms. Duncan, it will, if things continue as they have been. Those blasted leftist radical guerillas are focusing far too much attention on Bradford & Lehrer for my comfort. I want out, now, before it all blows up in your faces. You tell them that."

Footsteps clopped across the wooden floor toward the door. Thom scrambled into the adjacent hallway just in time to avoid being caught red-handed. A second later, Cassidy Morton strode past, the ridiculous Fedora pulled low over his forehead and a fierce frown tugging down the corners of his mouth. If he noticed Thom cowering in the side corridor, he didn't let on.

Once Mr. Morton was out of sight, Thom slumped against the wall. His heart threatened to pound a hole in his rib cage. Whatever the pitfalls of amateur sleuthing might be, he thought with a wry smile, he sure couldn't call it dull.

When the adrenaline rush had settled into a low hum in his blood, Thom pushed away from the wall and sauntered out into the main hallway, headed for his office. Ms. Duncan's door stood wide open. She glanced up as Thom strolled past. Thom gave her a casual nod. She grimaced and looked back down at the papers on her desk.

Thom grinned. *Leftist radical guerillas.* Phil was going to love that one.

Back in his office, Thom made sure the door was firmly shut before pulling his cell from its holder on his belt and dialing Phil's cell number.

Phil answered just in time to keep the phone from switching to voice mail. "Sorrells and Stone Half-Vegan Detective Agency. You dig 'em up and we plant 'em."

Thom laughed. "What does that even mean?"

"You know. Dig up cases, plant the perps in the clink?"

"You're crazy," Thom declared, grinning.

"And you wouldn't have it any other way, sweet thing."

Thom decided to ignore the smug tone of Phil's voice. After all, he was right.

"Listen, Phil, can I come over to The HO for lunch today? We need to talk."

"Babe, you know you can come over here anytime you want." Phil's voice dropped to a near whisper. "You got some information?"

"Yeah. I don't want to say anything on the phone, though."

"Good idea. C'mon over whenever you're ready. I'm helping out on the floor today but I'll take my break when you get here and we'll talk."

Guilt needled Thom like it always did when Phil was short on help. Mike had gone to part-time since classes resumed, which left Phil short one busboy on weekdays. It made no sense for Thom to feel guilty about that, but he couldn't help it. If he hadn't left, he could've filled in so Phil wouldn't have to.

"Would you stop with the guilt already?" Phil scolded. "You didn't leave me short. Mike did. And we all knew that was coming eventually. I got somebody else, she starts day after tomorrow."

Thom shook his head. It was eerie how well Phil could read him, even over the phone. "I'll be over about eleven thirty, will that work?"

"That's good for me. See you then, Bubbles."

"Yeah, see you." *I love you,* he added silently as he clicked the cell shut.

Lately, it was getting more and more difficult to keep from adding those three little words to the end of every conversation. He wasn't sure why he was fighting it so hard, to tell the truth. Instinct told him Phil returned his feelings. So why couldn't he just say it?

*Because you're waiting for him to say it first, you fucking coward.*

Sad, but true.

Thom swiveled his chair around to gaze out the big picture window at the Pack Square fountain glittering in the sunshine. Tomorrow night was Halloween. He and Phil were planning to hit the costume party at Belial's Basement, then go back to Phil's house for the rest of the night. It was the ideal opportunity to stop being afraid and just take the proverbial bull by the fucking horns. To drag the "L" word out of storage, dust it off and give it to a certain tall, sexy, delightfully warped restaurant owner.

Not exactly hearts and roses, but he didn't think Phil would mind. He wasn't any more of a romantic than Thom.

His mind made up, Thom spun around and turned his attention to the inventory spreadsheet he'd been working on before the trip to the men's room had morphed into an impromptu spy mission. Maybe by tomorrow night, the herd of buffalo stampeding through his chest would settle down enough for him to confess his feelings for Phil without having a heart attack.

He refused to think about what Phil might—or worse, might not—say in return.

༽ఒ

Phil was kneeling on the sidewalk outside The Happy Onion's large front window when Thom roared up. A spray bottle sat beside Phil's left knee. He was scrubbing at something on the window with a rag. Amused, Thom parked his bike, cut the engine and went to see what Phil was doing.

"Hey, Bubbles," Phil called, flashing a wide grin as Thom approached. "I'll be done in a sec."

"Okay." Pulling his helmet off, Thom tugged Phil's head back by the braid, bent and kissed him. "Have you demoted yourself to window washer now?"

"Hey, I've been my own busboy lately. You can't get much more demoted than that." He tapped at the glass, where a streak of something orange smeared across the lower corner of the window. "Some kid left a bit of his Halloween cupcake behind. I just figured I'd go ahead and wash it off before we got too busy."

Thom nodded, his fingers still petting Phil's hair. "I overheard a very interesting conversation this morning. I'm hoping we can put together what I heard with the information you already have and come up with something we can use."

"Yeah?" Phil swiped the last of the orange icing from the glass, then sat back on his heels. His hazel eyes shone with curiosity. "Sounds important."

"It is."

"Well, then, let's go back to my office and you can tell me all about it." Taking the spray bottle and rag in his left hand, he rose to his feet. "I found out a couple of interesting things myself."

"Cool. I can't wait to compare notes." Thom slid an arm

around Phil's waist and bit his shoulder through his long-sleeved Happy Onion T-shirt. "I like this whole talking thing. Communication is definitely good."

Phil's laugh rumbled against Thom's chest. "Much better than keeping stuff to ourselves and fighting about it later."

Smiling, Thom tilted his face up. Phil met him in a sweet, lazy kiss that set Thom's whole body buzzing. When they broke apart, Phil led Thom to the restaurant door and inside.

Just before entering The HO, Thom looked up to find a middle-aged woman staring at him from the sidewalk. It wasn't a "men kissing, how degenerate, they're going to hell" stare, or even a "men kissing, ohmygod that's hot" stare. It was more like an "I just saw someone I know do something unexpected and kind of gross" stare. Which was puzzling, since even though she looked vaguely familiar, Thom didn't think he knew her.

He and Phil were passing through the kitchen when recognition hit. Thom stopped, forcing one of the cooks to swerve around him and Phil. He muttered an apology to the young man, who didn't even spare him a glance.

"What's the matter, Bubbles?" Phil steered him through the door into the back room and gazed down at him with concern.

"Nothing. Just, I saw the evening concierge from Rosewood outside. She saw us kissing, and she had this kind of horrified look on her face." Thom shrugged. "I didn't recognize her at first. I remembered who she was just now in the kitchen, that's all."

Phil frowned. "You don't think she'll try to get you in trouble, do you?"

"I don't see how she could."

"Oh, she could. Remember Dave and Karen? Remember the real reasons they were fired? And they were worried about the same thing happening to you."

190

"I know. And it might, I'll admit that." Thom leaned against Phil's side, head on his shoulder. "If it comes to that, I'll deal with it. Right now, I want to tell you what I found out before I have to go back to work."

Phil kissed the top of Thom's head, let him go and unlocked his office door. Inside, Phil sat in the single chair and Thom plopped onto his lap.

"So." Phil wrapped his arms around Thom. "Tell me."

"Long story short, I saw Cassidy Morton in the building and followed him to Leta Duncan's office. He told her that he wouldn't be Bradford & Lehrer's whipping boy anymore, and that he wanted out. He seems to be afraid the shit's about to hit the fan and the company's going to be in major legal trouble."

Phil's eyebrows shot up. "Wow."

"Yeah." Thom snuggled closer to Phil's chest, one arm slung around his neck. "Duncan said something about an agreement between Morton and the company. And apparently people are starting to talk about how Mr. Morton's involved with Rosewood."

Phil snorted. "Kind of an understatement there. It's all over the local political blogs. Most people think he took money under the table to help Bradford & Lehrer get hold of public property for Rosewood. That's been the theory ever since the project was first announced."

"I know. And that's what I thought too, at first. But he said something about the company having some sort of evidence against him. Evidence of what, I don't know. But he said he'd rather them bring that forward than to have his involvement with Bradford & Lehrer come out."

"You think they're blackmailing him?"

"Who knows. But it sure sounds that way to me."

Phil's expression turned thoughtful. "I don't like this, Thom. You're getting too close. I think you should back off."

Thom shook his head. "I don't have anything solid yet. I need more time."

"We can bring what we have to the cops. Dave and Karen have legal representation and are about ready to serve Bradford & Lehrer with a lawsuit. That plus what I found out yesterday is plenty. It's not worth putting yourself in any more danger."

"What'd you find out?" Thom asked, partly because he was sincerely interested and partly to change the subject.

"Volunteer water-quality monitors have found toxic levels of pesticides and defoliants in the water downstream from Rolling Hills. In other words, hard evidence of wrongdoing, even if it's not on Rosewood specifically. And don't try to change the subject on me." Phil lifted a hand to caress Thom's cheek. "Please, pretty baby. Please don't do this anymore. Just...just leave that place, before they start getting suspicious and make you a target."

Thom let out a brittle laugh. "Yeah. Like I have anywhere else to go. I still need to work, Phil, and if I'm going to work I might as well keep on watching and listening."

"You don't think I'd give you your job back here? Babe, I'd take you back in a heartbeat, and not just because I...because we're seeing each other. You were a fantastic bartender and an all-round dream employee."

The hurt in Phil's eyes probably shouldn't have been a surprise, but it was. Contrite now, Thom leaned in and kissed Phil's lips. "I'm sorry. I know you would, and I truly appreciate that. But I just have to see this through. Please understand."

Their relationship had changed over the past few weeks. Without either of them consciously pushing it in that direction, it had moved from casual dating with only an implied promise of exclusivity to something more serious. Something that already felt stable enough to last. Putting themselves back on the inherently uneven footing of employer and employee might just destroy what they'd built, and Thom didn't think he could stand that.

He didn't voice any of it—wasn't sure he could even if he wanted to, which he didn't—but Phil knew him well enough by now to hear all the things he couldn't quite say.

With a deep sigh, Phil nuzzled Thom's throat. "Damn you and your noble impulses."

Thom smiled, some of his tension melting away in the heat of Phil's lips on his skin. "I'm not being noble. You'd do the same thing in my place."

"Are you saying I'm not noble?" Phil leaned back and planted a hand over his heart. "Ouch."

"Morton called you and your protesting crew 'leftist radical guerillas'. That sounds noble to you hippie types, right?"

"You jackass." Snickering, Phil gave the side of Thom's hip a smack. "Man, if Morton thinks we're radical, he's led a sheltered life."

"No kidding. You and your friends are total flower children. No pipe bombs or anything."

Phil's smile faded into a solemn, determined expression. "We're gonna bring them down, Bubbles. We have the facts on our side, and we're going to make sure those amoral assholes get to finally see the inside of a prison like they deserve."

The intensity in Phil's eyes made Thom's cock twitch and start to swell. Slipping a hand around the back of Phil's neck, he angled his head for a deep, thorough kiss. It didn't take long for the familiar passion to rise high enough to overwhelm the bit of Thom's brain that had no idea what he was going to do when he had to leave Rosewood.

୫

Thom was late returning to work. Muttering under his breath, he jogged toward the employee entrance from the parking garage to the building's basement, punched in the entry code and slipped into the utilitarian hallway. With any luck no one would spot him before he could get to his office and fix himself up a little.

He knew he looked like he'd just been fucked six ways from Sunday—lips cherry red and swollen, hair tangled, shirt still half-untucked. And just to top it all off, he thought he tasted a bit of dried semen at the corner of his mouth. He probed at it with his tongue. *Dammit, I should've taken the time to clean up at The HO.*

The problem being, of course, that he'd been forced to leave rather precipitously. He had a meeting with one of the Midnight Rose liquor suppliers in—he glanced at his watch—ten minutes.

Shit.

He hurried along the corridor to the stairs, stuffing the tail of his shirt into the waistband of his slacks as he went and cursing his inability to control his libido around Phil. At this rate, he wouldn't have to wait and quit when Rosewood was eventually shut down, because he was likely to get fired for turning a forty-five-minute lunch break into an hour-and-twenty-minute fuck-fest.

One of Rosewood's many office underlings was standing outside Thom's office door when he got there, shifting from foot to foot and looking about ready to bolt. The boy's eyes widened when he caught sight of Thom.

Crap.

Gathering the shreds of his dignity around him, Thom approached the young man. "Something I can do for you?"

"Um. Ms. Duncan sent me to tell you to come to her office at one thirty." A brown-eyed gaze raked up and down Thom's body, clearly wondering what in the hell he'd been up to.

Thom frowned. "Can it wait? I have a meeting with a supplier at that exact same time."

"She said to tell you she's sending someone else to take your meeting, just come to her office instead." The man took a step backward. "Sorry. Uh, sorry."

Sighing, Thom forced a smile. "It's okay. Thanks for letting me know."

Relief flooded the boy's face. He nodded, turned and practically ran down the hallway.

Thom shook his head as the young man vanished around the corner. "I know damn well I'm not that scary." He fished his keys out of his pocket, unlocked his door and stepped inside.

A little rearrangement of clothing, a few swift strokes of the brush he kept in his desk to smooth down his tousled hair, and he felt more or less ready to face his boss. He popped a mint in his mouth before leaving his office and trudging down the hall to hers. Whatever her reason for wanting to see him, he figured it would go better if he didn't have cock breath.

As he strode along the plush carpet, he wondered why Duncan had to see him now, of all times. She knew he had that meeting scheduled, and he couldn't for the life of him work out why she would want to send someone else just so she could talk to him instead. The supplier was expecting the Midnight Rose manager. Sending someone lower in the food chain in his place—even if it was the head bartender—wouldn't just make Thom look bad, it would make the whole company look bad.

*Just add it to the fucking list*, he thought with a bitter smile.

195

Thom forced himself to stop scowling as he approached Duncan's door. He was a few minutes early, but fuck it. Maybe he could get it out of the way and still make the meeting with the supplier.

Squaring his shoulders, Thom knocked on the door. There was no answer. Frowning, he knocked again. Silence.

*Dammit.* It would be just like her to not let him in until precisely one thirty.

He cracked open the door and peeked inside. The office was empty.

Empty.

Leta Duncan's office. Leta Duncan, who was up to her eyeballs in her bosses' dirty deals.

Hm.

Wondering how wise he was being, Thom slipped inside the office and shut the door behind him. He hurried behind the desk before he could lose his nerve, and/or get caught.

He had no idea what he was actually looking for, so he decided to start with her computer. To his utter shock, an email from Don Bradford was open on Duncan's expensive flat-screen monitor. Skimming the message, Thom saw something about "the CM situation" and "stop him before he stops us". His mouth went dry at the implied threat in the terse words.

He hit "print" before he could think about it too hard. The printer seemed to move in slow motion. Centuries later, the damned machine finally spit out the piece of paper Thom wanted. He snatched it up, folded it and shoved it in his jacket pocket.

The doorknob turned as he was reaching for it to exit the office. With a split second to decide what to do, he lunged toward one of the leather visitor chairs in front of Duncan's desk. He fell into it just as the door swung open.

If his heart hadn't been galloping like Secretariat at the Derby, he might've laughed at the look on Leta Duncan's face when she walked in and saw him there. As it was, he met her dumbfounded stare with a blank expression that was more the result of shock at his own boldness than any real calm.

"Mr. Stone," she sputtered after a tense moment. "What are you doing in my office?"

"I was told you wanted to meet with me. I got here a couple of minutes early, and your office door was open so I came on in." Thom was relieved that his voice didn't wobble even a little.

Her eyes narrowed, hard gaze darting around the office as if looking for evidence of Thom's misdeeds. Thom forced himself not to react. Unless she had a fingerprinting kit in her purse, there was no way she would be able to tell what he'd just done.

"Yes, well. I was called away for a moment. Next time I'll be certain to lock the door." She walked around to the other side of the desk, sat and folded her hands on top of the polished wood. "Mr. Stone, I'll come straight to the point. A certain matter has come to my attention that I feel needs to be addressed immediately."

Thom swallowed. He had a feeling he knew where this was going. "What matter is that?"

"Our evening concierge saw you this morning, engaging in a very public, very amorous display with a rather scruffy-looking man." She sniffed. "Frankly, Mr. Stone, you look as if you have been engaging in activities completely inappropriate for a professional on company time. Such lewd behavior reflects badly on this company and will not be tolerated."

Thom didn't bother pointing out that the "company time" bit was debatable, at best. He didn't think it would help his case any.

"So what are you saying?" he asked, though he thought he knew exactly what she was saying.

Her already-thin lips nearly disappeared. "I'm sorry, but we have to let you go."

"Because I kissed my lover in public? Or because I fucked him on my lunch break?" He tilted his head, ignoring Duncan's gasp at his crude language. "Or maybe it's because he's a he and not a she."

"Of course not," she insisted, though the way she suddenly couldn't meet his gaze spoke volumes. "Your preferences are your own business. My decision would be the same if you were involved with a woman."

"Really."

"Yes." She fiddled with a pen on her desk. "As I said, I'm very sorry for this rather precipitous decision, but—"

"I saw one of the housekeeping staff at the mall a couple of weeks ago," Thom interrupted. "He was practically fucking his girlfriend on a bench right in front of that place where you get the giant cookies. He still had his Rosewood nametag on. You gonna fire him too?"

It didn't surprise him in the least when, instead of asking for a name—which was a good thing, since he'd made the whole thing up—she shoved her chair back and leapt to her feet. "Out," she spat, pointing at the door. "Get out of my office, and out of my company, you...you *annoying* little man!"

Thom was almost disappointed she couldn't come up with anything more scathing. Phil called him worse things at least ten times a week, just to get a rise out of him.

"Gladly." Feeling strangely relieved, Thom rose and leaned over the desk. "My lawyer will be in touch."

The color drained from her face. Thom turned away before

the murderous spark in her eyes could turn into actual murder. He walked to the door as calmly as he could, opened it and strode out into the hall.

His legs were shaking by the time he got to his office. Dropping into his chair, he laid his head on the desk and took several long, deep breaths.

He'd just been fired. Fired! That had never happened to him before. The fact that it was happening now not because of any problem with his work, but because of his sexuality, of all things, filled him with helpless anger.

Of course, he couldn't *prove* he was being fired for being gay. But he knew that's what it was. Maybe the circumstantial evidence would be enough for a lawyer to work with.

And then there was the piece of paper in his pocket. That very incriminating piece of paper, which just might be the final downfall of Bradford & Lehrer.

Speaking of which, Thom needed to get said piece of paper to Phil, and they needed to decide what to do about it.

Snatching his few personal items out of the desk drawers, Thom left the office keys on the desk and hurried upstairs to the condo he'd been using. It only took a few minutes for him to pack his things into his duffle bag. Pretty sad, really, that he hadn't ever settled in. But then again he'd never felt at home here. He couldn't feel particularly sorry for leaving.

He took the elevator down to the parking garage, his bag slung over his shoulder. He rode straight to The Happy Onion and parked in the alley out back. Thankfully, Tory was exiting just as Thom realized he no longer had a key.

"Hey, Thom," she said, smiling. "Phil's out front bussing tables."

"I figured. Okay if I go in?"

"Sure." She held the door open with one hand. "See you."

"Yeah, see you." He slipped through the opening, giving her a grateful smile. "Thanks."

Inside, Thom hurried through the storeroom and kitchen and into the restaurant proper. After a moment, he spotted Phil wiping down a table in the corner. He strode over.

Phil straightened up when Thom tapped his back with one finger. "Hey, Bubbles," he said, a wide smile spreading over his face. "What're you doing back so soon?"

With so many things swirling in his head, Thom blurted out what was foremost in his mind. "I got fired."

Phil's mouth fell open. "What? Why?"

Glancing around the crowded restaurant, Thom took Phil's arm and steered him between the tables, through the kitchen and into the empty back room. "I think they fired me because I'm gay."

"Oh shit." Phil leaned against the wall, looking stunned. "Are you sure?"

"Well, no. I mean that's not what she said. But I'm pretty sure I'm right."

"Fuck."

"I know. But listen, that's not even the biggest thing."

"There's more?"

"Yeah." Thom fished the printed-off email out of his pocket, unfolded it and handed it to Phil. "Read that."

Taking the paper, Phil scanned it. His eyes widened. He looked back at Thom with an unfamiliar fear in his eyes. "Shit, Thom. Does this say what I think it does?"

Thom nodded. "I think so. I think they've threatened Cassidy Morton's life."

# Chapter Fifteen

Circe was waiting for Thom and Phil when they returned from the police station later that afternoon. Phil took one look at her bright eyes and fierce expression as they walked through the front door and stifled a groan. From the looks of it, she wasn't going to like what she was about to hear any more than Thom had.

Hopefully she wouldn't react the same way, though. Phil was no stranger to insults slung in anger, but he didn't think he'd ever heard some of the things Thom had called the hapless officer they'd talked to.

"Hi, guys," Circe called with a smile as they approached the bar, where she was using the usual late-afternoon lull to straighten up. "So what'd they say?" Her tone clearly said she expected the police to have rushed straight over to Rosewood like an avenging army and arrested the entire upper-management staff on the spot.

Phil winced, and Thom shot him an I-told-you-so look. Thom had argued against telling Circe anything until after they'd spoken to the police. She was smart, business savvy and a loyal friend, but she had an impressive temper when her idealistic values were challenged. Thom had been of the opinion that if they didn't get the response they wanted from the cops, Circe's righteous indignation might lead her to storm downtown and make unintentional trouble for them. Phil had insisted that the police would surely be able to act on their information, and pointed out that she couldn't possibly say anything worse than Thom had. Thom had continued to object, and Phil had told Circe anyway.

It was more than a little galling to realize that Thom had been right.

Phil squeezed Thom's hand. "I'll talk to her."

"Yeah." Hooking his free hand around Phil's neck, Thom rose on tiptoe and gave him a swift kiss. "I'll wait for you in your office."

Phil watched his back as he walked away. Aside from blowing up at the police station, Thom had handled the afternoon's events remarkably well. But Phil saw the melancholy behind Thom's smile, and it worried him. Not that Thom didn't have a right to feel down. It was just that Phil had never seen him look so dispirited before, and he had no idea how to make it better.

Something cold hit his throat and slid down into the neck of his T-shirt. He fished out the piece of crushed ice and glared at Circe. "What was that for?"

"I said your name and you just kept on staring at Thom's butt, so I just did what I had to to get your attention." Leaning over the bar, she leveled a deadly serious look at him. "So what happened, Phil? I can already tell it didn't go well."

Phil let out a sigh and sank onto the nearest barstool. "It wasn't all that terrible, actually, just not what we wanted."

"Disappointing rather than disastrous, huh?"

"Pretty much."

Circe reached under the bar and came up with a cold bottle of Dos Equis. She opened it and slid it across to Phil. "Tell me."

He picked up the bottle and took a long swallow. "There's not a lot to tell. The officer we talked to was nice, but basically he told us there's nothing much the police can do. He said we should get a good lawyer and go after them in civil court because we didn't have a criminal case."

Circe's mouth fell open. "You're shitting me."

"Nope."

"What about the chemicals in the water around Rolling Hills? What about Thom being fired?" She tilted her head, frowning. "Well, actually I kind of see that. Those kinds of cases belong in civil court. But what about the email? They threatened a city councilman, for fuck's sake!"

"Keep it down, would you?" Phil glanced around. Thankfully, there were only a few customers in the place at the moment and none of them were paying any attention. "They said the email was suspicious, but the way Thom got it meant they wouldn't be able to use it as evidence so it might as well not exist."

Circe leaned closer and lowered her voice. "So they're not doing anything? They're just letting it go?"

Phil shrugged. "They promised to look into the water contamination, and they said they'd keep an eye on the Rosewood management, whatever that means. But that's it, yeah."

"Those assholes." Circe's brown eyes blazed. "Thom was upset, I bet."

"More than the situation really deserved, I think."

"What'd he call 'em?" she asked, the glower vanishing behind a sudden grin.

"He started out with 'incompetent gelatin-brained bureaucrat' and it went downhill from there." Phil sighed across the mouth of his bottle. "He was damn lucky they didn't lock him up, to be honest. I've never seen him lose it quite like that, and you know how his temper is."

"Amen, brother." Tucking a stray curl beneath the scarf holding back her hair, Circe straightened up and wiped absently at the spot where Phil's beer had left a wet ring on the bar. "And I bet y'all thought I'd be the one to go postal, huh?"

Phil chuckled. "Yep."

"So you figure he overreacted?"

"I do, yeah. Not that I necessarily blame him. He'd had a hell of an afternoon. I think hearing that there's nothing he could do right this minute was the last straw."

"Oh. Well, I can see that." She sucked on her bottom lip for a moment. "I guess he's gonna get a lawyer then, huh?"

"Definitely. He already has the name of Dave and Karen's lawyer. He's gonna call her in the morning and make an appointment."

"Good." She glanced toward the front door, where a couple had just walked in and was approaching the bar. "Looks like I got customers. Tell Thom to let me know if I can help with anything, okay?"

"Sure." He covered her small hand with his large one and smiled. "Thanks, Circe. Love you."

"Love you too, handsome." She turned her hand in his, squeezed his fingers and pulled away to attend to her customers.

Pushing to his feet, Phil strode through the restaurant toward the back room, his Dos Equis bottle swinging from his hand. His office door stood open a crack. Phil smiled. Evidently Thom remembered where he kept the extra office key.

Phil nudged the door open with his foot, went inside and

bumped it closed again. Thom sat slumped in Phil's chair, his head resting on his folded arms. "Oh my God, I can't believe I called a cop a dickless, retarded warthog," Thom moaned before Phil could say a word.

Biting back laughter, Phil skirted the desk, picked Thom up and settled him on his lap. "I thought it was funny. Interestingly, so did several of the other cops."

Thom curled up and rested his head in the curve of Phil's neck. "Why didn't you stop me?"

"Oh, you mean there was actually a chance I *could* have stopped you?"

No answer, which was answer enough. Thom sighed and shifted so that his hair tickled Phil's chin. "What did Circe say? Is she gonna go ballistic?"

"Naw. She was way calmer than you were."

Thom snorted, but left it at that. "It looks like I'm homeless again. Can I use the apartment upstairs? Just for a little while?"

"Sure, if you want." Tilting Thom's face up, Phil gazed into his eyes. "But I'd rather you stayed with me."

For a second, Thom just stared, and Phil was sure he was going to say "no". Then he smiled, and Phil breathed again. "Okay, yeah. I'd like that. Thanks."

Relieved, Phil echoed Thom's smile. "My pleasure, believe me."

He pulled Thom closer and kissed him. Thom's lips parted, a soft moan escaping as his tongue slid into Phil's mouth. God, it was sweet. Phil wished this moment could last forever.

"It'll be okay, baby," Phil whispered when the kiss broke. "Everything'll be all right."

Thom didn't answer, just settled back into Phil's embrace.

Phil tightened his arms around Thom and hoped like hell life wouldn't make a liar out of him.

ℭℰ

"Thom!" Phil peered up the stairs, brow furrowed. "Aren't you ready yet?"

Obstinate silence for a moment. Then, "No."

"Come on, Bubbles. It can't possibly take that long to put that costume on."

"Oh it's on. That's the fucking problem."

Sighing, Phil glanced at his watch. Seven thirty. It was Halloween, and the party at Belial's Basement was just now starting, but Phil was anxious to get there. The way he figured it, he and Thom deserved a little mindless fun tonight. He was determined to snap Thom out of the funk he'd been in since the previous day and bring back that sweet, sunny smile.

"What's wrong with the costume?" Phil called, plucking a bit of lint off his snug black leather pants.

"You've got to be fucking kidding me, right?"

Thom's voice was closer now. Phil looked up. Thom stood at the top of the stairs, arms crossed over his bare belly, radiating a sense of wounded dignity. He wore a pair of skin-tight dark purple velvet pants slung low enough to show the jut of his hipbones and a long purple coat whose only reason for existing seemed to be to showcase Thom's alabaster skin and sculpted abs to best advantage. A black leather choker and Thom's ever-present boots completed the outfit. His hair was slicked back and tied with a strip of leather.

If Phil's knees hadn't gone watery, he would've rushed up the stairs and molested the man.

Phil licked his lips. "What's the problem? You look fucking hot."

"I look like an undead pimp," Thom countered, scowling.

"Nope, you look like a vampire, which is kind of the point." Phil mounted a couple of steps and peered closer. "Nice makeup, by the way. Didn't know you knew how to do that."

A rosy blush colored Thom's cheeks. "I used to be sort of a Goth when I was in high school."

Phil snickered. "Babe, you're just full of surprises."

"Yeah, well, here's one for you. I'm changing." Thom whirled and stomped off toward the bedroom.

After a shocked second, Phil bounded up the stairs in Thom's wake. "No, Thom, c'mon. Leave it on." He caught up to Thom at the bedroom door, spun him around and grabbed his upper arms so he couldn't get away.

Thom glared up at him, those blue eyes looking bigger than ever lined in black and set in a face baby-powdered to an unearthly pallor. "Let go."

"No." Phil dragged him closer and wound one arm around his waist. "Going as vampire master and slave was your idea, why's it suddenly a problem now?"

Thom leaned against Phil's chest with a deep sigh. "I just didn't realize I was going to feel this stupid. Or this...visible."

Phil had to laugh at that. "Trust me, Bubbles, we'll be wearing the conservative costumes in this bunch."

Thom raised his head to give Phil a skeptical look. "Even you?"

"Even me, yeah." Phil fingered the thick silver chain around his neck and the painted-on vampire bite just above it. "I'll have on a jacket, and my ass doesn't hang out of my pants, so yeah, I'm pretty conservative."

"That's good." Thom slid a hand around to cup Phil's butt. "Because no one but Master Thom gets to see your ass."

Grinning, Phil thrust his leather-covered cock against Thom's lower belly. "Babe, if you wear that outfit for me now, my ass is all yours later."

"Your ass is *always* mine," Thom pointed out.

"Hm, true. How about I let you play with that crop and leash you got for our costumes later tonight?" Phil shot Thom his best lecherous leer. "What about it, Master? Dress like a vampire now, tie me up and whip me later?"

Thom's gaze turned heavy. "You have a deal." Pulling out of Phil's embrace, Thom produced the aforementioned leash from somewhere inside his jacket and clipped it to Phil's chain. "Let's go, slave. We have a party to get to."

Phil obediently trailed Thom downstairs, shrugged on his jacket and pocketed his car keys. Thinking of all the kinky fun they could have later had him hard as a rock inside those so-tight leather pants.

Thom shot a smoldering stare at Phil as they left the house, and Phil fought back a dizzying wave of lust. He grinned. This promised to be one hell of a party.

ॐ

It was one hell of a party. Phil had sworn up and down it would be, and damned if he wasn't dead right.

*Dead right.* Thom giggled into his fourth whiskey and Coke. Maybe it was because he was well on his way to being drunk for the first time in ages, but he'd been making those accidental vampire references in his head all night. It was funny as hell.

Thom glanced around looking for Phil, who'd gone to the

bathroom. No sign of him. Which wasn't surprising, really, considering how packed the place was and how much everyone seemed to be drinking. There was bound to be a long line.

A willowy young man wearing a white loincloth and not much else bumped into Thom's shoulder as he passed, leaving a smear of silver glitter on Thom's coat. "Whups, sorry," the boy slurred, attempting to brush at the glitter and missing by several inches.

Thom watched him stagger off, taut little behind peeking out the back of the loincloth with every step. Phil hadn't been kidding about the two of them having the most conservative costumes. Last time Thom had been here—*when I first met Phil*, he thought fondly—it had looked like any other neighborhood pick-up joint. Tonight it resembled nothing so much as a gay S&M disco. In hell. He giggled again.

Long arms slid around him from behind. Phil's beard rasped the shell of his ear as Phil brushed a soft kiss across his temple. "You're a cute drunk, angel face," Phil observed, plonking onto the barstool next to Thom's with a wide grin.

Thom aimed a stern glare more or less in Phil's direction. At least, he hoped it was a stern glare. So far this evening he'd shown a rather alarming propensity for goofy smiles and most un-vampire-like giggles. "That's *Master* Angel Face to you, slave boy."

Chuckling, Phil stole Thom's glass and took a long swallow. "Well, *Master* Angel Face, wanna dance?"

Thom considered. He didn't recognize the song playing, but it was loud and primal, with thundering drums and a bass line that throbbed and pulsed like a heartbeat. It sounded like sex interpreted as dance music. In other words, perfect for dirty dancing.

"Yeah, okay." Hopping off the barstool, Thom looped Phil's

leash around his wrist and dragged him off into the heaving throng on the dance floor.

A crowd of sweaty men in various stages of undress closed around them about two steps from the bar. Thom molded his body to Phil's and gave himself up to the driving rhythm. Phil moved against him, arms looped across his shoulders and one long leg insinuating itself between Thom's.

Hard, leather-clad muscle met Thom's crotch, and *damn* it felt good. Moaning, Thom rocked against that firm thigh. He felt wonderfully uninhibited, in spite of being surrounded by a bunch of strangers. Maybe because it was a bunch of strangers just as lust-crazed as himself, everyone happily grinding against each other and having a good time. It had been far too long since he'd let go like this. Just had fun dancing with his lover.

His lover. Phil. For whom he planned to confess his feelings later tonight.

Maybe that's why he'd hit the whiskey so hard. Liquid courage was a magnificent thing.

One of Phil's arms slid snug around Thom's hips beneath his coat, pushing his groin even harder into the thigh rubbing against it. "Oh, fuck," Thom groaned, hands digging into Phil's back while his cock swelled to near bursting against Phil's leg. "Phil. God."

Bending, Phil ran his tongue up Thom's throat. "You're so hard for me, pretty baby," he breathed in Thom's ear. "You want to come? Right here on the dance floor?"

*Not in public!* "Fuck, yes."

Thom frowned. Had he just said that?

Apparently so, because now Phil's hips were undulating against his, Phil's arm strong and sure around him, holding him so close their mingled sweat glued their bare skin together.
210

Deciding he could ignore his sense of propriety just this once, Thom arched his neck for Phil's bites and kisses and let the heat spread through him.

Lost in a haze of pleasure, Thom barely noticed the song switch to something slower but no less sexual. Phil's hand slid down the back of his pants, one finger dipping into the crease of his ass. It felt deliciously filthy to be doing this here, in the middle of a packed dance floor. The long purple coat hid Phil's exploring hand from the rest of the bar, but still. Anybody who looked close enough could tell what was happening.

Thom whimpered when Phil's fingertip brushed his hole. "Phil. Close."

A low growl rumbled from Phil's throat, raising gooseflesh on Thom's arms. "Come, baby."

That magical, wicked finger penetrated him. The hot dry burn shot through him like lightning, and he came with a keening cry that was drowned out in the bone-rattling thump of the music. Phil held him, murmuring nonsense in his ear while he shook and moaned through his release.

"Oh my fucking God," Thom gasped when he'd recovered enough to talk. "I can't believe I just came in my pants in the middle of a bar."

"With my finger up your ass," Phil reminded him, wiggling the digit in question and making Thom squeal. "That was soooo hot, pretty baby."

"You can say that again," said a booming voice from behind Thom.

Thom twisted his neck to see who the hell the voyeur was. A big, muscular middle-aged man wearing leather shorts and a harness stood there leering. The man grinned and waggled his eyebrows. "You're a pretty little thing. Your daddy there let you out to play?"

"No," Phil answered before Thom could correct the man's perceptions about his relationship with Phil. "He's all mine."

The man just shrugged and turned back to his dance partner. Thom gaped up at Phil, who was still glaring daggers at the back of the stranger's head. "Hey, who's the master and who's the slave here?"

Phil blinked, and his expression relaxed into a sheepish smile. "Sorry. It's just the thought of any other man touching you makes me see red."

Thom felt one of those goofy grins spread across his face. Reaching up, he cupped his palms around Phil's cheeks. "I don't want any other man touching me either. Just you."

"Good."

They stared at each other. The look on Phil's face was warm and tender. He opened his mouth. Closed it again, and shook his head.

Something in Phil's eyes made Thom's breath hitch. For a heart-stopping second, he thought Phil might actually say you-know-what right there in the bar, with his finger still lodged in Thom's butt. Before Thom could decide if that was refreshingly different or just plain weird, Phil bent and captured his mouth in a deep, whiskey-flavored kiss. Thom opened wide and sucked Phil's tongue in, relieved that Phil's sense of timing wasn't completely whacked after all.

By the time they drew apart, the music had changed again, to something bouncy and infectious that was better suited for actual dancing than the simulated fucking which had been going on before. Thom dismounted Phil's thigh, forcing the insistent finger out of him. Phil's hand slid up to sit possessively on Thom's hip.

"I'm gonna go to the bathroom and get cleaned up a little," Thom shouted over the music. "Meet me back at the bar?"

"Sure thing, Bubbles." Smiling, Phil brushed a soft caress over Thom's cheek. "Hurry up."

Phil sloped off toward the bar, smacking Thom's ass on the way. Thom clutched his coat around him to hide the big wet splotch on the front of his pants and made his way through the sweaty crush of humanity to the bathroom.

To his relief, the place was nearly empty. One of the bartenders exited a stall and headed to one of the sinks without so much as a glance in Thom's direction. Thom edged over to the sink farthest from the other man and turned the hot water on, wondering how long he could procrastinate. He didn't much like the thought of some stranger watching him swab the spunk off his crotch and pants.

The bartender left. Thom grabbed a handful of paper towels and dampened them in the running water. Just as he was about to shove them down the front of his damp pants, two more men burst in, leaning on each other and laughing. Thom let his waistband snap back and pretended to be washing his hands. His new companions didn't seem to notice. They staggered over to the two urinals, unzipped and started pissing. Thom took the opportunity to hold the thin, clingy fabric away from his groin and scrub the coagulating fluids from his skin.

An eternity later, the two men finished their business and shuffled out again without washing their hands. Grimacing, Thom turned his attention to his pants. Coming on the dance floor was a heady rush. The consequences? Not so much. The night was young. He didn't particularly care to spend the remaining hours cold, sticky and uncomfortable.

He didn't even look up when the door opened again. It was a bar, after all, and a popular Halloween party. He could hardly expect to have the bathroom to himself for long. At least he was done with the exposing-himself part. He could live with people watching him clean his pants.

At the periphery of his vision, he saw a very large man dressed all in black lean against the door. The man wore what appeared to be a Mardi Gras mask.

Thom frowned. Something didn't feel right. Deciding maybe he could live with damp, stained pants after all, he shut off the water and turned to leave.

A demon with three horns and a lolling red tongue stood behind him. Thom jumped back against the edge of the sink, heart in his throat. He barely had time to register the cold but very human eyes through two holes in the mask before a Latex-gloved hand shot out and dealt a crunching blow to his jaw.

His head snapped sideways. The room spun in a sickening arc. When everything stopped moving, he realized he was flat on his back on the dirty tiles with the demon standing over him. He started to scramble backward. Demon Man reached down, flipped him over and hauled him up by his arms.

When his assailant started dragging him into one of the bathroom stalls, Thom's shocked paralysis broke. He squirmed and kicked, but couldn't break free of the man's grip. "Let me go, asshole!"

In answer, Demon Man swung Thom's body like a rag doll. His head connected with the metal frame of the toilet stalls. For a second, everything went gray. When his head cleared, he was in a locked stall, slumped on the toilet while the masked man loomed above him. His hair had come loose to tickle his face. It took him a moment to realize that his attacker had taken the leather tie and bound his wrists behind his back.

Thom drew breath to scream. Attracting the attention of someone outside looked like his only option at this point. Before he could make a sound, the man in the demon mask shoved a rag into his mouth and tied it in place with a large bandana.

Gagged and restrained, head whirling and stomach churning, Thom could do nothing but keep kicking and hope his best death glare would suddenly be able to kill for real.

Demon Man grunted when Thom's boot connected with his kneecap. "Goddammit! Little bastard."

He hit Thom again. The punch sent Thom spinning off the toilet and onto the floor. He lay there panting, his heart pounding so hard and fast it made him dizzy. Or maybe that was just the repeated blows to the head.

A big hand fisted in his hair and yanked, pulling him to a half-sitting position. He couldn't help the pained mewl that escaped. It fucking *hurt*, and not just because of the headache already jackhammering his skull apart.

The feel of cold metal against his throat stopped all thought of renewing his struggle. He went still, staring up at the man now holding a very large, very sharp knife to his jugular.

"You shouldn't have done that," Demon Man growled. He pushed the tip of the knife harder against the groove on one side of Thom's windpipe. Thom felt a sharp pain, felt blood well and trickle down his skin. "If you hadn't done it, I wouldn't have to be in here killing you."

For some reason, the fact that he had no idea what the fuck the guy was talking about made Thom angrier than the man's apparent desire to murder him.

Furious, Thom twisted in the demon's grip. The knife slid along his skin just above the leather choker. He ignored the pain of hair ripping loose at the roots, ignored the dizziness and nausea and the burning ache where the knife had cut him. Surging onto his knees, Thom rammed his head into Demon Man's crotch with all the force he could muster. The agonized howl he got in return was worth the renewed surge of pain thumping through his skull.

"John?" a voice called. The man guarding the door, Thom guessed. "You all right?"

Before he could answer, Thom head-butted Demon John's crotch again. This time, the man bent double, both hands cupping his injured privates. Seeing his chance to disable the bastard, Thom levered himself onto the toilet seat and kicked his attacker in the face.

"Son of a *bitch*!" the man roared, moving one hand to cover his bleeding nose. "Joe! Get the fuck in here!"

Footsteps clomped toward them. Demon John unlocked the stall door, and it swung open. Mardi Gras Joe pushed in beside the demon, shut the door behind him and locked it.

Thom considered his options. On the one hand, the door to the bathroom was now unguarded, and it was only a matter of time before someone came in. On the other hand, in a gay bar he doubted anyone would even blink at noticing three men in the same stall.

On a hypothetical third hand, Phil would eventually come looking for him. The question was, would he find Thom bruised but alive, or dead in a pool of his own blood?

The demon raised his head and pinned Thom with an enraged glare. "You little fucker," he spat, pointing a thick finger at Thom. "I am going to *enjoy* gutting you, boy."

Mardi Gras moved to one side, grabbed Thom's bound arms and jerked him to his feet. Demon John and his knife closed in with grim purpose.

Thom wanted to fight them. He didn't want to die, but if that's what was about to happen, he wanted to go down swinging. So to speak. But his legs felt like rubber, and he couldn't make himself move, no matter how much he wanted to. Everything sounded muffled, as if his ears were stuffed with cotton.

His vision tunneled, and he felt himself losing consciousness. As the world slid away, he wondered if he imagined the sound of a door slamming open, or a familiar voice calling his name.

# Chapter Sixteen

After Thom left for the bathroom, Phil headed to the bar. He needed a cold beer, and he figured another drink would help dull any regrets Thom might develop about letting Phil bring him off in the middle of a crowded bar.

"Give me a whiskey and Coke and a Dos Equis," he yelled once he'd caught the bartender's eye.

Waiting for the drinks, Phil thought about what had just happened out on the dance floor. The memory of Thom's face, sweet mouth slack and eyes glazed with orgasm, made Phil's insides quiver. He'd shot like a fucking teenage virgin just from the sight of Thom coming in his arms. He probably should've gone to clean up as well, but he hadn't wanted to. Maybe he'd regret that later, when he tried to unglue the leather from his skin. For now, though, he planned to enjoy the physical evidence of how Thom affected him.

"Phil-licious. Long time no see."

*Shit.* Phil looked to his right. Brad grinned at him and raised his nearly empty glass in greeting. "Hi, Brad," Phil said, managing not to grimace. "You look, um...interesting."

*There, that was polite enough.* It was the best he could do. A Tinkerbell outfit was a little over the top, even for Brad. At least the dress matched his hair.

"You look edible, as always." Brad grabbed the bartender's

218

sleeve when he brought Phil's drinks over. "Get me another Green Fairy, please, honey. Put it on my tab."

Phil handed the bartender a wad of ones and a handful of change, then turned to search for Thom. There was no sign of him yet. "Uh, I'm here with someone, so..."

"Hm, yes, I know. I saw you dancing with him earlier. Are you cruising middle schools now?"

Shaking his head, Phil picked up his beer. "Why don't you go find somebody to dance with? Other than me," he added when he saw the predatory gleam in Brad's eye.

Brad sighed. "I have to pee."

Phil gave him an incredulous look. "Maybe this is a stupid question, but if you have to piss why don't you go to the bathroom instead of the bar?"

Scowling, Brad took the Neon green beverage the bartender handed him and sipped it. "I can't get in. Someone's blocking the door."

An unpleasant feeling curled in the pit of Phil's stomach. "What do you mean?"

"I mean what I said. I pushed on the door, it ran into someone big, and said big person told me to fuck off." Brad stirred a finger through his drink. "They're probably in there fucking. Hopefully they'll shoot fast and I can get in there before my bladder explodes."

Brad kept prattling on, but Phil had stopped listening. The seemingly disparate elements of the situation were coming together in his head in a way he didn't like one bit.

Thom had gone to the bathroom several minutes ago.

Thom hadn't yet returned from said restroom trip.

Brad couldn't get in the bathroom where Thom presumably still was.

Something wasn't right. Phil felt it in his bones.

Setting his beer on the bar beside Thom's drink, Phil slid off the barstool and started pushing his way through the mass of people. He heard Brad hurling insults in his direction, but he didn't care. His gut told him Thom was in trouble, and he couldn't think of anything but getting to him.

When he reached the bathroom, he kicked the door as hard as he could. Expecting the door to be blocked like Brad had said, Phil lost his balance and nearly pitched forward when it flew open and hit the wall with a clang. After a surprised moment, he recovered and raced into the bathroom.

"Thom!" he called. "Where are you?"

There was no definitive answer, but the faint moan and scuffling sounds had Phil lunging toward the last toilet stall. Three pairs of feet showed beneath the door. Phil saw Thom's boots and the bottoms of his purple pants in the midst of the trio, and that was all he needed to know. Yelling like a berserker, he rushed at the stall door and drove his shoulder into it with his full body weight behind him. To his relief, the so-called "locks" on the doors were just as flimsy as he remembered them being. Metal screeched, and the door jerked open.

As his momentum drove him forward into the three bodies huddled together, Phil had an impression of black clothes, a feathered mask and a Halloween demon. Then he spotted Thom, white-faced and bleeding, a makeshift gag tied in place in his mouth, and Phil's vision went red.

He wasn't sure exactly what happened next. He thought he punched someone in the face, and he was pretty sure he broke someone else's wrist. The mental image of a bone snapping, followed by a scream and a knife skidding behind the toilet, seemed very real. In any case, when the blind rage passed, Phil found himself on the bathroom floor outside the stall, struggling against the grip of the five men holding him down. Someone was sobbing nearby, and someone else was spitting a steady stream of colorful curses. The whole room seemed to be packed with people, but Phil couldn't see Thom anywhere.

"Thom?" His voice sounded panicked and barely sane, but he didn't give a shit. If anything had happened to Thom, those motherfucking bastards were going to *die*, right here and now. "Baby, where are you?"

"Right here."

The crowd gathered around Phil parted, and the face Phil wanted to see most in the world came into view, battered but intact. The gag was gone. Blood trickled from a thin cut running across the front of his throat above his choker, but the wound appeared to be superficial.

Phil had never been more relieved in his life. Shaking loose of the restraining hands, he sat up and pulled Thom into his arms.

"It's okay," Thom whispered, cuddling against Phil's chest and running his hands up and down Phil's back in long, soothing strokes. "I'm all right. Just a little banged up, is all."

"God, I was so fucking scared." Phil clutched Thom as tight as he dared, not knowing where he was hurt. He buried his face in Thom's soft, fragrant hair. "Jesus, pretty baby. What if I hadn't come in? What...were they..."

"I don't know. They were going to slit my throat, I think. But damned if I know why." Pulling back a little, Thom planted both hands on the sides of Phil's face and met his gaze. "It doesn't matter. We'll figure all that out later. All that matters now is I'm fine, you're fine and those two bastards are going to jail. Okay?"

Phil managed an anemic smile. "Yeah. Okay."

Hal, the bar's owner, shooed the crowd away and helped Thom stand. "Police and paramedics are on the way. Should be here any minute." He glanced up at one of the bartenders who was standing by the sink. "Charlie, you go out front and wait for the cops. I'll get Phil and Thom to a table to wait."

"What about the guys who attacked Thom?" Phil asked as he clambered to his feet and pulled Thom close to his side. "What do we do with them?"

To his surprise, Thom snickered. "I don't think that'll be a problem."

"Huh? Why not?"

Hal took Thom's free arm and steered him and Phil toward the bathroom exit. "Well, they're restrained now, and of course we'll leave a couple of our best men in here to watch them, but you, my friend, put both of 'em pretty much out of commission."

"Um. What'd I do to them?" Phil wasn't sure he wanted to know, but he was going to have to find out sooner or later. Might just as well be now.

"One of the guys has a goose egg where you apparently knocked him down and he conked his head on the toilet. He was down for the count when we got in here. The other one was screaming bloody murder 'cause you'd broken his wrist." Hal cracked a wolfish grin. "Damn fine job, if you ask me. No more than the stupid fucks deserved."

Phil nodded, relieved he hadn't killed anyone. He thought a person really ought to remember it if they committed murder.

Outside, Phil set Thom down in the first empty booth and slid in beside him. Lifting Thom's chin, Phil planted a gentle kiss on his lips. "You sure you're okay, baby?"

Thom shrugged. "My head feels like someone used it for a battering ram, but other than that I'm fine."

"Yeah, well, you're getting checked over by the paramedics when they get here." Hal pointed a stern finger at Thom when he started to protest. "No arguments. You were out cold when Charlie got to you, and that cut on your throat's still bleeding."

"But I..." Thom trailed off, his gaze cutting from Phil to Hal and back again. He sighed. "Okay, okay. But only because Phil wants me to."

Phil smiled as Hal hurried to the bar to help wrangle the crowd. "Thanks, Bubbles."

Someone passing by snickered. "Bubbles?"

"Drop it," Phil warned, noting the barbed glare Thom shot at the poor guy. Phil kissed the blossoming bruise on Thom's jaw. "What happened?"

"I went in the bathroom, and those two guys came in a couple of minutes later. The guy in the Mardi Gras mask blocked the door. The one with the demon mask decked me and dragged me into that stall." Thom's eyes took on a haunted look. "I fought back, but it wasn't enough. They had me, Phil. They were going to kill me, and if you hadn't shown up when you did I think they would've succeeded."

A hard chill shot up Phil's spine. He buried a hand in Thom's hair and rested their foreheads together. Thom's slight body trembled in Phil's embrace. Now that the immediate danger was over, reaction had set in and Phil was shaking almost as hard as Thom.

*I almost lost him. He almost died in here tonight. And I've never once told him how I feel about him.*

The shock of it was enough to dissolve the fear which had kept Phil silent for weeks on end. Tilting Thom's face up, Phil stared straight into his eyes. "I love you, Thom."

Thom blinked a couple of times, then burst out laughing.

Of all the reactions Phil could've imagined, this wasn't one of them. A hot blush rose in his cheeks. He looked down, feeling ridiculous. At least they were alone.

Cold hands pressed to Phil's cheeks. "Phil. Look at me."

Phil did, albeit reluctantly. Thom smiled, eyes shining. "I'm laughing because you just stole my thunder. I'd planned to tell you tonight, after the party."

The light dawned, and Phil felt a big grin spread over his face. "You love me?"

Laughing, Thom leaned in and kissed Phil's lips. "Yes, you big goof," he murmured, stroking Phil's cheek. "I love you."

Phil let out a whoop that drew every eye in the bar to him. Ignoring the laughter and stares from the other patrons, he wrapped both arms around Thom's waist and lifted him into his lap. They kissed to a chorus of catcalls and whistles.

When they drew apart, Thom laid his head on Phil's shoulder with a happy sigh. Phil rested his cheek against Thom's hair. The two of them still had a long night ahead. There would be endless questions to answer, and Thom needed to be examined to make sure there were no serious injuries. Right now, though, they were alive, and together, and in love.

*I love him. And he loves me.*

Phil smiled. Life was good.

ॐ

"Uh-huh... Uh-huh... Uh-huh... Yeah... Yeah... Uh-huh... Say again?... Oh, I see... Uh-huh..."

Phil yawned. Thom had been on his cell phone for at least fifteen minutes, and most of it had been less than enlightening for Phil. He glanced at the clock beside his bed. Eight thirty a.m. On a *Saturday*, yet. Maybe the cops had been awake for hours, but he and Thom had been sound asleep when they called.

Another yawn nearly split Phil's face in half. Grumbling under his breath, he wriggled over to where Thom sat cross-legged in a nest of rumpled bed clothes, wound his arms around Thom's hips and curled up with his head pillowed on Thom's thigh. He closed his eyes and smiled as Thom's fingers threaded through his unbound hair.

Phil drifted into a doze while Thom continued his lopsided conversation with the police. In the three days since Thom's attack, the cops had called him every single morning at what Phil considered an absolutely ridiculous hour. They'd also called most afternoons, and they'd both had to go down to the police station the day before. It was disruptive as hell, but Thom never complained so Phil kept his own irritation to himself. After all, the police were doing their level best to make sure the two repeat offenders who'd attacked Thom weren't the only ones to see the inside of a prison.

"Okay. Thanks, Detective. I really appreciate all you've done... Yeah... Okay, I'll talk to you soon. Bye."

Phil opened his eyes and looked up as Thom clicked his phone off and set it on the bedside table. "Good news?"

"Very." Nudging Phil off his lap, Thom lay down and went straight into Phil's embrace. "Leta Duncan confessed early this morning. She hired those two muscleheads to kill me."

"Bitch," Phil growled. "Did she say why?"

Thom nodded, his sleep-mussed hair tickling Phil's shoulder. "Apparently she had a security camera in her office, and it caught me printing off that email."

"Oh. Not good."

"You can say that again. She decided to have me whacked

225

instead of saying anything to the head honchos, because she was afraid I'd go public and she'd be fired for being so damn careless with such sensitive information."

Phil snickered. "Whacked?"

Thom smacked Phil's shoulder. "Shut up, you ass."

"Okay, okay." Phil leaned in to brush a light kiss across Thom's lips. "So she really was working alone, like Bradford and Lehrer claimed?"

"Yeah. They're both still in trouble, for lots of things, but she's the only one who'll be charged with attempted murder."

"Hm." Phil ran a hand over the curve of Thom's T-shirt-clad shoulder. "What about that email threatening Cassidy Morton?"

Thom shrugged. "According to Don Bradford, he didn't intend any physical threat. He just meant for her to offer Mr. Morton more money."

Phil snorted. "Oh sure, he'd say that *now*."

"Hey, bribery and blackmail are plenty bad enough." Grinning, Thom raked his fingers through Phil's hair. "Don't worry, my great big he-man protector. Rosewood's being sold, and the Rolling Hills project is off now, thanks to your detective work and my cleverness in pissing off the right person just enough to get her to try and kill me."

"Don't joke about that." Phil pulled Thom closer and kissed the purple bruise on his forehead. "You want to go back to sleep now? You haven't gotten nearly enough rest in the last three days."

Thom wrinkled his nose. "Are you kidding me? I haven't spent so much time in bed since I had chickenpox when I was five. And," he added with a pout that made Phil's crotch tingle, "we haven't had sex even *once* since Wednesday."

Phil swallowed. "The paramedic said you had to rest and

not exert yourself."

"For a few days, she said." Thom's hand wandered down Phil's spine, slipped inside the back of his pants and curled around one butt cheek. "Three days is plenty. Let's fuck."

"Oh shit," Phil panted as Thom's fingers crept into the crack of his ass. He told himself he didn't point out that it hadn't been three *whole* days yet because Thom wouldn't listen. "B-but, your head. You...you were knocked out."

"Only for a few seconds." Thom slung a leg over Phil's thighs and canted his hips forward. And *oh God* Thom was hard, his cock digging into Phil's hipbone through their pajamas. "I'm fine, honest. Even the headache's gone now." He latched his mouth onto Phil's chin, tongue stirring the hairs of his beard. "Please, Phil. I want to see if sex is any different now that we've both said the 'L' word."

Phil laughed, a bit breathlessly. "You know what, if you're desperate enough to try and justify it that way, then how can I say no?"

"You can't." Thom squirmed until his body was pressed against Phil's from chest to toes. He kissed Phil's throat, warm lips lingering on his skin. "C'mon. Make love to me."

The blood rushed to Phil's cock so fast it made him dizzy. "You...you want..."

"I want to ride your cock," Thom purred, sounding unforgivably cool and collected. "I want to come with your prick so deep up my ass I can fucking *taste* it when you shoot inside me."

*Sweet Jesus on roller skates.* Phil licked his lips. "I could go for that."

"Figured you might." In a movement too quick for Phil's lust-fogged brain to follow, Thom shoved him onto his back and straddled his hips. Thom grabbed the hem of Phil's shirt and dragged it upward, fingers trailing along Phil's ribs. "Take this off."

Phil did as he was told. The T-shirt came off inside out. Phil threw it on the floor, then reached for Thom's shirt. Together, they got the garment off and tossed it over the edge of the bed. Phil ran both hands up Thom's chest. God, his skin was so smooth. Pale and silky and so fucking perfect.

"You're so beautiful," Phil whispered, rasping the pads of his thumbs across Thom's little pink nipples. He trailed his fingers upward to brush the thin red line marring the white skin of Thom's throat. "Those bastards deserve to die for touching you."

Thom's smile faded. "Let's not talk about them. I don't want to think about that right now."

"Of course not. I'm sorry." Gathering Thom into his arms, Phil buried a hand in Thom's baby-soft hair and sealed their lips together.

Thom's mouth opened with a tiny sigh. His tongue slid out to twine with Phil's, and *God* it was good. Thom always kissed as if his continued existence depended on tasting every corner of Phil's mouth, and Phil loved it.

Sometimes he wondered how he'd ever lived without this. Every other relationship he'd ever had seemed gray and empty compared to the way Thom made his spirit soar just by being near.

Phil's dick was hard enough to knock holes in concrete by the time Thom pulled back, sucking on Phil's bottom lip for a moment before letting go. Thom planted a trail of kisses down Phil's chest, stopping on the way to give both nipples a quick suck. A warm, wet tongue delved into Phil's navel before following the line of hair over his belly. Phil moaned, his body arching into the touch.

Sitting up, Thom curled his fingers into the waistband of Phil's green striped pajama pants. "Lift up."

Phil obediently lifted his hips so Thom could slide the pants to his thighs. Rising onto his knees, Thom reached through the V of his legs to push Phil's pajamas down as far as he could. Phil managed to worm them down to his ankles, pull them off with his toes and kick them out of the way. He stared up into Thom's face. Thom's gaze raked up and down Phil's naked body. The heat in Thom's eyes was enough to set Phil's skin on fire.

"Now you, baby." Phil ran a finger under the edge of the thin black pants Thom had been sleeping in. "Take 'em off."

Thom stood, wobbling a little on the pillow-top mattress, and stripped off his pants. Staring into Phil's eyes, he took his flushed and leaking cock in a loose grip and stroked it from base to tip. His tongue came out to trace the line of his lower lip in a deliberately seductive caress.

Phil let out an honest-to-God whine. "Shit, baby." He clamped his fingers around the base of his cock, trying to keep himself under control long enough to actually get inside Thom. "Come back down here. I'm gonna shoot if you keep teasing like that."

"Don't you dare," Thom ordered, blue eyes blazing. Dropping to his knees, he reached over and fished the lube out of Phil's bedside table drawer. He handed it to Phil, then stretched himself out on top of Phil's body, legs splayed to either side of his hips. "I think you know what to do."

Phil struggled to coordinate his hands as Thom's mouth attacked his. After a moment's fumbling, he managed to open the lube. It didn't matter that he got as much of the slick stuff on the bed as on his hand, or that the bottle wasn't quite closed when he dropped it beside him on the mattress. All that mattered was Thom's exuberant tongue in his mouth, Thom's needy little noises when Phil slid two slippery fingers inside him.

Two and a half days, Phil decided, was *way* too long to go without the feel of Thom's bare skin against his.

Phil plunged his fingers as deep as he could into Thom's ass, twisting and scissoring to stretch the tight muscles. Thom gasped and arched when Phil's fingertip zinged over his gland. "Oh God. Fuck. Phil. Now."

*Are you sure?* Phil almost managed to ask out loud. *It's been a while since I topped, your ass is about tight enough to snip my fingers off and I don't want to hurt you.* Sadly, all that came out was, "Nnnuhgh."

Giggling in that adorable way he did when he was too far gone to keep his guard up, Thom reached behind himself and tugged Phil's fingers free of his hole. "You won't hurt me, worrywart. I'm ready. Fuck me."

Phil couldn't have answered right then if the lives of a bus full of orphans depended on it. Grabbing the lube, he poured a palmful and coated his shaft in the viscous fluid. Thom sat up, grasped Phil's prick and impaled himself in one swift movement which tore identical cries from both of them.

For several long moments, they both held still, breathing hard. Tremors ran in waves down Thom's back, where the muscles stood out hard and tense beneath Phil's palms. Phil's body wanted to rut like a moose in heat. He fought it with everything he had. Thom was so *tight.* Phil could feel the blood pulsing through his cock where Thom's sphincter clamped down on his shaft. If he gave in to his screaming instincts and ended up hurting Thom, Phil would never forgive himself.

After a torturous eternity, the near-painful grip on Phil's cock eased. Thom leaned forward, braced both hands on Phil's chest and rocked his hips.

"Oh fuck," Phil breathed as Thom's muscles rippled around his shaft. "Oh God. Oh fuck."

Nodding, Thom moved again, another slow glide that sent electricity arcing along every nerve in Phil's body. "Feels so good. So fucking good."

Phil agreed, but his capacity for lucid speech had flown the coop. Lacking the ability to tell Thom how he felt, Phil compensated by slipping one hand around Thom's waist, curling the other hand around his cock and thrusting up into his ass.

Thom let out a ragged moan. His fingers dug into Phil's pecs. "Oh. Oh yes. Phil."

Phil stared, entranced, at the man straddling him. God, he loved Thom like this, his heart-shaped face flushed and his voice breathy with desire. Biting his lip, Phil dug his heels into the mattress and canted his groin upward.

After a couple of fumbling false starts they fell into cadence with one another, hips rocking together in a languid rhythm. Thom's insides clutched Phil's shaft in a hot living grip that magnified the slightest movement into an explosion of sensation. He stroked Thom's cock in time with their mutual thrusts, creating a soundtrack of moans and sighs from Thom.

It was obvious Thom wasn't going to last, but that was okay since Phil was already teetering on the edge himself. They could always go again. They had all day to play. All weekend, in fact, since Phil had given himself some time off.

Actually, Phil mused, they had not just a day, or a weekend, but an entire lifetime. Months and years and decades to learn all there was to know about each other, physically and otherwise. To discover all the little joys a shared life could hold.

Growing old with someone had never been one of Phil's goals for his life. Now it *was* his life, and he couldn't think of

Ally Blue

anything better.

"Ooooh, fuuuuuck," Thom groaned, snapping Phil back into the moment. "Gonna come."

"Yeah," Phil growled, finding his voice at last. "Come on, baby." He tightened his grip on Thom's shaft and pumped as hard and fast as he could, watching Thom's face the whole time. "Do it, sweet thing. My pretty baby. Let go."

Whimpering, Thom lifted up and slammed himself down, over and over again, driving Phil's cock in as deep as it would go. Phil met him thrust for thrust, one hand firm on his hip and the other a blur on his prick. Just as Phil felt his release building in his lower belly, Thom went still. His cock pulsed in Phil's palm, his body bowed and he came with an echoing cry. His hole clenched around Phil's shaft, sending Phil tumbling over the edge into an orgasm so intense his vision grayed at the edges.

Thom tumbled forward onto Phil's chest. Semen squelched between them, and Phil's half-tumescent cock popped out of Thom's hole. He let out a squeal before relaxing into Phil's embrace. "Damn. I really, really needed that."

"Mmm-hmmm. Me too." Closing his eyes, Phil buried his face in Thom's tangled hair and drew a deep breath scented with apple shampoo and fresh come and the lingering traces of sleep. "You okay?"

"I am fan-fucking-tastic." Raising his head, Thom gave Phil a heart-stopping smile. "I could get used to waking up in your bed. In fact, I think I already *am* used to it. It's not gonna be easy to leave when the time comes."

"Then don't leave."

Thom stared, his eyes wide and surprised. Phil swallowed, but didn't take it back. He hadn't planned to say that, but now that it was out there, he knew he wanted it. He loved Thom.

Wanted to spend forever with him. If they were going to share their lives, why not share a home?

Thom licked his lips. "Phil, I...I don't know what to say."

"Say you'll live with me." Phil laid a hand on Thom's cheek, thumb caressing the corner of his kiss-swollen mouth. "C'mon, Bubbles. You need a place to live, and I have a house that's way too big for just me. We're in this thing for the long haul, yeah?"

"Yeah." A glowing smile flashed across Thom's face and faded into seriousness. "I still don't have a job, Phil. No income means I can't pay you any rent, or even pay for my share of groceries and utilities."

"I've been thinking about that, actually."

"Oh?"

"Mm-hm."

Thom arched a pale brow at him. "And what have you come up with?"

Nervous now, Phil twisted a lock of Thom's hair between his fingers. "Well, you know I want you to come back to The HO."

"Phil, you know I don't want to work for you again, and you know why." Thom's voice was as gentle as his fingers stroking Phil's chest. "Especially now. I can't be your lover—your life partner—and be your employee. I just can't."

"I know that."

"So why bring it up, then?"

*Now or never, Phil. Just spit it out.* Phil drew a deep breath. "I want you to be my partner. My business partner, I mean. In The HO."

Thom's mouth fell open. "You...you mean... What?"

"I've been thinking about this for ages. You're smart, you've got one hell of a head for business and you're a born manager. I

233

do all right, but so far The Happy Onion's made it mostly on luck and some amazing cooks. We can't keep coasting forever. I need a partner who can help me make the place rock solid. You're that person, Thom." Brushing away a stray platinum lock from Thom's eyes, Phil searched Thom's shocked face. "So what do you say? Will you do it?"

Thom's mouth opened and closed a couple of times. When he spoke, his voice was faint. "I... How do... I mean, I don't have the capital, I, I don't—"

"Hey. Stop." Phil touched a fingertip to Thom's lips. "I don't really know the legalities of making you a partner. But don't let the money worry you. Whatever you can spare, that's what I'll take. Hell, I'd give it to you, except I know you wouldn't let me."

"Well, you're right about that." Thom worried his lower lip between his teeth. "Wow. Damn. Are you sure this is what you want?"

"More than anything." Phil grinned. "Does this mean you're saying yes? You'll live with me, and be my business partner?"

A thousand-watt smile spread across Thom's face. "Okay, yes."

"Yes to both?"

"Yes, you pest. Both."

"Awesome." Cradling the back of Thom's skull in one hand, Phil pressed his head downward until their lips brushed. "Kiss me, partner."

Laughing, Thom did. It was a lazy, unhurried kiss this time, full of the promise of kisses to come. When it broke, Thom drew back to meet Phil's gaze with a solemn, thoughtful expression. "It won't always be easy, you know."

"I know. Most good things aren't."

"I know how I am, Phil. I'm difficult to deal with sometimes.

I can be a bastard sometimes."

"Oh yes, I'm well aware of that. So can I, sometimes." Phil craned up to kiss the tip of Thom's pert little nose. "Stop trying to talk me out of wanting you in my life. It's not going to work."

Thom's cheeks flushed. "I know. I'm not trying to do that, believe me." He shrugged, looking sheepish. "It's just, you're the best person I know, and you deserve someone perfect. I wish I could be that for you, but I know I can't."

A warm, tight feeling coalesced in Phil's chest. Bringing both hands up to frame Thom's face, Phil stared into his eyes. "I don't want you to be perfect, baby. Nobody can be that. I just want you to be *you*. That's all I need."

Thom's smile outshone the sun pouring through the window. "I can do that."

They kissed again, slow and sweet, then Thom snuggled against Phil's chest, his head tucked into the curve of Phil's neck. Smiling, Phil looped his arms around Thom's waist and let his eyes drift shut.

# Epilogue

*Asheville Citizen-Times*

*Monday, December 31st, 2007*

*ASHEVILLE—In a surprise decision yesterday evening, Judge Maris DeMarco denied former Asheville City Councilman Cassidy Morton's request for leniency in the Rosewood bribery case.*

*Morton resigned in November after former Rosewood general manager Leta Duncan revealed his role in Bradford & Lehrer's illegal acquisition of land for the Rosewood complex. During the explosive final day of Morton's trial, his attorneys made an impassioned plea for mercy, claiming Morton was blackmailed into falsifying property deeds and other official records in order to ensure the City Council's approval of the Rosewood project. However, the information which prompted the blackmail ultimately worked against Morton. Don Bradford, co-owner and CEO of legally embattled Rosewood developers Bradford & Lehrer, surrendered photos of Mr. Morton purchasing and injecting heroin in West Asheville last winter. Judge DeMarco, a known anti-drug crusader, is expected to hand down the maximum possible sentence for a city official convicted of accepting bribes.*

*In related news, Leta Duncan will be transferred to the North Carolina Correctional Institution for Women in Raleigh today to begin her sentence for the attempted murder of Thomas James Stone, former manager of Rosewood's on-site nightclub Midnight Rose. She received fifteen years with the possibility of parole after ten years in exchange for her testimony against her former employers, Don Bradford and Keith Lehrer. Mr. Bradford and Mr. Lehrer are both currently in seclusion after having been released on bond. Both men are awaiting trial on a variety of charges related to environmental and building-code violations on the Rosewood site and the now-defunct Rolling Hills development in West Asheville, as well as blackmail and a multitude of other charges. Bradford & Lehrer's company assets have been frozen pending the trials. The bulk of the company's money is expected to eventually be awarded to the former Bradford & Lehrer employees who are suing the company for discrimination based on religion and sexual orientation. Mr. Stone, whose violent assault on Halloween night precipitated the downfall of Rosewood and Bradford & Lehrer, is one of the plaintiffs in the lawsuit.*

Disgusted, Thom tossed the newspaper across the desk. It fell over the other side and scattered all over the floor of The HO's office. "Those fucks. Why the fuck did they have to put that in about me being part of the lawsuit?"

"It's news, baby," Phil answered from the storeroom, where he was double-checking supplies for The Happy Onion's very first New Year's Eve party that night.

"Yeah, but that reporter *swore* she wouldn't put that in."

"I guess she lied."

"She sure did. Bitch." Scowling, Thom kicked the leg of the desk. "Reporters have no scruples."

Laughter floated from the outer room. "That's not fair and you know it."

"Yeah, whatever."

Ally Blue

Phil's grinning face popped around the edge of the door. "Have you already forgotten how they made you look like a hero for breaking the Rosewood case?"

Thom sighed. Phil was right. He *hated* it when Phil ruined a perfectly good rant by being right.

Still grinning, Phil sauntered into the office, perched on the edge of the desk and twisted his upper body around to meet Thom's gaze. "You look good behind that desk, sweet thing."

Heat rushed into Thom's cheeks. God, he wished he wouldn't keep blushing like that. One day, maybe he'd get used to Phil telling him how sexy he looked in his shiny new role as restaurant owner.

Thom pushed to his feet, skirted the desk and went to stand between Phil's knees. He looped his arms around Phil's neck. "You know what I like best about being your partner?"

"What?" Phil's hands rested on Thom's hips, pulling him closer.

"Fucking on *our* desk instead of *yours*."

Chuckling, Phil leaned forward to plant a lingering kiss on Thom's lips. "We have almost five hours before the party starts."

"I know." Thom nipped at Phil's lip, then soothed the sting with his tongue. "There's lube in the bottom drawer."

Phil's grin kicked up a notch from merely mischievous to outright evil. "Why, Mr. Stone, are you planning to take advantage of me?"

"Absolutely." Tilting his head, Thom stole another kiss, this one more aggressive than the last. "Drop your pants and assume the position, Mr. Sorrells."

He had to laugh when Phil went tumbling to the floor in his haste to obey.

ॐ

Six hours and forty minutes later, the party was in full swing. Thom watched the happy, laughing crowd with a smile from his perch on a stool at the end of the bar. Throwing a New Year's Eve party had been his idea, but he hadn't been at all sure how it would turn out. *Looks like Phil was right about this too,* he thought, pulling his man's arms tighter around his waist.

Warm lips brushed Thom's temple, and a thick golden brown braid fell over his shoulder. "Told you this party would be a hit," Phil rumbled in Thom's ear. "You shouldn't worry so much."

"Yes, I know." Thom tipped his head back to kiss Phil's neck. "And I'm really glad you were right."

"Hey, it was your idea." Phil wound his fingers through Thom's and pressed their entwined hands to Thom's heart. "I knew you'd do great things for this place."

Thom laughed. "Is that something else you were right about?"

"Hell yeah."

A squeal sounded from behind the bar. Thom turned to see Circe haul herself up onto a chair and wave both arms over her head. "All right, everybody, it's almost midnight! Time for the countdown, y'all ready?"

Whoops and cheers rose from the crowd, along with a chorus of yeses and a few nos. Grinning ear to ear, Circe held her hands over her head and began to count backward from ten.

"Ten!" she shouted, and the crowd joined in.

"Nine!"

Phil nudged Thom off the stool.

"Eight!"

Thom turned to face his lover.

"Seven!"

Smiling softly, Phil wound his arms around Thom's waist...

"Six!"

...And pulled him close.

"Five!"

Thom slid both hands up Phil's chest to cradle the face he'd come to love more than any other in the world.

"Four!"

*I love you, Bubbles*, Phil mouthed.

"Three!"

Thom felt the goofy, love-struck smile that only Phil could bring out of him spread across his face. *I love you too*, he mouthed back.

"Two!"

The look in Phil's eyes was the sweet, tender one that made Thom think maybe they really could have a lifetime together. Phil bent closer, head canting sideways and lips parting...

"One! Happy New Year!"

...And their mouths met in a kiss that sent pure joy swooping through Thom's soul. The sounds of singing and New Year's wishes faded around him, leaving him floating with Phil in their own little private bubble. He clung to Phil's broad shoulders and prayed to whoever might be listening to please, please never let this feeling end.

When they drew apart at last, Thom leaned against Phil's chest, head spinning like he was drunk even though he hadn't touched a drop of booze all night. He figured if he looked in a mirror right then, he'd see himself glowing like an incandescent bulb.

Phil's hand cupped his chin, lifting his face to meet Phil's gaze. Smiling, Phil kissed his nose. "Happy New Year, sweet baby."

"Happy New Year." Rising on tiptoe, Thom rubbed his cheek against Phil's. "This is it, isn't it? We'll always be together."

Phil's breath hitched in Thom's ear. "Forever."

*Forever.* Thom smiled. "I can live with that."

# About the Author

Ally Blue used to be a good girl. Really. Married for twenty years, two lovely children, house, dogs, picket fence, the whole deal. Then one day she discovered slash fan fiction. She wrote her first fan fiction story a couple of months later and has since slid merrily into the abyss. She has had several short stories published in the erotic e-zine Ruthie's Club, and is a regular contributor to the original slash e-zine Forbidden Fruit.

To learn more about Ally Blue, please visit www.allyblue.com. Send an email to Ally at ally@allyblue.com or join her Yahoo! group to join in the fun with other readers as well as Ally! http://groups.yahoo.com/group/loveisblue/

*Dreams don't always come true. But sometimes nightmares do.*

# Closer

## *© 2008 Ally Blue*

*Book Four in the Bay City Paranormal Investigation series.*

After nine months of tumult, Sam Raintree is ready for some peace and quiet. A beach vacation with his boss and lover, Dr. Bo Broussard, promises to provide the serenity and reconnection they both need. Bo's business and his children command a good deal of his time, and Sam is looking forward to two weeks of his lover's undivided attention.

Then a new case for the Bay City Paranormal Investigations team puts a crimp in Sam's plans. Fort Medina, a seventeenth-century citadel guarding the mouth of Mobile Bay, is less than five miles from their vacation beach house. Bo invites the group to stay with them while investigating the place, promising Sam he won't get involved. But Sam knows better. Sure enough, Bo can't resist joining the investigation, and talks Sam into doing the same.

Events take an alarming turn as Bo's behavior becomes more erratic each day. Puzzled and frightened, Sam scrambles for an explanation while the man he loves turns into a volatile and unpredictable stranger.

When the truth comes out, it may already be too late to save Bo from a force neither of them can control.

*Warning: This book contains explicit male/male sex (including spanking and rimming), graphic language, violence, ghosts and monsters.*

*Available now in ebook and print from Samhain Publishing.*

*Enjoy the following excerpt from* Closer...

Sam jolted awake, his heart slamming against his ribs. The first dawn light leaked around the curtains to lend a dim illumination to the room. Sam sat up and looked around, trying to figure out what had woken him. The dream he'd been yanked out of was just as horrible as the one from the previous morning, but it wasn't what had disturbed Sam's sleep. It was something else, some sort of noise or movement in the bedroom.

A low, ragged moan drifted from the pile of covers bunched on the other side of the bed. Bo's body jerked, throwing off the corner of the bedspread which had obscured his face. His brows were drawn together in fear or pain, or both. Little whimpers bled from his open mouth. When Sam laid a hand on Bo's bare shoulder, he could feel Bo trembling.

Sam frowned. In the short time he'd shared Bo's bed, the man had never suffered nightmares. The fact that he seemed to be having one now of all times made Sam feel cold all over.

"Bo, wake up." He gave Bo's shoulder a shake.

With a sharp cry, Bo shot to a sitting position, panting like he'd just sprinted a mile. His wide-eyed gaze darted around the room. The fear melted from his eyes when they met Sam's.

"Fuck." He flopped onto his back. "God, I'm glad you woke me up."

"You've never had nightmares before," Sam pointed out, keeping his tone carefully neutral. He lay down beside Bo and propped himself up on one elbow. "What was it about?"

"Damned if I know." Bo tugged at a lock of tangled black hair lying across his chest. "I don't remember anything specific.

Just…weird images. They were terrifying when I was dreaming them, but I couldn't even tell you what they were now."

"Strangely enough, I just woke up from another dream like I had yesterday morning. And now you're having them too." Sam licked his lips, hoping his next words didn't touch off an angry tirade. "Was this nightmare anything like what you saw at the fort?"

"Not really, except for the general sense of fear, and not being able to breathe properly." Bo darted a pointed look at him. "I know what you're thinking, Sam, but I really don't believe the two are related. I don't usually have nightmares, that's true, but I have had a few in my life. The hallucinations I had last night probably triggered one, that's all."

A hard chill raced up Sam's spine. "I thought you said it only happened once."

"It did."

"Then why did you just say 'hallucinations', plural, like it happened more than once?"

A muscle twitched in Bo's jaw. "I didn't mean to say that. I meant to say 'hallucination', singular."

"But—"

"For God's sake, Sam, drop it!"

Anger and frustration boiled up inside Sam and bubbled over. He kept his voice calm with an effort. "I will not drop it. This is important. I'm sure of it."

Sighing, Bo pressed both palms to his eyes. "Look. I know you're worried, and I understand why. But *one* strange feeling during the investigation and one nightmare do not add up to anything dangerous, or even concerning."

"Even though I had a very similar dream yesterday morning, and again just now?" Sam persisted. "Even after the dreams at Oleander House?"

"This is nothing like Oleander House." Turning onto his side, Bo folded an arm beneath his head and gazed into Sam's eyes with a pleading expression. "Don't you think I'd tell you if I felt this was anything to worry about? Do you really think I'd put everyone in danger by keeping it to myself?"

"No, of course not." Sam tucked Bo's hair behind his ear, fingers brushing his neck. "But I don't think you're seeing this situation clearly."

Bo's fingers curled, bunching the sheet between them. He looked away. "What makes you think I'm not being clearheaded about this?"

"I don't know, exactly." It was hard for Sam to say, but it was true. He couldn't lie to Bo, no matter how difficult it might be to tell the truth. "All I know is, you're not acting like yourself. And that worries me."

With an impatient noise, Bo kicked the covers aside and started to get up. Sam wrapped both arms around his waist and rolled on top of him, pinning him to the bed.

"Let me up," Bo growled, dark eyes flashing.

"No."

"Sam..."

Fisting a hand in Bo's hair, Sam leaned down and kissed him until the angry tension melted from his body and his mouth opened beneath Sam's.

The kiss went on for endless, blissful minutes. Sam didn't break it until Bo's legs opened to cradle Sam in the space between his thighs. Drawing back, Sam stared down into Bo's heavy-lidded eyes. Bo's pupils were dilated, his breath coming short and quick. The sight made Sam's chest ache.

"I love you," Sam said, putting his whole heart into the

simple sentiment. "Maybe these dreams and visions of yours mean something, and maybe they don't. I think they do, but I don't know for sure. All I know is, I'll do anything to keep you safe. Even risk you hating me."

The lingering anger in Bo's eyes faded into a familiar affection. He reached up and laid both palms on Sam's cheeks. "I could never hate you. I'm grateful every single day to have you in my life."

Sam's throat closed up. He couldn't say what he felt right then, but he thought Bo understood.

Bo's gaze dipped to Sam's mouth. When he looked up again, lust had replaced the tenderness in his eyes. Sam's body responded with a predictable rush of desire. He tilted his hips, rubbing his naked prick against Bo's equally bare crotch. Bo moaned, low and rough. His thighs slid against Sam's ribs, one heel lodging in the small of Sam's back. Sam could feel Bo's cock filling, the hardness pressing against Sam's own growing erection.

A tiny corner of Sam's brain wanted to disentangle himself from Bo's arms and legs and continue the conversation Sam was beginning to realize Bo had successfully distracted him from. But the clutch of Bo's limbs around him, the increasingly frantic movement of Bo's hips and the needy little sounds he made, silenced that part of Sam's mind. One arm beneath Bo's neck and the other braced on the bed, Sam took Bo's mouth in a bruising kiss as they thrust against one another.

# GREAT CHEAP FUN

## Discover eBooks!

THE FASTEST WAY TO GET THE HOTTEST NAMES

Get your favorite authors on your favorite reader, long before they're out in print! Ebooks from Samhain go wherever you go, and work with whatever you carry—Palm, PDF, Mobi, and more.

Samhain Publishing, Ltd.

Printed in the United States
151009LV00002B/16/P

9 781605 042930